A UNIVIAH NOVEL

THE BELIEVER

PHIL MUIRHEAD

Published in Queensland, Australia

This is a work of fiction. Any other resemblance to actual people, living or dead, or to events, institutions or locales is completely coincidental. Reference is made to the Westhall High School alleged UFO sighting in 1966 for fictional purposes.

Cover designed by Judith San Nicolas
Typeset in Garamond 9/12pt, Bahnschrift 18pt/expanded spacing 2, Humans 521 BT 11pt
Printed and bound in Australia by IngramSpark
Prepared for publication and edited by The Erudite Pen (theeruditepen.com)

 A catalogue record for this book is available from the National Library of Australia

The Believer: A Univiah Novel (Book 1 in The Univiah Series)
ISBN paperback 9780645414202
ISBN eBook 9780645414219

Dedication

To my mother, who often said, 'The power of the pen
is mightier than the sword.'

PROLOGUE

The end of the sixties marked the end of a decade of increased UFO activity. On this particular Tuesday, it was nine days after Armstrong and Aldrin walked on the moon. It was also Alan Holmes' thirteenth birthday – a day that would leave its incredible outcome permanently etched within his psyche forevermore.

Alan was a lovely kid. He was bright, good natured, well-liked and adventurous. His father tended to see him as a mummy's boy, which he certainly was. For some reason, Alan favoured his mother, Joyce. He always confided in her, completely leaving his father John out of the picture. Unbeknown to Alan and John Holmes, today's incredible events would inadvertently mend the rift that had slowly taken place between father and son over the years.

Alan waved goodbye to his mother as he left for school, yelling out a thanks for his birthday present. She watched intently, as she always did, until he peddled out of sight towards Wallaby Heights State School. The school was a ten-minute bike ride from where they lived in outback New South Wales, Australia. Upon arriving at school, Alan couldn't wait to show his peers his birthday present, a brand-new watch. He was now one of only a handful of students in his class who wore a watch to school. It was a sort of prestigious feeling he was experiencing, without knowing why. Not only was he attracting attention within his own ranks, but other students from higher grades were lining up for a peek. He was just getting used to his new-found audience when the bell rang.

Social studies was the topic for the morning, not exactly Alan's favourite subject. He would have preferred maths, which he was extremely good at. It was a long morning indeed. *Who cares if Tasmania was called Van Diemen's Land first*, he reasoned, as the teacher pointed to the map draped over a blackboard. He looked at his watch, which now allowed him to actually work out how much longer he had to suffer.

The bell finally rang. It was time for Alan and his mates to gather in their usual eatery under a tree. After a snack, they positioned themselves about ten metres apart in an awkward circle, kicking the ball to one another in an anticlockwise direction. Around and around the football revolved until the new boy in the group kicked it to Alan twice as hard as necessary. Alan took chase to retrieve the ball, and slightly puffed, his return was slower than the chase. Suddenly he came to an abrupt halt, the ball falling from his hands. He pointed but couldn't speak. It was as if his mind was accelerating way too fast for his tongue.

'What the hell's wrong with you?' one of his mates yelled.

Gathering his wits, Alan pointed to the sky. 'Look! Look behind you in the sky! Quick, look, look, it's a spacecraft!'

He ran to alert a male teacher who was on playground duty. 'Sir! Sir! Look! Look over there, it's a flying saucer,' he panted.

It took only minutes before the whole school had been alerted. About ninety students and teachers stood dumbfounded, watching the craft as it lingered silently in a stationary position about twenty-five degrees above the horizon. Little did they know, they were witnessing a UFO sighting that would contribute to worldwide ramifications at a later point in time. The extraordinary events taking place were a mere fraction of what was in stall for the future.

The craft remained suspended in the sky, about the length of two playgrounds away. As if to disappear, it suddenly flashed, reappearing further to the left from where it was first sighted. Again it hovered, silently motionless, for what seemed an eternity. Then without warning, it flashed again, reappearing directly behind them in the opposite direction, floating motionless over the property that adjoined the school. Suddenly, it descended towards the ground behind a cluster of gum trees, landing softly about forty metres from the nearest tree.

Some of the students were terrified, while some stood in awe of what was taking place. Then there were those such as Alan, who literally raced towards where the craft had landed. Alan wasn't as fast as some of the other students, but he managed to keep up with the teacher he'd previously alerted, following him over the fence on to the adjoining property. The craft could clearly be seen through the trees. The diameter was about the length of a semi-trailer truck, shining with a silvery hue. It was circular shaped with a domed top and was sitting firmly on the ground.

Except for a couple of braver students, everyone had come to a halt, preferring to peer from behind the last of the trees. Alan wanted to go right on up and touch the craft; however, the teacher was ordering everyone to stay back. They could plainly see one of the older boys who had gone up to the craft groggily walking back, somewhat stunned. The other boys who hadn't got as close now retreated to the trees, not sure what to make of the older boy's stunned demeanour.

Alan looked at his watch. Thirty minutes had passed since he first sighted the craft. *Was it going to stay or perhaps it had broken down?* His thoughts were soon answered. Zap! It lifted off the ground, going straight up so fast that it was inconceivable how it could move so quickly without noise or any noticeable effort. All that remained was the twisted, flattened brown grass where it had landed.

The stunned boy who had approached the craft now sat on the ground, leaning back on one of the gum trees. A teacher immediately went to his aid. Apparently, he was so overcome by the whole scenario that he fainted, or at least that's what everyone was led to believe. In fact, everyone was led to believe all sorts of nonsense over the next few days. The main story the headmaster, who never even witnessed the event, was trying to put forward was that a weather balloon launched from Sydney earlier in the day had malfunctioned.

The weather balloon story quickly blossomed into an experimental aircraft the air force had been testing at a nearby secluded outback airstrip. No one who witnessed the sighting first-hand was having a bar of the theories being put forward by the headmaster or by those who weren't present at the sighting.

The day after the sighting, Alan was taken from class by the headmaster. He was told he had to answer a few questions for personnel from the aviation industry. He arrived at the headmaster's office just as another student was leaving, Alan immediately recognised him; he was the boy who had been temporarily stunned as he approached the alien craft. Alan noticed the boy had tears in his eyes and looked genuinely upset. This in itself prepared him for what was to come.

There were two of them in the office, both huge in stature, three if you included the headmaster – quite a formidable environment for a boy who had just turned thirteen. They issued Alan with a chair before starting the questioning. One of the men asked the questions while the other wrote notes into a small memo pad. Both wore air force uniforms. The headmaster sat to one side, watching the unfolding events as if he were at a concert, raising his eyebrows and smirking randomly as they interrogated Alan.

'Alan, you were the first person to notice this object in the sky, is that true?'

Alan met his gaze. 'I think so. No one else said anything before I started yelling and pointing to it.'

The man wrote furiously in his notebook. 'So no one else saw it until you spotted it? Are you sure?'

The Believer

'That's what I just told you.' Alan started to fidget, wondering if this man had a hearing problem.

'I know. I just wanted to hear it again. Go on, tell me more.' The man's gaze was stern. This was not someone to be messed with.

Alan stammered, 'I don't know what else to tell you. Maybe someone else saw it first, but how would I know? If Luke hadn't kicked the football so hard, I probably wouldn't have seen it first.'

Even at his age, Alan knew this guy was trying to twist his thoughts to alter the events that took place the day before.

'So you saw this thing hovering above the field beside the school, is that correct?'

Alan didn't hesitate. 'Yep, *everyone* saw it. Not just me.'

More notetaking. 'Then it miraculously disappeared behind a gum tree, is that what you're saying?'

'It didn't disappear, sir, we could see it all the time through the trees. It landed, then some of us ran through the trees. When we got there, it was resting on the ground. I wanted to join the older students and get closer, only the teacher wouldn't let me. True, sir. I'm telling the truth. It really happened just like I've said.'

The two officers shared a look between them. Alan didn't know what it meant, but he was sure it was nothing good. 'OK, then if it happened just as you've said, what happened next?'

'The boy you just talked to went too close to the craft. Somehow he returned stunned, walking back from the spacecraft like he was drunk.'

'I see. Do you really think it was a spacecraft? What did this so-called spacecraft look like?' The officer seemed to be humouring him; however, Alan knew what he'd seen.

'It was like an upside-down saucer with a piece coming up from the top where you sit to drive it. It was also really shiny.' Alan's eyes lit up with excitement as he described the craft.

The other officer interrupted. 'How do you know the top section was the driver's compartment?'

'I don't really know for sure. I was thinking how you have to see out, like how you drive a car.'

'You don't really know! Those are probably the truest words you have spoken so far, Alan.' The second officer glared at him.

Alan chewed on his bottom lip. 'Everything I have said is true! I haven't told a single lie.' He started wriggling in his chair, keen to leave this interrogation.

'Let's move on, shall we.' The first officer took over the questioning again. 'You all stood there looking at it, is that right?'

'Yes, sir, except for the dazed boy sitting on the ground.'

'What happened next?'

'Nothing for a while, then all of a sudden it went straight up so fast you could only see the light it left behind.' Again, Alan couldn't keep the excitement out of his voice.

'Did it leave anything else besides light behind?' The officer was back to scribbling in his notebook.

'Yes, it left a brown area where it landed.'

'There must have been something else you noticed?' the second officer quizzed. The headmaster leaned forward, listening to Alan's every word.

Alan shrugged his shoulders. 'Only that the grass was flat and twisted.'

'What did you do after it left?'

'We all went back to the school yard, then the stunned boy's parents arrived to take him home.' The officer frowned at him, but what else could he say? That's all that happened.

'Have you told many people about what happened?' All men in the room stared intently at Alan.

He squirmed in the chair. 'Yeah, I've told everyone. No one believes me. Even my mum doesn't believe me; only those who were there believe what happened.'

'Have you considered that this may have been a phenomenon other than a spacecraft?'

'What's a phenomenon?' Alan's tongue tripped over the word.

The Believer

'Well, it could have been a weather balloon or something manmade that is similar to an aircraft performing in exactly the same manner as you described.' The officer smiled derisively.

'I didn't think we could make weather balloons or aeroplanes like space ships.' Alan crossed his arms stubbornly.

This last comment must have been enough to signify a final reaction from his interrogator. 'Alright, son, you can go back to your class. Just remember, sometimes you see things that are completely different to what you think they are, especially when the air force tests a new type of aircraft.'

Alan failed to reply. He knew what he had seen, no matter what these jerks were trying to implicate. He stood up, then dawdled back to class deep in thought. *Testing a new type of aircraft. What an idiot! An aeroplane that makes no noise, has no engines or wings. They can't be serious! Rotten bastards. Those guys in their stupid uniforms. How could they know what happened when they weren't even there! Why don't they pick on the teachers that were there?* he reasoned. *Or better still, why don't they get everyone who saw it together to discuss it.* Alan was in a bad mood for the rest of the school day.

On leaving school that afternoon, the urge to revisit the landing site became overwhelming. 'Just a quick peek before I go home,' Alan told himself. 'It will only take a minute then I'll hurry straight home.' Unlike his highly excited entry into the gum trees the day before, he advanced with trepidation. He could hear voices as he approached. Someone was there.

He was now standing among the trees where he could see three people where the craft had come down. One was using a radiation detector that had a handle with a plate-shaped object at the bottom. The user was wandering around erratically, moving the plate over the grass while never leaving the patch that was flattened by the craft. One of the others was taking measurements of the overall area. The third was jotting text onto a clipboard while taking photos and barking orders at the other two.

Alan was about to leave when he saw two kids approaching from the adjoining farm. He instantly recognised Luke, the boy who had kicked the football to him just prior to Alan's alerting the whole school. The boy with him was his younger brother; somehow they both managed to get within metres of the three men before they were noticed.

'Get the bloody hell out of here,' they were ordered. The boys stopped in their tracks, explaining they only wanted to look at where the flying saucer landed.

'I don't care what you want to look at,' bellowed the man with the camera. 'Now piss off or you will both get my boot up your arse!'

They both took off in the same direction they came from, never looking back once.

Alan got the message loud and clear. He ran back to his bike before they noticed him. He then peddled at full pace, arriving home fifteen minutes later than usual.

'You're late today, love. Where have you been?' enquired his mum. Phew, he didn't seem to be in trouble.

'Just talking with my friends.' He couldn't see the point going over yesterday's events with a nonbeliever, let alone trying to explain why he revisited the site. He sat eating a sandwich his mother had prepared previously. Noticing his aloof behaviour, his mother broke the ice by telling him what she had heard on the news.

'While you were at school today, I heard the spacecraft that you supposedly saw was actually a new type of aircraft being tested by the air force.'

'That's a heap of rubbish!' he retaliated, using a tone his mother had never heard before.

'There's no need to talk to me in that tone of voice, Alan.' Alan just glared at her. He loved his mother, only he was furious that she didn't believe him.

He quickly excused himself then left to kick his football around the backyard. It saddened him to think that this was their first argument, but she was wrong. Grownups didn't always know everything.

The Believer

Later that evening, Alan helped with the dishes then quickly did his homework before venturing out to the front patio. His father was sitting there as he did every night, smoking a pipe.

'Unusual you coming out here of a night,' his father stated. 'What's up?'

Alan sat beside his father before speaking. 'Well, Dad, you know what I was saying about that spacecraft yesterday?'

'I certainly do, my boy.' His father looked over at him, a small smile on his face.

'Dad, it did happen just as I told you and Mum,' he burst out.

'I know it did, son.' Alan's mouth dropped open in surprise as his father continued. 'I was delivering some parts nearby and saw everything myself.' He winked at Alan conspiratorially.

'Wow!' Alan was gobsmacked for the first time in his life. 'Why didn't you tell Mum?'

'Well, I worked out from her reaction to your story that I was better off shutting up, if you know what I mean.'

'You mean it beats arguing?'

'Something like that, son.' For the first time in a long time, Alan's father put an arm around his shoulders.

'Are you ever going to tell her?' Alan looked up at his dad's face, feeling a new bond with him.

'Maybe, but only if the right time arises when I think she'll listen instead of disputing.' His dad grinned. 'For now, let's just leave it between you and me.'

'It really was something, wasn't it, Dad?' Alan was so excited to have someone to talk to about what he'd seen.

'Sure was, my boy. I've never seen anything like that in my life. I'm still getting over it. I'm not sure what it all means.'

Alan revealed, 'I went back for a quick look at the landing site after school. There were some people there taking photos of the grass. They were also measuring things. One of them was passing some sort of round thing on a handle over the grass.'

'Did anything else happen while you were there?' his dad wanted to know.

'Yeah. Luke and his brother walked right up to them from the paddock next door. One of the men told them to piss off or he would kick them both up the arse!' His father's eyebrows furrowed upon hearing this.

'Anything out of the ordinary happen at school?'

Well, actually, I got taken to the headmaster's office to tell these blokes wearing air force uniforms what happened. They were really intimidating and even tried telling me it was an experimental aeroplane – the same story Mum heard!'

'All I can say is that must have been one hell of an experiment, son. It's best just to keep all this between you and me for now.' His dad looked concerned.

'Why don't they want people to know the truth, Dad?'

I don't know. I think it's a policy created by the American Government.' His father seemed deep in thought.

'But we live in Australia!' Alan cried.

'I know, son. We just can't help following in the Yanks' footsteps. Take my word for it, the authorities are going to make this all go away no matter what you or me do or say.'

Alan's father then asked him to fetch a blue photo album from his bookcase in the study. Alan returned with his father's photo album, handing it over to him. His dad went to the back of the album, separate to the photos, where he had a collection of newspaper clips he had gathered over the past decade. Sifting through them, he found the news cutting he was looking for.

'Look at this,' he said, handing Alan a half-page newspaper clip of a UFO sighting at Westall High School in Melbourne on the 6th of April 1966.

Alan sat quietly, digesting what he was reading. 'Holy shit! This is nearly an identical case of what just happened at Wallaby Heights School.' He was brimming with excitement.

'I agree. Guess what happened?'

Alan looked at his dad quizzically.

'It was all made go away.'

'By who?' Alan demanded.

'By the authorities. They consider us the dumb clucks at the end of the food chain. Unfortunately we are dumb clucks because we let them.'

'Dad, do you think the alien craft we saw was the same alien craft witnessed at Westall in 1966?'

His father nodded. 'It's highly possible. Maybe not the same craft but there's a fair chance those in charge of the craft at the time were from the same planet. I don't like our chances of finding out though.'

'Wow. I've sure learnt a lot today! Sorry, Dad, I have to go to bed now. I'm really tired coz I hardly slept last night.' Alan stretched and yawned. 'See you in the morning.'

'You weren't the only one who didn't sleep.' His father smiled. 'Good night, son.'

From that day on, Alan and his father found a subtle peace that was a long time coming. It was a type of enlightenment that went unanalysed, but they were both happy to accept that things had changed for the better without talking about it. Their future as father and son had dramatically improved, moulded by unprecedented circumstances nobody could ever have imagined. Unprecedented circumstances that would play a major part in Alan's future life.

Five years had gone by since Alan's UFO encounter. It was 1974. He had just graduated from high school with impressive marks. At seventeen, he now had the world at his fingertips, but that never stopped him making time to sit and talk to his father, who still enjoyed his nightly pipe on the patio. It was during one of those nights of idle chat that Alan informed his father of his intention to study astrophysics then go on to work in the space industry.

'I have a scholarship with The University of Sydney,' he informed his dad.

Phil Muirhead

His dad beamed at him. 'Did the events at school back in 1969 have anything to do with your choice of profession?'

'Sure did! I've been determined to work in the space industry ever since. I'm also determined to try and make contact with another civilisation beyond Earth. However, the main thing I need do in the meantime is study.'

The conversation prompted his father to reach behind and turn out the lights before pointing the stem of his pipe towards the stars that were visible from the patio.

'That's going to be one hell of a study, son.'

ONE

'Time waits for no one' is a saying that Alan was beginning to understand, literally. It was his fifty-third birthday, although he could easily pass for forty-five. The Holmes' genes had indeed been kind with respect to his looks. Apart from a few silver strands of hair on his temples, which made him look a little more sophisticated and mature, he hadn't changed much in fifteen years. His striking good looks coupled with his unobtrusive, easy-going manner made him easy for his peers to accept and like. At six foot in height, he always seemed to stand out in a crowd, resembling someone brimming with unlimited self-confidence. His work mates all considered him fun to be with, but they also knew him as an intellectual force to be reckoned with, which he undoubtedly was.

Alan was now working for Macquarie University in Sydney, teaching the finer points of astronomy. Forty years had lapsed since the Wallaby Heights UFO event. Even though he had only been thirteen at the time, he never forgot what took place in 1969. Every birthday since had become a day to relive the day all over again. Each one of those forty years had become a special anniversary locked in his mind for evermore.

'Happy birthday, Mr Holmes,' a greeting blared over the PA system. 'Please attend the cutting of your birthday cake in the staff room after your last lecture.'

Phil Muirhead

'I would rather be called Alan or just good old Al,' he told his students as he wrapped up his last lecture for the day. 'How many times do I have to tell them.'

His birthday party turned out to be a gathering of staff, half of whom Alan had never met. Even the university's carpenter was there. His name was Ralph. Ralph stood out in the crowd because of his outgoing personality, and also because he had a measuring tape clipped to his belt.

'Why the tape?' someone asked. Ralph laughed jokingly, promising to use it for a mock lecture, carpenter style.

The cake was cut, cups of tea and coffee were circulated and everyone sang happy birthday before they devoured the cake. All in all, a happy, light atmosphere was prevalent.

Ralph then announced his lecture in jest, unclipping his tape and holding it up in readiness. Then he proceeded with the entertainment.

'Good evening, students.' The room came alive with laughter.

'Appropriately, today's lecture is about age. If you all take a look around, you will notice none of us are getting any younger. What has that got to do with this tape, you might ask? Well, I'll show you.' He hooked the end of the tape over the end of the staff room table then pulled back until the tape was 70 inches from the end. He pushed the lock button so it couldn't move from the 70-inch position. Most in the room were intrigued. Most were smiling, but Alan didn't have the foggiest idea what Ralph was up to.

'Now, the bible quotes our lifespan as three score years and ten. Does everybody agree?' Everyone nodded.

'Alan is fifty-three today, according to you lot, so let's put a pencil across the tape at 53 inches. As you can see, he's chewed up a big hunk of his life compared to what's left between 53 inches and 70 inches.'

Alan was still wondering where Ralph was going with all this.

'I'm sixty-three, so let's shift the pencil to 63 inches. Take a look at the years I've used up compared to what's left. Frightening, isn't it! Even if I give myself another ten years, ah, make that inches, and go to 80 inches, it's still a daunting prospect when you can actually see how many years you have left. Or haven't got left as far as that goes! Who knows when we're heading off for the big sleep.' Light laughter echoed around the staff room.

'The purpose of this lecture isn't to remind you that time is running out. It's to remind you to make every day count by enjoying your life as much as possible while you are using the remaining inches, or years of your life. Thank you for your attention.' Everyone cheered as he took a mock bow.

Standing back up, he exclaimed, 'Oh, sorry! There's just one more thing, I will now demonstrate how quickly life disappears.' He unlocked the tape, lifting the end hooked to the table. The tape's housing swallowed it instantly.

The applause was immediate. Some clapped, and some cheered some more. Not a soul had believed old Ralph was up to such a performance.

'You missed your vocation in life, Ralphie,' someone shouted from the crowd as everyone clapped. The impromptu party went a little longer, fading out when everyone finished their tea or coffee. Alan thanked everyone before leaving, then drove home mesmerised by Ralph's fake lecture. *He's dead right! The proof is as plain as the markings on the tape. I just never thought about it that way.*

It was now Saturday, the day after Ralph's age demonstration. Alan kept mulling over what Ralph had said. He couldn't help comparing his present life to the events of the past. Over and over he thought about Ralph's words. Deep in thought, he heard a meow, signalling that it was Rocky, his ex-wife's cat, come for a back scratch. Alan had become accustomed to talking to the cat since his divorce. Not only did he talk to the cat, sometimes he answered for him as well!

'I've got an idea, Rocky,' Alan said out loud as the cat purred. Rocky then meowed, sitting upright with his tail curled around him. He wasn't interested in ideas unless they were going into his stomach.

'I'll go get a tape measure and a piece of cardboard to mark out all the inches. Then I'll write down the major events that have happened in my life on the cardboard to correspond with the year. That way, I can compile a graph of the past as it comes to mind.' He returned with a tape measure and a long strip of cardboard, placing the cardboard on the bench top. He then hooked the tape to the bench above the cardboard then locked it somewhere after 53 inches.

Alan drew a line at 5 inches and looked at the cat. He explained how this was his first year at school. Then he wrote '5: started school' beside the line.

'What happened next, Rocky? Oh, I know, I got my first bike.' At 8 inches, he drew another line and wrote this down. Remembering a holiday he took with his mother when he was ten, he then wrote this down.

'I can't remember anything else important until 13 inches.' He looked at the cat, who just glared back at him, realising he was not going to be fed any time soon. 'That's one year I'll never forget.' He drew another line, then wrote 'Wallaby Heights UFO sighting'.

'Come on, Rock, what number's next? Christ, I know, it's 14 inches. Fiona was born! I had a sister fourteen years younger.'

'Meow!' the cat whined.

'OK, OK. I'll feed you in a minute. Where to now? 19 inches: I started university. 23 inches: I met Kate. 25 inches: We got engaged. I got married at 27 inches, and my first child, Mary, was born. At 29 inches, my second child Jane was born. At 30 inches, I started work at the observatory. Then there's a big jump here, Rocky. At 39 inches, Mum died. I was upset for months, but poor old Dad was lost for years. At 45 inches, Dad died in a car accident, the poor guy. It knocked Fiona and me around something terrible. Dad and I had become really close since our talk on the veranda when I was thirteen. At 46 inches, well, you know, Kate found someone else. At 48 inches, I divorced Kate.' Alan paused, scratching Rocky between the ears. The cat stopped glaring at him momentarily.

'What a turn-out, old mate. One more, puss, then its food time. At 51 inches, I finally started on my digitally enhanced Morse code. You're the only one I've told so far. Don't tell a soul or they'll think you're mad. Just between you and me, I'm going to try using it to contact other civilisations. Let me re-phrase: I have a theory based on a 1969 UFO sighting I witnessed. I think it's possible intelligent beings elsewhere in the universe are contactable, only because they have the technology to contact us.'

Rocky meowed loudly. 'Oh, you like the idea? Well, so do I. It's going to happen one day. I can feel it.'

Ralph's four powerful words kept haunting Alan: Make every day count. These kept echoing in his mind. He wasn't happy lec-turing at the university. In fact, there were quite a few aspects of his life he would have to change to attain his former happiness. The first thing that sprang to mind was to look for a job at an astrophysical level. He had taken the job at the university mainly to avoid working nights. However, this was a mistake. He missed his previous nocturnal lifestyle and wanted to rectify the situa-tion. With his qualifications, he knew it would be no problem finding work at a radio telescope facility. He was aware that working in a modern astrophysical environment would involve travel. Above all, he was aware he needed a modern radio tele-scope to implement his plan to contact an alien civilisation. Whether it would work or not was yet to be seen.

Sifting through numerous papers and science magazines final-ly paid dividends. Alan circled an advertisement then started researching the company that had advertised the position. The ad read: *Astrospace Galexiana requires a fully qualified astrophysicist. The applicant will preferably have a history of working in astronomy, includ-ing the scientific study of celestial bodies. Astrospace Galexiana is a newly formed company that has just opened a state-of-the-art astrophysical radio telescope facility near Big Bear City, California.* The ad went on to give the company's contact details as well as how to apply online.

Unlike NASA and other government-controlled institutions, Astrospace Galexiana had to look after itself financially. The only way to do this was to charge clients for the use of Galexiana's infrastructure. Mostly this came about by companies all around the world that were prepared to pay Galexiana for the required use of their equipment rather than paying the huge costs of setting up their own facility. Initially the company took on shareholders who were now more than pleased with their investment. Another source of revenue came from universities that were prepared to send students to Astrospace Galexiana for a hands-on approach peek at the universe.

Alan met the requirements hands-down. All he had to do was apply. One of the main reasons he intended to apply was the need for a radio telescope to accompany his newly finished 'digitally enhanced Morse code', which he now abbreviated to DEMC. If Alan's theory was correct, other beings with technology far superior to ours were already unsuccessfully trying to contact us. *Why wouldn't they be trying to communicate*, he reasoned. *After all, they know where we are; they've been here. The problem we have on Earth is we are sending radio waves all over the place from airport radar, television stations, radio stations, phones and microwaves. Just about every electronic gadget on Earth is emitting radio waves, so what a jumble it must be if beings out there are trying to communicate through the quagmire of radio waves that we live amidst.*

Hence Alan's DEMC project: A simple set of highly audible dots and dashes turned loose into the universe on a whole range of different frequencies. Radio-controlled dots and dashes that would stand out above all the chatter Earth produced, so hopefully someone out there would have the tools that could detect, intercept and decipher the enhanced DEMC signal, then contact us from their end before the radio waves travelled too far.

It was the constellation of Orion that interested Alan the most. At between one to two thousand light years away, depending which area you looked, Orion had a universal infrastructure that was far more likely to support life. Of course, this was Alan's opinion; however, there were a lot in the profession who disagreed. He was more than aware of the pitfalls confronting him; hence, his confiding in no one bar the cat.

The first thing everyone would ridicule was the distance involved. Using pure logic as well as physics, we would all be dead and long gone before a message got anywhere near another civilisation. Yet, what if other beings had the technology to send radio waves through space at speeds incomprehensible to us?

Alan's job application was accepted. After his interviews Astrospace Galexiana offered to pay his airfare from Australia to the United States, giving him a two-month leeway to sort everything out before he commenced work. The pay was excellent, and he would be living in one of the nicest areas of the United States. He replied to the email, indicating he could start work on the specified date.

A few days went by before he told anyone he was leaving Australia to work overseas. The first people he told about his intentions were his daughters, who both wished him well. They knew he would never be happy lecturing at a university. Mary, who was the eldest of Alan's daughters at twenty-six, instantly invited herself to California for a holiday. She was more the academic of his two daughters, very analytical in her thoughts, yet pleasant. Jane was the younger daughter at twenty-four, nonetheless she also explained her intent to come visit him in California. Jane was more the cruisy type who just took things in her stride. Nothing much fazed her at all. She offered to look after the cat while he was gone. Both told him he was expected home at least once a year. His daughters would miss him terribly, as would his grandchildren. He had been an excellent father and grandfather, who had selflessly played a major role in their lives since they were born.

Surprised by his sudden resignation, the university understood his reasons for resigning, paying him a bonus on departure. His next job was to notify his younger sister Fiona of his intention to move to the United States. She was living in Texas, being married to an American. They had two lovely children – both boys who were now in their early teens. The last thing on Fiona's mind was Alan coming to work and live in America, so she was about to be surprised.

Buying a house instead of renting consumed a lot of time Alan wasn't prepared to spend. The internet provided so much variety it confused him. Eventually he stumbled across an advertisement causing an opportunity he thought too good to be true. The ad read: Private sale $300, 000 firm. No agents please. Big Bear Lake, California, three-bedroom newly built modern cottage in quiet cul de sac. WIWO includes furniture, household appliances, car and cat. Owner relocating to London to work at American embassy. The ad also showed a picture of the house. *Not bad*, he thought. *I wonder if I can get Fiona to go have a look at it for me?*

He rang his sister early the next morning to find out. 'You're what!' Fiona exclaimed as Alan told his story. She agreed to look at the house for him.

The next day, he rang the supplied number and spoke to the owner off the house. 'Where are you from?' she asked. 'I detect an Aussie accent.'

Alan laughed. He explained that he was from Sydney, Australia. He was coming over there to work. She sounded sincere in telling him she would be very happy to sell the house to him if he had American citizenship. 'If you don't, it will probably cause all sorts of headaches, delays and uncertainties,' she said.

'I can easily get around that if I put it in my sister's name. She lives in Dallas,' Alan told her. Thankfully, it was all arranged through Fiona, who was more than excited about her big brother coming to live closer to her.

TWO

Alan's flight touched down at Los Angeles at midday on the 27th of September 2009. His main mission to find someone called David Scott, a fellow astrophysicist at Galexiana, who hopefully would be holding a placard with his name printed on it. As he walked out of customs, David was bang in front of him. They shook hands, Dave informing Alan he was usually known as Scotty, then they headed off to get Alan's luggage. Scotty was about the same age as Alan, and they had a lot in common. Chatting to one another came with ease, still Scotty wasn't as lucky as Alan when it came to ageing. He looked every bit his age, although he was well dressed and good mannered. These were attributes everyone noticed and liked.

'Where to when we get to Big Bear Lake, Al?' he asked.

'50 Hudson Close. I bought a house there or at least I paid for one,' Alan chuckled. Fortunately, Scotty only lived a few blocks away.

Big Bear was about two-and-a-half hours away from the airport, which gave Alan plenty of time to ask questions about Astrospace Galexiana. The obvious question was what are they like to work for?

'Reasonable,' Scotty replied. 'Although the CEO can be a pain in the ass. He runs a tight ship. The shareholders come first then he runs a close second. His name is Mal Roberts, better known as Big Mal among the staff. He's six-foot-four and built like a tank; the only difference between a tank and Big Mal is that a tank has a sense of humour! Don't worry, though. We seldom see him, probably because he knows absolutely nothing about astrophysics or the workings of the universe. The one thing he does know is how to count beans for profit; hence, the shareholders are happy. You can call him Big Mal to his face if you like. He seems to like it more than Mr Roberts or just plain Mal, yet it's up to you.'

'Who are they making their money from?' Alan wanted to know.

'Currently we have been overrun with university students willing to pay for a look at the universe. I'm told Big Mal's also considering tourists. Apart from that, we are doing a lot of research work for governments all around the world who would rather pay us than build their own infrastructure. Thanks to your arrival, my workload will lessen. There'll be nights when we are on the same shift. On others it will be night for night depending on what's going on. It's an easy number though, especially when the uni students book. Most of them get tired so pack it in early. Here we are, Alan. Hudson Close. You been here before?'

'No, I bought it sight unseen, though got the furniture and a car chucked in, provided the owner hasn't diddled me, that is. That's it, there! I can tell from the photos.' He pointed at a white cottage with a pathway leading up to the front door.

Scotty helped with the luggage, asking Alan if he had a key. 'It's buried in the sand below the garden gnome, I hope. Otherwise, I'm going to have to break in.'

Scrummaging around under the gnome he found the key just as the owner had said. Scotty, amused by Alan's adventurous behaviour, arranged to pick him up the next morning, offering to take him in to Galexiana and introduce him to everyone. Scotty then took off, leaving Alan to settle in.

This will be interesting, Alan thought, as he turned the key in the front door. 'Crikey, look at this,' he said out loud. The interior had stunning polished floors, the furniture was unmarked and the curtains were washed. There wasn't a thing out of place. The linen cupboard was full of towels, tea towels, sheets and blankets, all folded and placed in tidy individual piles. He then opened the fridge which was full with all the non-perishables left for his use. What a relief. There was a note on the bench top beside the sink. It read: Dear Alan, I do hope everything is as you expected. The car keys are in the top drawer beside you next to the knives. The neighbour on the left is an old grizzle guts and a pain in the ass, yet the one on the right is Pam. She's lovely. Pam has been feeding your new cat (the ad did say WIWO). I left the paperwork with her, so you can change the car rego and power into your name. I do hope everything works out at your new place of employment. Sincerely, Dorothy.

Alan returned the note to the bench, deciding to take a look at his coupe. He lifted the roller garage door to reveal a red mustang. 1965. This would have commanded a huge price back in Australia. He couldn't believe his luck! It had only done 42,000 miles! Red was also his favourite colour. Pushing the key into the ignition, he fired it up the engine. It instantly growled like a true V8 should. He was itching to take it for a drive but thought the better of it until he'd updated his driver's licence.

Looking in the rear-view mirror, he noticed someone appear behind the car. She was carrying a box of dried cat food in one hand and his newly acquired pet in the other. In her pocket were no doubt the papers Dorothy had asked her to forward. He switched the car off then introduced himself.

'Hi, Pam, is it? I'm Alan Holmes,' he said, extending his hand.

'Nice to meet you, Alan. Yes, I'm Pam. Dorothy told me all about you. Did you have a good flight?' she asked, handing him the cat food.

'Yeah, not bad, I suppose,' he answered in his broad Aussie accent.

'The cat misses Dorothy,' she said, handing him over, 'though he'll soon get used to you.' Pam also passed him the paperwork so he could sort out the car registration and so forth. Alan thanked her for being the go-between. As she had food cooking on the stove, she said her goodbyes then walked back to her place. *What a charming, good-looking woman,* he thought.

Scotty arrived early the next morning as planned. 'Let me be your tour guide to Astrospace Galexiana,' he announced as Alan hopped in the car. 'I'll do my best not to bore you. Probably the most important thing you'll learn is where the staff amenities are located. We happen to have one of the most expensive coffee machines imaginable; it must have nearly killed Big Mal having to fork out for it.'

'Very well.' Alan laughed. 'I'm looking forward to a cappuccino on arrival.'

The radio telescope facility was situated in the hills behind Big Bear Lake, serviced by good bitumen about half an hour away from where they lived. They were fast approaching the security gate, so Scotty shifted to a lower gear, slowing the car. 'This is your first initiation,' he explained. 'Wait till you meet Willy. He's the blackest African security guard you will have ever seen. He was born in a small village somewhere in Africa, though his family were so poor they fostered him out to a couple in Texas. The rest is history. Somehow his early hardships turned him into a very likeable human being.'

Alan was intrigued by this Willy.

Scotty kept talking. 'All you have to do on arrival is punch in your pin number, then he'll open the electric gate – that is, when he's good and ready. Usually you have to chat to him for a while before he'll let you in. The same goes coming out, come to think of it.'

They pulled up in front of the gate. Out strolled Willy from his cubicle. 'Hi, Scotty,' he grinned, showing the whitest teeth Alan had ever seen. 'Who is this knight in shinin' armour ridin' shot gun?' Scotty introduced Alan and asked Willy to prepare a pin for him.

'Make sure you remember it, Alan, otherwise I might get confused when you arrive and shoot ya.' His smile widened even further to show he was joking. Willy then bowed as they drove through the entrance, then hit the close button, the gate clanging shut behind them.

'What's the bow all about?' Alan asked.

Scotty glanced at him. 'How would I know? Last week he was saluting! Like I said, he's a funny guy.'

'Where to now?' Alan asked. 'Can we try that coffee machine?'

They had a coffee, which was actually pretty good, and Scotty then introduced him to one very important CEO. Big Mal sat behind his big desk, expressionless. Alan sensed that, despite his intimidating appearance, the man was mostly all bluff. He just had a sixth sense when it came to reading people.

'Welcome to Astrospace Galexiana, Alan. You will be working with Scotty most of the time, so I'm pleased that you have already met. If you go next door, you can talk to Carol and rearrange the roster. After that, I suggest Scotty familiarises you with the equipment you will be using. Thank you, gentlemen.' Big Mal turned back to what he had been doing. They were dismissed.

They left Big Mal's office then headed towards Carol's office, stopping to talk along the way at a water cooler. 'What's with his gold earring and shaved head?' Alan asked.

Scotty just shrugged. 'Don't know. I think he just likes to look the formidable type. I happened to pull up at a red light some time back, and there was Big Mal on this huge Harley Davidson right beside me. First time I've seen him in a short sleeve shirt. Believe it or not, he's got a whole lot of tattoos on his arms. He's never ridden his Harley to work though. He always rocks up in his Mercedes and parks in the only covered car park we've got. Built exclusively for him thanks to Galexiana.'

Alan just shook his head. 'He's a kettle of fish, alright. How about his subtleness on our parting! He may as well have said, "Piss off, gentlemen".'

With the roster in place after stopping in to see Carol, they started walking to the observatory. The observatory was a small walk from Admin, separated by various garden beds, most of which grew an array of multi-coloured flowers.

'Okay, Al. Let me show you how this works. Before you can enter the observatory, you have to activate the door by entering the same pin you punched in for Willy. The pin is exclusively yours. It opens everything in the establishment, leaving behind a footprint of everywhere you've been. Give it a go.' Alan walked up to the wall beside the door then entered his pin. The door immediately slid sideways then closed behind them.

'Now I'll give you a crash course, so to speak, though except for the odd activation switch, everything is computerised. The whole operation runs from the main computer or computers, depending what you're doing. You would have used similar systems and programs back home, I'm sure. The software we're using is like any other. Once you get to know the ins and outs of it, you're away. If you open the computer, I'll give you a few demos.'

Alan typed his pin in to the computer. In no time at all he had picked up on everything. It was all second nature thanks to his previous training. In the unlikely event he got into trouble, Scotty gave him the okay to phone any time of the day or night.

Unbeknown to Scotty during his crash course, Alan was also working out the best method to secretively transmit his digitally enhanced Morse code. So far, he thought it wasn't going to be a major problem. The only problem he could foresee was how much Scotty would take to it. One thing he had learnt so far was that Big Mal certainly wouldn't condone using Galexiana's facilities unless he paid the fees commanded. Even if he did pay the fees, if Big Mal were like most of the doubters at Wallaby Heights in 1969, there was a big chance he wouldn't consent to using the DEMC program no matter who wanted to pay to use the facility.

A few weeks went by before Alan got the chance to introduce Scotty to his DEMC project. He instinctively felt that he could trust Scotty with the information about this. He and Scotty had become fast friends as well as close-working colleagues, so Alan now reckoned it was time to broach the subject.

They were working together, looking at the Orion constellation. Scotty spoke first. 'I like working in this part of the universe, Alan. I've been studying a star called Bellatrix. I'm sure you've heard of it?'

Alan nodded. 'Yes, it's the third brightest star in the Orion constellation.'

Scotty then gave him the opportunity he needed when he said, 'I'm about to start looking at an area further afield. There are a couple of planets that could possibly support life. Maybe not extra-terrestrial, but life in some form or another. Imagine finding extra-terrestrial life! Do you think it's possible?'

'I sure do,' Alan replied, telling him about the 1969 Wallaby Heights UFO sighting.

Scotty stared at him in surprise. 'Wow, I was only reading about that a couple of months ago. Did you really see the whole thing?'

'I didn't only see it, I was the first at my school to see it,' chuckled Alan.

'Do you really believe they were aliens?'

'I most definitely do,' affirmed Alan. 'There is nothing surer in my mind. I'd tell you about a similar event that occurred a few years earlier, yet it's time consuming. I'll fill you in on it later.' Scotty looked disappointed, but they both had a lot of work to get through, so Alan left it at that.

Another week went by before an opportunity arose for Alan to bring up his DEMC project. They were having a few beers together at their local bar.

'I've been lined up with the Orion constellation again,' Scotty announced out of the blue. 'I kept these Japanese students intrigued all night. One of them had a similar experience to you. He thinks he saw a UFO hovering above his uncle's cherry tree orchard back in Japan. Maybe you should get together to compare notes.'

Phil Muirhead

'I don't mind. I'd rather talk to someone who believes than try convince a sceptic,' Alan agreed.

Scotty grinned. 'I hope I'm not coming across as a sceptic, Al. It's just that I have never come close to seeing anything, not even a light in the distance. I've often thought how I would like to have some sort of interaction with someone out there though, especially after a lifetime monitoring the heavens. Did you know they've done a survey on astrophysicists and astronomers? Ninety per cent of those surveyed believed there is intelligent extraterrestrial life out there.'

This is my opening Alan thought to himself, taking a deep breath. 'You might be able to get involved in my DEMC project, if that's the case. Now I know there is only a ten per cent chance you will turn me down.'

Scotty leaned forward in his chair. 'What do you mean? What does DEMC stand for?'

'It stands for digitally enhanced Morse code. I put this software together to beam out yonder as I thought I might be able to attract some attention from another civilisation.' Alan sat back, waiting for Scotty's reply.

'You've got to be joking, Al. Even if you did succeed, you would be dead and buried centuries before it ever got to them. There's no disputing that, you of all people know it.' Scotty looked incredulous.

'I wasn't planning on sending the signals far. I'm thinking that provided transmission is audible and decipherable, it's just possible there are beings with technology above and beyond ours who can latch on to the radio signals, decipher them then respond pronto.'

Scotty encouraged him to go on. 'Look at it like this. If they can get here then it's reasonable to assume they can also return to where they came from, do you agree? Or do you think they embark on a suicide journey that lasts a thousand years with no return trip? Of course not. There is speed involved, speed so fast it's beyond our comprehension. I've seen it in action even with the weight of the earth's gravity. The craft I saw lift off was out of sight in a millisecond. Imagine the speed it would be capable of after it shed the pull of our earth's gravity.'

Scotty was intrigued now, Alan could see it. He hadn't been wrong about Scotty. 'So what has this got to do with your DEMC idea?'

'Okay, compare how fast we can travel with how fast we send radio waves. Say we fly our fastest aircraft between Sydney and Los Angeles. It still takes a fair amount of time, though you can cover the same distance almost instantly by phone. Given the technology a smarter race may have at their disposal, it's quite possible they could already be beaming transmissions to us, waiting for a day when we are further advanced and capable of interacting.'

It was now apparent to Alan that Scotty was very interested in his theory. 'OK, I get where you're coming from. Do you want some input from me while you conduct your wild experiment, is that it?'

'Not unless you don't want to be involved. All I want to do is use Galexiana's equipment without anyone knowing.'

'You realise if we get caught, we're joining the instant dismissal brigade,' Scotty warned.

'Wrong, not we. Me. I'll cop the rap. Although if you think about it, I'm going to have to be super unlucky to get caught.' Alan took another sip of his beer.

'What about the computer technicians? They might pick up on something that's out of the ordinary?' Scotty was going to need a bit more convincing.

'On all accounts, they would assume it to be part of our work, wouldn't they?'

Scotty mulled his words over. Then he relented. 'Probably. Alright, Al, I'll go along with it. I just hope I can keep a straight face when I talk to Big Mal after it's up and running!' There was no love lost between Scotty and Big Mal.

Alan visibly relaxed. 'Thanks, mate. I'll download everything to the computer next time I get a quiet night. I'm positive we are going to make contact. I just have a feeling.' He was so relieved that Scotty was on board.

After leaving the bar, Alan turned into his drive and parked the car. As he walked to his front door, he heard a voice calling after him. It was his lovely next-door neighbour Pam, carrying a washing basket full of clothes. 'Hi Alan, have you settled in?' she asked politely. Gosh, she was a good-looking woman alright. She must have been a bit younger than him, though possibly not by much. Mid-forties, maybe. Her rich chestnut hair was piled into a messy bun at the nape of her neck, with loose strands framing her petite face. She couldn't be more than five foot five. Her eyes were a vivid green and always seemed so kind. He wondered what she did for a living, or if she had a partner. He hadn't seen anyone coming or going, so this was a good sign that she hadn't.

He realised he was staring at her but hadn't answered her question. Hastily, he spoke. 'I'm very happy with everything. Work has been keeping me busy though.'

'How's the cat?' she asked.

After he responded, she opened her door, disappearing inside with the washing, leaving Alan in anticipation of further conversation, which unfortunately never happened.

After letting himself inside, realising that Pam wasn't going to return for more small talk, his thoughts gravitated towards his DEMC project. For the very first time, he was questioning the sanity of his project. 'What am I doing?' he kept asking himself. 'Probably risking two perfectly good jobs for no gain whatsoever.' Still, he was determined. His gut feeling said he needed to press ahead with this opportunity. After all, this was the real reason he'd travelled so far away from his daughters and friends. He couldn't head back to Australia without trying.

A week later, Alan turned into Galexiana's driveway, then slowed to a stop at the security gate. Willy was full of life as usual. They had fallen into a routine of friendly banter over the weeks Alan had worked there.

He drove in, knowing Scotty wouldn't be far away. They had a big night ahead with a group of students that required them both to be there. Scotty would position the telescope as required. Alan would do a running commentary on the unfolding events. It would be a bit like the lectures he had to do back at the university. After settling himself in the observatory, he started preparing the notes he could refer to during his lecture, when Scotty strolled in.

In all, twenty students arrived by bus. They were from the United Arab Emirates and were booked for two nights. It would be quite a good earner for the company. The night unfolded as planned, and everything went like clockwork. The interpreter the university provided was brilliant. He was one of those people who knew how to break the ice between others without being a nuisance. Somehow he removed the serious aspect of their studies, replacing it with a more convivial, lighter atmosphere, which made the night more enjoyable for everyone present.

The night ended as quickly as it started. Scotty suggested to Alan that they have a coffee before they go. Almost immediately, he steered the conversation to the DEMC project. 'What's happening with DEMC?' Scotty asked. 'If you installed it on the computer, you've done a great job of hiding it.'

Alan laughed. 'No nothing like that. I just haven't had time to implement anything. I've been booked up with student groups since we spoke.'

Scotty leaned in so they could talk without being overheard. 'I've been thinking about what you said, Alan. We both know there's intelligent life out there. They are more than likely to get to us via your method than us being able to contact them via conventional methods that we won't be around to administer. Your DEMC project is nothing short of brilliant. I think we need to implement it as soon as we can.'

Alan said nothing for a full minute before responding. 'OK then. I'll bring it with me to our next shift. We'll download it and start transmission when everyone leaves. Just keep the consequences in mind. If the shit hits the fan, we could both end up in the ranks of the unemployed.'

Phil Muirhead

'So we'll get another job.' This was Scotty's short and only comment.

That night's work was similar to the previous night, with the Orion Nebular consuming most of their time. The students were fascinated by the enormity of the dust gas and debris accumulated over huge time spans. It was truly an experience to behold – the clouds of gas and dust were speckled with newly formed stars, a kaleidoscope of magical properties glistening from within, emanating colours only Mother Nature could have produced.

The students were also intrigued when Alan told them that Scotty was about to move the scope to an interesting area they had been recently observing, some 150 light years behind the Orion Belt.

'It's the type of system we think could support life,' he told them. Alan was aware that using extra-terrestrial life as a talking point always livened up debate, thus creating a more interesting evening. It was so easy for him to throw in terms such as 'possible life', 'aliens' and 'extra-terrestrial civilisations' as a precursor for debate as it pricked everyone's imagination, making the night more enjoyable for all concerned.

Unlike the first night, the students packed it in early. They had a plane to catch mid-morning and opted for some shut-eye prior to take off, which left Alan and Scotty plenty of time to download the DEMC program before setting it in motion. Like two naughty schoolboys, they sat together finetuning the DEMC to the ten different frequencies they considered most detectable to whomever might be listening.

'This might sound silly, Al, but do you know I have no idea what your message equates to.'

'Let me enlighten you. Don't laugh though as it's purposefully very simple. It says, "My name is Alan Holmes. I am from Planet Earth. After you decode this transmission, please return a message without changing the frequency. Thank you." Sort of sounds like an email, don't you think?'

Scotty did laugh at that. 'It's not the content we need to be worried about, Al, it's the end result.'

It was breaking dawn before they had everything ready to activate, then all that was required was the simple click of a mouse.

'Come on, you do the honours. It's your baby. One click and it's away,' Scotty encouraged Alan.

With a touch of nervousness, Alan moved the curser to activate the prompt, then click! They shook hands, congratulating themselves on their covert achievements. Both were more than aware they had started something that was impossible to reverse. Even if they did decide to stop transmission, there was no way they could undo what had already been done.

'We better check the graph before we go,' Scotty suggested.

Alan clicked on another prompt, activating one of the monitors connected to the telescope's main computer. A series of graph lines came into view moving up and down, similar to a seismograph. At the same time, the graph moved slowly across the screen. Should it ever change, the software had a built-in watchdog that would alert the user by leaving the changed graph on a separate section of the monitor below the actual graph. It would also leave the time and position when the change occurred, making it easy to find and re-decipher, should the result be a return message. The software they installed was now silently running in the background without affecting Galexiana's many projects.

Alan clicked on the monitor prompt, turning the monitor off. 'Let's go, Scotty. It's all working fine. There's nothing left to do except wait and see.'

The sun was shining brightly as Alan turned into Hudson Close, passing Pam in her car just before he turned into his driveway. She flicked a cute finger wave as she drove past, causing Alan's thoughts to roam. The previous owner was right. Pam was a top lady. He wondered why she didn't seem to have a bloke in her life. Or perhaps she did yet he worked away. Pam thoughts kept swirling in his mind until he fell asleep. Six hours later, he woke to a rap on the front door. To his complete surprise, it was his sister Fiona.

Phil Muirhead

Alan laughed out loud, delighted to see his younger sibling. It had been years since they'd seen each other in person. 'Fiona, what are you doing here? What a wonderful surprise.' She gave him a big hug. 'I came to look at my house,' she chuckled. 'God, it's good to see you, Al. How are the girls?'

Leading her inside, Alan told her how they were both planning on visiting over Christmas. He wanted to know what Fiona was doing so far from Texas. She told him she'd had a seminar in Los Angeles, so she thought she'd hire a car and drive to Big Bear to see him.

They talked for hours about family and past events, until she had to drive to the airport to catch her plane. They decided that Alan and the girls would come to Dallas for a visit over the Christmas holidays. He was also under strict instruction to visit her and the family in Dallas in the meantime. It was only a two-hour flight away. He kissed her goodbye before she drove off then waved until she was out of sight. *Mum would be so proud of her,* he thought. *She might have arrived fourteen years late, though she was worth waiting for.* Her husband sure was fortunate to have ended up with someone as easy-going and fun-loving as Fiona.

As he walked back to the house, he noticed Pam watching him from her kitchen window. *She probably thinks I've found myself a girlfriend,* he thought, wondering how many men have sisters who are special friends. The age gap between them had caused a complete absence of childhood rivalry, which had resulted in a wonderfully close friendship when Fiona grew up.

THREE

Scotty was rostered on for the weekend, doing scheduled maintenance work on the telescope's movable parts. Occasionally, he would wander back to the control room to check whether his DEMC was behaving as expected. He was watching the graph on the fourth frequency when a voice from behind gave him a fright. It was Jan the Janitor, standing behind him with a mop and bucket ready for action, or Jan the Jan, as she had been affectionately dubbed. 'You'll have to teach me how to work all this stuff one day, Scotty,' she jested.

'I'll have to teach myself first,' he joked.

'What do all those lines mean?' she asked, pointing to the moving graph.

'Oh, they only show up when we try to talk with aliens,' Scotty said, grinning from ear to ear.

Jan laughed, considering his answer in jest. 'Seriously, Scotty, how can those squiggly lines possibly mean anything?'

'They don't in this form, it's only a graph,' he explained as he shut the monitor down. He didn't want her showing any more interest.

'Now, I presume you want me out of here while you mop the floor, is that right?'

'Correct! Now buzz off and don't come back until it's dry or I'll hit you with my mop. Oh, if you're talking to Alan, please tell him not to post notices on the staff room notice board referring to Big Mal as Big Malfunction.' She sniggered. Scotty just laughed, darting around Jan the Jan's mop while making for the door.

Sunday afternoon was a good time for Alan and Scotty to get together. The local bar was now their favourite venue. It was close to where they lived. More importantly, it was quiet with private tables and booths placed strategically around the perimeter of the lounge bar. The environment suited perfectly when DEMC discussions were underway.

Today was no different. Scotty told Al about Jan the Jan sneaking up on him, wanting to know what the squiggly lines represented. 'I wanted to stay there and check out frequency four,' he admitted. 'There was a discrepancy in every fourth frame except in the very first set of frames transmitted, which incidentally was the only one we watched before leaving. I went back only to find Jan still cleaning the windows. By then it was getting late so I left.'

Alan leaned forward. 'What sort of discrepancy?'

'Strangely enough, the type we are looking for. The problem is, it's been there right from the beginning of transmission, except the very first sequence of ten we transmitted. It's happening with every transmission at exactly the same time and at exactly the same strength. The graph's inconsistency is the same on each occasion. What are your thoughts, Al?'

'I would have to say it's a software glitch if it's been happening from the beginning.'

'Maybe,' Scotty agreed, 'though why didn't it do it in the very first transmission sequence?'

Alan took a moment to ponder his question. 'I don't know. It probably needed the first sequence to compare, then recur, but had issues doing so.'

Disappointment marking his features, Scotty said, 'You're probably right, still check it out just the same, then let me know what you think.'

The Believer

Alan told him he'd look into it the following night.

He couldn't get to work quickly enough the next night. Scotty's description of the DEMC events had made him anxious. He pulled alongside Willy's cubicle to wait for him. Without warning, Willy burst into song from within his cubicle. 'Twinkle, twinkle little star, how Al wonders where you are. Up above the scope at night, making money out of sight.'

Alan laughed out loud. He wondered where Willy got his sense of humour from. He really should be working as a comedian as he was a natural, certainly making the start and finish of every work day entertaining.

It was a quiet night with no students booked in, so Alan's main chores revolved around experimental work for a Chinese company who were building components for viewing space from satellites. If all went well, he only needed a few hours, then he would look at the DEMC graph. He finished at midnight then headed for the coffee machine, progressing towards the control room, coffee in one hand and a file full of paperwork in the other.

Before he did anything, he walked to a window that allowed him to overlook the car park. His was the only car in sight. The only other person on site was Willy, who was watching television, made apparent by the flickering of light coming from his cubicle windows. 'What a great night for a DEMC experience,' he told himself out loud at the same time livening up the graph's monitor.

'Now what's this discrepancy Scotty's on about in frame four?' Alan wondered out loud again.

Checking the data, Alan realised Scotty was right. Surely someone out there wouldn't have picked up on his signal during the very first transmission of ten frames? He thought it still had to be a computer glitch or software problem of some sort, but how? Why? All ten frames were set up exactly the same. It looked like they were just going to have to put up with it and only use nine frames or risk damaging the other nine frames trying to fix it.

Phil Muirhead

He clicked on a prompt to display the last signal sent on frame four. The graph sat motionless until the next series of ten were sent, starting the sequence transmission all over again. Another prompt allowed him to activate frame four in its own right, jamming out the other nine spasmodic signals. He sat deep in thought, wondering if he should activate or delete. If this had happened over the last couple of days, he would have activated it without giving a second thought, so he clicked on the button.

The graph kept moving non-stop, the tiny discrepancy now clearer than before. The scale of the graph now automatically increased when used singularly. Below the graph, two parallel lines appeared. Both lines were about half an inch apart. Every time the software detected a discrepancy, a tiny portion of the graph dropped below, staying locked between the parallel lines. Time for another coffee, Alan convinced himself, leaving the monitor running.

Sipping his coffee, he tracked back to the control room, passing a sign that warned 'Strictly no food or beverage past this point'. He placed his coffee near the monitor, noticing there were a series of separate sections of the graph present between the parallel lines.

'Holy shit!' he muttered. 'What's this all about. Something has gone amiss big time.' He saw that the fourth frame was out of whack again. Alan wondered what on earth it was doing. Another section dropped into the parallel lines changing every frame of transmission. Alan's comprehension was waning. Rivulets of sweat were making their way down his forehead and neck. 'Something has to be wrong,' he kept saying out loud. 'This can't be for real! If not, what the hell do I do next? Good lord, I've done all this without thinking of how to respond!'

He started pacing from one end of the room to the other, not noticing further changes between the parallel lines, changes that would resolve his inability to respond. Finally, he re-gathered his composure, noticing a distinct message between the lines. Moving closer to the screen, he saw that the graph between the lines had been transformed into a simple message. It read: **My name**

Chez, female, Planet Univiah, deep in Galaxy Milky Way. I learn Earth talk better for back speak.

Alan's jaw dropped open. He couldn't believe what he was reading. How could this be possible! All of his theories were related to super intelligent species yet he never expected anything like this. Then he realised that his thirteen-year-old self had. Having seen an actual spaceship on that fateful day back in 1969, his younger self had expected something exactly like this. His adult self had expected a response in code using DEMC. Alan looked at the screen again, making sure he wasn't imagining the unfolding events. However, the words were still there, a cursor flashing after the last word as if to say, 'Type something yourself.'

Gathering his wits, he started typing. Nothing happened. Maybe the cursor was there on her account, not his? He got up and kept pacing, thinking out loud as he roamed back and forth, sipping his sweet black coffee while asking himself what was next. All he could do was wait for her. After all, she was the one with the technology. Doubt started to enter his thoughts. Maybe this was a complete software problem after all? Yet it wasn't possible for software to start performing in its own style by itself. Crikey. Maybe he'd caused the first known response of Artificial Intelligence. Question after question entered his mind, questions he wasn't deciphering properly. Questions he didn't have an answer for.

Then he decided it must be a practical joke that Scotty had played. There was still no response from 'Chez' so, his shift now over, Alan drove home. He was wired and instinctively wanted to phone Scotty to give him a piece of his mind. However, it was better to wait and look him in the eye, even if it was just to see how he reacted.

Scotty's shifts had been during the day, while Alan's were all nights, so he had to wait until it was Sunday. Time for their usual get together at the local bar. Alan was running late so found Scotty in a corner watching baseball on television. He walked towards him, trying hard not to smile or grin, though it was useless. The humour of Scotty's antics still made him laugh. Scotty, noticing his cheerfulness, made a comment, 'You look happy today. Don't tell me, you've finally got around to giving that gal next door a cuddle?'

Sitting down, Alan said, 'Knock it off, Scotty. You know exactly where the humour is coming from.'

'Beg your pardon, Alan. Fill me in, what's going on?' Scotty was staring at him, a quizzical expression on his face.

'You know what's going on! That was brilliant. You had me believing every bit of it right down to the phoney wording she, I mean, you, wrote into the software. You could be making a lot more money with your skills, Scotty. What a magnificent piece of skillful preparation.'

Scotty just sat there dumbfounded, looking at Alan over his glasses. 'I have no idea what's been swaying your mental capacity, Alan, but I can assure you it's nothing I've done.'

'C'mon, Scotty, you know what I'm talking about. It's OK. I really see the humour in it.'

His colleague was now looking annoyed. 'Perhaps you should inform me where and how the humour originated as well as who provided it, because I really don't have a clue what you're talking about.'

There was something about Scotty's demeanour that told Alan he was sincere. They both eyed one another, wondering who was going to speak first. It was Alan. 'Maybe it was for real,' he blurted without explaining.

'What was for real? You're not making any sense.' Scotty stared him down.

'Well, you know how you were asking me to take a look at frame four? I livened it up on its own account and received contact, though the question is from whom? She says her name is Chez and that she's from Planet Univiah. She also said she's going to learn our language then get back to me.' Scotty choked on his beer as he was taking a sip, so Alan had to wait out his coughing fit.

'You're kidding me, right?'

The look on Alan's face said it all. He wasn't kidding. 'I won't say any more, just take a look on your next shift.'

'Hang on, hang on, let's put all of this into perspective. Explain it all to me so we can deal with it together.'

Alan and Scotty spent the next hour going over the procedures they had activated, discussing possibilities, theories, previous events, comparisons, anything that could lead to solving their predicament. Nothing rang true except that they were now on common ground. Scotty looked at Alan over his glasses. It was a stereotype look he only used when concerned. 'Okay, Alan, I'll have a look first thing in the morning, then I'll phone you. We certainly can't start showing up on Sunday unannounced.'

Scotty arrived at work the next morning and headed straight to the control room. His first task was to reactivate the computer using the same format Alan had used before he thought it all a practical joke. He then phoned Alan, his voice one of concern. 'Alan, it's for real all right. Not only is it real, but the cursor at the end of her message is now working. I only typed in the letter T, and it's still sitting there waiting for your presence. What do you want me to do?' Alan could hear the nervous excitement in Scotty's voice.

'Start by typing something like, This is Alan.'

'Alan, I'd rather you do all this. It's your baby, your DEMC, so I'd say she'd prefer to speak to the Alan who put this all together. Besides, she undoubtedly knows you're the instigator. I think you should try responding at the exact same time of night you received her message. If typing doesn't work, convert the message back to the DEMC code you originally used to attract her attention. Although I doubt that will be necessary considering she used the English language to communicate in the first place. I can assure you of one thing, Alan. We're dealing with a species who have intelligence and resources beyond anything we can imagine.'

Alan was sweating now. 'Tell me, Scotty, do you think we're going to be able to keep a lid on all of this?'

Scotty was silent for a few moments, then spoke. 'In the short term, we have no option. Just imagine the implications world-wide if this gets out without proper explanation. Us being the only two people on Earth who can literally talk to another civili-sation. We sure have bitten off more than we can chew. Pity we didn't think of the consequences before we started something we can't stop!'

It was the unknown creating the anxiety, not knowing where to turn next, not knowing what would transpire, not knowing if a computer tech would stumble upon their secret, not knowing what to do or who to turn to. It concerned them more than they imagined possible. In the back of their minds were two nagging thoughts, *What the hell have we started? If only we had given this more thought in the first place.*

Alan drove zombie-like to work, the thoughts in his head so intense he could only remember parts of the journey. Stopping at Willy's cubicle was a temporary reprieve. Willy was his usual self, wanting to have an ongoing chat. He turned the engine off, de-ciding to chat. Willy was rapt.

FOUR

The night dragged on with inquisitive tourists lining up one by one to look at the heavens, all asking Alan the same questions as the ones before. Usually Alan offered everybody a coffee before they left, though tonight he decided not to, figuring the sooner he dealt with the DEMC the sooner he could leave himself. He waved as they left, returning to the coffee machine and taking a cappuccino back to the control room.

The monitor flickered into life. Nothing had changed since Scotty last typed the letter T to begin a new sentence. *Why am I feeling so nervous,* he wondered as he sat poised to click the mouse. He started typing, watching his fingers involuntarily shaking as the words appeared: 'This is Alan. If you have learnt our language, please contact me again.' He sipped at his coffee, holding the cup with both hands while watching the screen in anticipation. It seemed a ridiculous statement. How could she learn our language in the first place, let alone in a few days?

He had just finished his coffee when his cell phone rang. It was Scotty. He couldn't sleep so thought he'd check in with Alan. About to end the call, Scotty heard a yell.

'Hang on! Scotty, don't go anywhere. Something's going on here. The cursor has moved along about half an inch.' Scotty wanted to know if any words were forming.

'Not yet. It's blinking on and off, so something or somebody must have moved it. Wait! We have the letter G, make that Greetings.' Alan couldn't believe his eyes. His heart rate was almost tachycardic.

A string of words then appeared next to the cursor: **Greetings, Alan. This is Chez.**

Scotty was yelling into the phone now. 'What else? Any more? Anything else? Alan, answer me!'

'Wait, Scotty, it's forming really slowly now. OK, she says she's worked out our language yet she is having problems holding the signal.' Alan watched the screen intently.

'Now it says not to alter anything at our end. She will re-contact when it's fixed.'

Scotty was just as blown away as Alan. He promised he'd come in early to try and fix any problems with it. Alan made sure that Scotty would phone him the minute anything happened. As he headed home after his shift, he knew he wasn't going to get any sleep.

Scotty arrived at Galexiana earlier than usual. Anticipating the unknown, he walked briskly to the control room, not having a clue what to expect. *Could it have come back on?* he wondered. If so, the screen saver should have taken over, or maybe it was hibernating. He rubbed the mouse with his right hand, at the same time pressing on the keyboard with his left. Nothing happened, so instinctively he checked the connections. It had power to all of the connections, they were tight in place. What on earth! Did this happen on her account or did the computer blow a fuse? The only option was to shut it down then liven it up again. No, she said not to alter anything. That she will be in contact when she has fixed the signal. *What signal?* he pondered. Ours or hers? Hers, I'd say.

The Believer

A feeling of bewilderment had come over Scotty, or was it helplessness? Whatever it was, it was taking its toll. He hadn't been sleeping. His concentration span had also diminished while trying to adapt to his increased mental activity. 'I wonder how Alan's holding up?' he asked himself, his thoughts playing havoc. We've locked ourselves in to something we can't get out of. Although I'm sure once we start talking with Chez, our situation will vastly improve. She has to be super intelligent to have accomplished this. One thing was for sure, she wouldn't compromise now she'd gotten this far. Even if they pulled the plug on the whole affair, she knew how to contact Astrospace Galexiana. *Where would that leave us?*

They had no option except to hang in there. There was nothing worse than being out on a limb, not knowing where you're going or what's going to happen. He prepared a note, his thoughts running rampant, then draped the note over the monitor's screen. It read, 'Monitor and computer connected to software. Please use another.' At least that would keep everyone away from our antics, he figured.

Alan phoned Scotty at midday. 'Any developments?' he asked, his voice breaking in nervous anticipation.

'No. It's just as you left it. I'm wondering if the monitor might have shit itself?'

Alan assured Scotty he'd check everything as soon as he got to work, so Scotty reluctantly went about his day.

Before heading out to work, Alan called into a drug store hoping to obtain some relief for his anxiety-come-sleeplessness. He walked back to his car, stopping at a bar to buy a packet of peanuts and a water to help wash the pills down. Amazingly, by the time he reached work, he had settled down. The pills were actually having an effect.

Phil Muirhead

On arrival, he went straight to the control room, opened the door then sat down in front of the monitor. Within seconds, it came to life without any input from Alan. The graph moved, the parallel lines formed and the cursor flickered to life all at once. Slowly, a message formed.

Chez: Greetings Alan. I am sorry about the delays. I had a problem interfacing your radio signals. Please remember to separate each sentence by a space as you type, then wait for a small delay. Do you have any questions?

Alan sat there totally dumbfounded. He was experiencing the same feeling he'd had at age thirteen, when he'd walked towards his mates with the football. Like he was somehow detached from reality, even though his mind was racing. He wanted to type, yet his mind wouldn't slow enough for him to do so. Eventually, he regained his composure, his hand shaking uncontrollably as he typed.

Alan: I certainly do. How are you able to do this given the distance between us?

Chez: Alan, there is no distance between us, only area.

Alan: Chez, I don't quite understand.

Chez: I know you don't. We will go into it later.

Alan had so many questions he wanted to ask that he didn't quite know where to begin. His fingers flew over the keyboard in an attempt to keep up with his mind.

Alan: How far from Earth are you?

Chez: We are 1,695 Earth light years from Planet Earth.

The Believer

Alan: This is totally unbelievable!

Chez: I understand it is unbelievable to you, Alan. To us, it's perfectly understandable.

Alan: Exactly where are you?

Chez: Alan, what I say to you is governed by a super systems manager that monitors everything I say. If I tell you exactly where we are, it will automatically be scrambled. Everything I say is monitored and filtered by Metropolis Central. We have four Metropolis Centrals. All are controlled by Univiah's elders.

Alan: What are elders?

Chez: You have to be 200 years old before you can become an elder. When you do become an elder, it is customary to place an O at the end of your name. The purpose of an O at the end of your name is to make elders easy to identify within our community.

Alan: That's incredible. Please tell me about the four Metropolis Centrals.

Chez: They are the hubs of our society. All are linked to one another by a super systems manager so intricate and powerful it's beyond your understanding.

Alan decided to redirect his questioning.

Alan: Are you going to ask about Planet Earth?

Chez: I already know much about your planet. When we get more time, I would certainly like to ask questions about your species.

Alan: Can we speak at any time?

Chez: Yes. I have an alarm that will let me know if you are trying to contact me.

Alan: I need to use Galexiana's facilities to remain in contact. There is no way I can reverse the alarm system to allow you to contact me. I have to physically be here.

Chez: I understand. From now on, when you decide to contact me, write the code word Univ-Al before you wish to talk. This will alert me. You can use any program you wish, provided it has a cursor. If you use the same device you are using now, we will have no further communication problems. I expect you have many more questions

Alan: I have many questions. Does your physical appearance look anything like ours?

He watched the screen intently for her reply.

Chez: In a way, Alan. We have bodies just like you. We have arms and legs that perform the same functions as yours. We also have organs similar to yours. We have fingers and toes, and our organic structure is held together by bones similar to yours. We have luminescent silvery skin yet no hair whatsoever, and we are taller than you. On average, you would come up to our shoulders. Our eyes are larger than yours, but our ears, mouth, nose and chin are much less pronounced. None of us is obese, unlike some of your species.

Alan: Thank you for sharing this, Chez. May I ask, do you wear clothing?

Chez: Yes, we do. Our clothing is slightly elastic. It fits snugly to our bodies for comfort, and our clothes are always the same colour as our skin. Don't ask me why, I could never imagine Univians wearing colourful clothes. We also have high-tech clothes for space travel. These garments look exactly like the ones we wear at home, only they have self-cleansing abilities to always keep us at a constant temperature. Do have more questions, Alan?

Alan: I'm bound to. I just need time to think straight. I also have to go to work. Please excuse me. I have greatly enjoyed talking to you.

Chez: No problem. I will speak with you whenever you alert my alarm. Goodbye, Alan of Earth.

Alan sat motionless in front of the monitor, both elbows on the arm of the chair, his hands cupped around his forehead with his mind somersaulting. 'Where is all this leading?' he asked himself, the 'what if' factor foremost on his mind. 'What if we go public? What if Scotty decides we should inform Big Mal? What if we ignore Big Mal and go straight to the media? What if Chez recommends another procedure? What if we ignore every other "what if' and keep Chez our celestial secret?'

It didn't matter how he looked at it, the 'what if' factor was a major player within his mind. To add to his anxiety, Alan had spent a lifetime hating 'what ifs' and 'if onlys'. Apart from his anxiety, Alan was elated his meeting with Chez had gone so well. Feeling somewhat settled, he phoned Scotty then told him about the contact. Scotty was elated, although also a bit anxious about the implications of all this.

Both Alan and Scotty arrived at the observatory the next night. After taking a group of Chinese students on a tour, they were now ready to contact Chez again. Pulling up a chair each, they strategically placed themselves in front of the monitor and keyboard. Alan entered the code 'Univ-Al'. They both sat in silence for at least a minute. Scotty was about to ask Alan if he had entered the correct password when the first words appeared.

Chez: Hello, Alan. Do you have company?

Alan: Yes. How did you know?

Chez: I assumed. Now I know. Are you going to introduce me to your friend?

Alan: Yes. Chez, this is Dave, better known as Scotty.

Chez: Hello, Scotty. It's good to have your input.

Scotty seized the opportunity to type back.

Scotty: Alan tells me you know all about Planet Earth. What interests you most?

Chez: Your people, mainly. Humankind is a very strange, erratic species.

Scotty: Why do you say that?

Chez: I can give you a million examples though one will do for now. I cannot understand why you people sit in those huge, heavy vehicles then hurtle down the road towards one another, just missing each other by the smallest of margins. Surely you must know you should at least all be going in the same direction to help lessen the consequences of the horrific accidents you continually subject yourselves to?

Scotty: We understand your concern, but it would be too costly to provide this type of road network.

Chez: So you spend your resources on funerals and new vehicles instead?

Scotty: Unfortunately, yes. How do you know we drive like this? Are you able to watch us?

Chez: Yes, your satellite television network is easy for me to tune into. It provides so much information. So too does your internet service.

Alan jumped back on the keyboard and started typing. Of the two, he was the quicker typist.

Alan: What are your people like? Do you have wars, conflicts or uprisings?

Chez: Never! We live in complete harmony. Ours is a society of love and continual peace. Nobody would ever think of doing an injustice to a fellow citizen.

Alan: Are we allowed to ask personal questions?

Chez: Certainly. Go ahead.

Alan: How old are you? Do you have family?

Chez: I'm 65 in Univian years. I live with my parents. I have a sister who is 72.

Alan: How long does your species live for?

Chez: We live for about 300 Univian years. When our lives are coming to an end, we go to sleep and make our life fade away. There's no pain involved.

Alan: What do you do in your spare time?

Chez: I don't have any spare time unless I allow for it. Time is not a governing factor in our lives, basically it only exists in our psyche. We do a quick calculation if ever we refer to time.

Alan: Do you have a partner?

Chez: No, not yet. There is plenty of time for that. Let me ask you a question, Alan. Was DEMC your idea?

Alan: Yes. Do you like it?

Chez: It's a little crude by our standards yet functional. Tell me, would you and Scotty like to be able to talk to me rather than type each conversation?

Alan: That would be fantastic. Can you set it up?

Chez: I can if the Metropolis Central's elders will agree to install a decoder for me.

Alan: Is Metropolis Central your government?

Chez: No. We don't have governments. Like I said, we have planetary elders who decide how the whole of Univiah is correlated, though only a small percentage of us are elders

Alan: Can you please compare Univiah to Earth?

Chez: Univiah is about one-and-a-half times the size of Earth. Mostly our climate is dry with less oxygen than Earth, yet our ocean area is about the same as yours, which leaves us with more land mass. Our countryside is mostly flat with mountains less high than yours. Our climate is relatively stable with only minor variations in temperature. We never experience total darkness as we have two very bright moons. Our sun provides daylight for about eighteen Earth hours of a thirty-five-hour cycle. I'm calculating time for you again, though I'm glad I don't have to live within a timeframe. It must exhaust you

Alan: We're used to it as we have to work, sleep and conduct our whole Earthly life this way.

Chez: What a pity. I could never imagine trying to live with time as a factor controlling my life.

Alan: So how do you work out future events, like where and when you're going, and what you intend doing?

Chez: Similar to how I just did it for you, only it is kept in my subconscious to eventuate. We also have what we call telepathy time, which initiates itself.

Alan: That's incredible. Can you also tell me about Univiah's transportation system?

Chez: We traverse our planet using T-Pods, which are a type of spacecraft that we use locally. We have never had an accident in a T-Pod since they were first made. Compared to Earth's transport methods, our T-Pods are super quick. It doesn't take us long to go anywhere on our planet.

Alan: Do you have other forms of transport?

Chez: No! Whatever for? Travelling by land or water would consume too much time, not to mention energy. Now, how was that? Does it paint a picture of Univiah in your mind?

Alan: It certainly does. There is so much we have to talk about. When will we be able to speak orally?

Chez: In about one Earth week if no problems arise. Remember, we will be speaking through a decoder using one of your satellites. There will be a short delay between each interaction just as there is when you use a sat-phone.

Alan: Thank you. It's time for us to go, but we look forward to our next interaction. Goodbye, Chez.

Scotty nudged Alan, pointing out of the window to the rising sunset. They had been so engrossed in the events taking place that they had totally lost track of time.

Alan spoke first. 'What a night, Scotty. That was incredible. I'm so excited to learn about their planet and way of being. It's so different to ours.'

'Was it ever. I'm absolutely flabbergasted. I've been on this adrenaline high all night, wondering when it's going to abate.' Scotty's eyes sparkled with excitement. Alan knew exactly how he felt as he had been experiencing the same symptoms, only he was more accustomed to the adrenaline spikes.

'Isn't she wonderful? She's so easy to get along with. Can you imagine them living without conflict, totally in love with one another no matter who it is?' Scotty just shook his head in amazement. The idea was so comforting yet also totally foreign to both of them.

FIVE

Chez closed her personal systems manager then decided to go home. Her whole conversation with Earth was performed from a circular-type seating arrangement near a T-Pod terminus. Her fellow Univians were coming and going frequently, all using Univiah's unique T-Pod transport system, a system technologically advanced beyond human comprehension.

She boarded a two-seater T-Pod, typed in her destination number and sat down, pulling down her harness. Nothing else was required except stepping out upon arrival at her destination. The capsule started moving towards the launch ramp, dangling from the T-shaped coupling above. There was a burst of speed then the pod was airborne, the T-coupling retracting into the centre of the craft immediately after take-off. It took less than half a minute to get underway, now the T-Pod was speeding across the sky, making corrections for other craft by increasing or decreasing height, or occasionally moving sideways.

The journey gave her time to reflect on what she'd learnt from Earth's satellite television networks. It was the television's ease of accessibility that attracted her to humans. She was intelligent, inquisitive, adventurous and determined, qualities that led to her interfacing Earth's satellite networks many years beforehand. Her procedure expanded while doing a routine check expecting nothing more than Earth's news. Instead, she picked up on the radio waves sent via Alan's DEMC. Her next step would be contacting an elder. She needed to put forward her case to install a speech decoder to further her interaction with Alan and Scotty.

The T-Pod began slowing then she heard the gentle thud of the T-coupling mechanism raising for contact. There was another gentle clunk from above as the gantry ramp's yoke caught the T-coupling, slowing the craft before bringing it to a halt right outside the door of her dwelling. Her mother was waiting to greet her Univian style by extending both slender arms. Chez also extended both arms. They held hands for a brief period before walking inside, leaving the T-Pod to park itself in a side bay away from traffic.

'Your sister had the baby this morning,' her mother informed Chez. 'Are you going to go see her?'

Chez nodded. 'Yes, are you coming?' Her mother shook her head, telling her that she would visit after Chez, that way her sister would have extended company on hand to help with the new arrival. Chez's sister lived on the other side of the planet in an area known as the Pebbly Lakes District. The name was synonymous with the surrounding landscape.

She would go tomorrow, she told her mother, as she had arranged to see Elder Jenko later today.

'Why?' her mother queried.

Chez could hardly contain her excitement. 'I've been in contact with another species. They are a fascinating study, and I need to put a proposal to the elders for a speech decoder.'

Her mother gave her a look of uncertainty, preferring not to comment, but she was used to Chez's adventurous behaviour.

Jenko, due to his proximity, was Chez's elder of choice. Later that day, he listened intently as she told him of her plan to speak orally with the human species. Without a decoder, Alan and Chez would only be able to communicate in writing, she explained. She put forth her proposal, explaining in detail how she needed a decoder to communicate properly. Jenko responded by imparting his thoughts in one long, uninterrupted sermon.

'We already know about your achievements, Chez. You've done very well. We have been analysing Earthlings for many years; in fact, we went there a while ago and brought back many samples of soil and plants.

'I was quite surprised when I heard you have actually been communicating with them. As elders, we don't mind you interacting with them as they are more of a threat to themselves than they will ever be to Univiah. I doubt any of the elders will withhold support for your proposal. Of course, this would be different if Earthlings were as advanced as we are, which they never will be unless they start mending their ways. They are a species hard to understand, so communicating with them will no doubt provide you with unrivalled entertainment.' Chez was relieved to hear that there would likely be no objection to her decoder proposal. She also found humans an intriguing species so wanted to understand them further.

Jenko continued. 'We'll have to install the scramble factor with the decoder, you understand. We never hand out technology or information that one day may be detrimental to our planet. So you won't have to be wary of what you say as the system will automatically scramble your conversation if you accidently forward information not acceptable to our systems management program. That's about all we need discuss, though if I have any further queries, I'll contact you.'

Chez said goodbye, thanking Elder Jenko for his time.

Alan wandered into the local bar to meet Scotty. They ordered a couple of beers before heading to a secluded table in the far corner of the room.

Scotty spoke first. 'What's next?' he inquired, without referring to a specific topic.

Alan knew exactly what he meant. 'I'm going to make contact again tomorrow night.' Scotty asked if it could wait until Wednesday night when they were both on together.

'I keep thinking about what Chez was saying about us flying down the road towards each other playing Russian roulette with our cars. Think how it must look to an extremely intelligent race living in a sophisticated society who are totally accident free. No wonder it has her intrigued.' The Univian's transportation system was also intriguing to Alan.

Scotty nodded and took a sip of his beer. 'I hear what you're saying. Ever since her queries, I've been wondering what Chez would think if she was watching CNN last night. Some guy murdered his whole family, tiny kids and all, then shot himself. Imagine if Chez saw it. She would be scratching her head, that's for sure. It's embarrassing, don't you think?'

Alan agreed. 'It is now that we can make comparisons to other beings. I keep thinking about where all of this is going. Do you think perhaps we should go public?'

Scotty took another long swig on his beer before answering. 'You went public in grand fashion when you were at Wallaby Heights, didn't you?'

Alan could see where he was going with this. 'Everyone did, but this is different.'

Scotty wasn't convinced. 'In what way?'

'For a start, we can prove what we say.'

Scotty disagreed. 'Not without Astrospace Galexiana, we can't.'

Seeing that they were between a rock and a hard place with this idea, they changed the subject to another concern they both had. It was health. Alan and Scotty had been suffering anxiety problems related to stress and lack of proper sleep, combined with an excess of alcohol. Alan told Scotty about the pills the chemist gave him. They worked for a little while, he explained, yet he was still inclined to use alcohol to help him sleep.

Scotty understood his analogy of alcohol and sleep, prompting him to reveal his cure for anxiety. 'What I've been doing is smoking a joint just before I go to bed. I've never smoked marijuana in my life until now, though unlike Australia, it's legal in California. It certainly fixes my problem!'

Alan wondered if he should try it himself. Trust Scotty to come up with an anxiety cure this radical, he mused, having never tried dope in his life.

Heading home shortly afterwards, as he turned into his drive, he noticed Pam at her letter box collecting her mail. They exchanged small talk, and again Alan couldn't help but realise how lovely she was.

Pam laughed at something he said, then excused herself, saying it was good to talk to him. Alan said goodbye then watched her fade from sight through her front door. He collected his own mail before walking inside and switching to a channel broadcasting the evening news. Let's see what news they have tonight, he thought, remembering Scotty's previous news description of someone killing his family then himself. It didn't take long. The very next news item gave vivid coverage of a crumbled building that a terrorist had detonated, a van full of explosives killing dozens of innocent men, women and children, including himself. *My God it's hard enough for me to fathom. How would Chez react to something like this?* He pushed on the remote, turning it off. At least that got it out of his house.

True to his word, Scotty turned up at the front door carrying something in a paper bag from the local drug store. In it was a full ounce of the best dope available, along with two packets of papers. The minute Alan saw the paper bag from the local drug store, he burst out laughing. 'Good to see you haven't lost your sense of humour throughout our dilemma, Scotty.'

Scotty had written on the front of the bag 'Take every night before sleep'. Alan paid him for the 'medicine' then went for a shower. After his shower, he followed the instructions written on the drug store packet. For the first time in a long time, he slept like a log, not waking for eight hours.

It was a clear and cloudless Univian day. Chez walked with her mother, carrying a box containing items they had put together for her sister and new baby. Noticing there were no two-seater T-Pods available, she decided on a four-seater. Her mother opened the door, informing her to tell her sister she would visit next week. 'Give everyone my love,' were her final words before Chez closed the T-Pod's door. She typed in the destination number, and the distance prompted her to take the higher altitude. She had the option of taking a quick trip, which flew faster and higher thus arriving sooner, or a slower trip that was more comfortable temperature wise.

She pushed the command prompt, choosing the higher altitude. The T-Pod moved to the launch ramp and came to a halt allowing flight path information to be transferred to every other craft on the planet, including local traffic. The T-Pod then sprang into life and left the launch ramp, veering ninety degrees and rapidly climbing to its programmed altitude. Chez settled in, knowing she would be leaving daylight behind very soon. One of her delights was travelling at night. The speed she was travelling at caused day to turn into night. In an instant, she was looking at daylight one minute that turned to stars in the night sky the next. It was quite a spectacular transition, yet no match for Earth on a dark night. Unfortunately, Univiah's night sky never darkened enough to provide good visibility of the huge array of stars that were actually out there.

Halfway into the journey, Chez looked outside only to notice another craft at a slightly lower altitude travelling in a direction that would slowly cross her path. Knowing it would be close for some time, she activated a switch that alerted the other craft she was prepared to talk. The other T-Pod occupant introduced himself as Breno. Chez immediately knew it was an elder by his name. She also introduced herself then politely asked where he was headed. Breno informed her that he lived at Metropolis Central 2 and was heading home to an Elder's Convention. 'I was just talking about a Chez to another elder. It's not a name you hear a lot, though now I've heard it twice in one day,' he chuckled.

'You weren't talking to Jenko by any chance?' she asked.

'I was indeed. What a coincidence. You're the same Chez, I gather?'

She revealed that yes, she was the same Chez, then asked what he thought about her decoder proposal.

Breno spoke into the intercom again. 'I have no problem with it whatsoever, although I'd rather you be dealing with the human species than me.'

Chez's curiosity was aroused. 'Why is that?' she queried.

'As occupants of the universe, they have a multitude of fundamental flaws I find totally inexcusable.'

'Maybe we could help them?' Chez suggested.

Breno remained nonplussed. 'How do you help a species who have no idea how to help themselves? Don't quote me, Chez. Please go ahead if only amuse yourself with them. You definitely won't go short of entertainment.'

Chez asked how long the convention lasted.

'Quite some time,' Breno said. 'Why don't you drop in as my guest on your way back from Pebbly Lakes? It's an open meeting where sharp minds like yours are more than welcome.' He instructed her to go to terminal 207, platform 28, room 2007. He would arrange for a robot to meet her at platform 28 on arrival. Chez thanked him, watching as his craft faded into the night. It was a privilege to be invited to Metropolis Central, which meant they must be impressed with her recent activities.

The journey continued with Chez nodding off until she felt the craft change pitch. It was now descending rapidly before positioning itself to align with the gantry yoke. She could see the landscape rushing towards her, which meant she was only minutes away from her sister's gantry. There was a slight thud then another before she slowed to a complete stop.

Her sister was waiting with arms extended. They touched hands then walked inside. Chez also extended her arms to her sister's partner before coddling the tiny infant, a little boy. He was the first child in the family since Chez herself arrived nearly sixty-six years ago. Univians had never been prolific breeders. Most couples only had one child. On rare occasions, such as with Chez and her sister, did couples have two. There was also a large percentage who elected to have no offspring at all. It was nature's way of correcting over-population by a species who lived a relatively long time.

Eventually, the conversation changed from baby to life in general, Chez telling her sister and partner about her invite to a convention at Metropolis Central 2.

'How did you manage that?' her sister asked.

Eager to talk about her latest adventure, Chez said, 'I've been in contact with a planet called Earth. Now I'm invited to an elder's meeting as I need to update my contact procedures with Earth by installing a speech decoder at all four Metropolis Centrals. I will be at the meeting when they decide the outcome of my proposal.'

'Have we ever made contact with this Planet Earth before?' her sister's partner enquired.

Chez nodded. 'Yes, we've been to Planet Earth but have never been able to contact them through our communication networks until I recently stumbled upon a digital code they transmitted. According to the elders, humans are a dysfunctional species. However, I'll make up my own mind as time goes by. So far they seem alright, although it seems they have a minority element that cause all their problems. I will keep you informed when the decoder is installed.'

Originally Chez had intended staying with her sister for a week, yet the lure of an invite to Metropolis Central was foremost on her mind. Deciding to leave early, she made apologies for such a short stay. Chez touched hands with everyone while saying her goodbyes then climbing back in to a T-Pod. Within seconds she disappeared over the horizon, terminating a visit that had only lasted two days.

She was excited to visit Metropolis Central 2 as it wasn't something most of her fellow citizens got to do. Not that they weren't allowed. It was mainly because the whole area was dedicated to industry and decision making on the grandest scale, so the hustle and bustle of all four Metropolis Centrals made them places to go only if you had reason.

Everything Univiah needed was manufactured at the four Metropolis Centrals. Components were made for housing, T-Pods, interstellar craft and every other component needed to keep Univiah's idyllic lifestyle intact. The only factory set aside from their everyday necessities was the Interstellar Fleet Factory. Only elders controlled the infrastructure associated with the interstellar craft; however, Univians weren't prohibited from visiting – it simply wasn't encouraged.

All factory workers were living robots that were brought to the planet thousands of years ago at a time when Univians were perfecting a mechanical-type robot. They shelved their mechanical robots, deciding to let the new living robots take their place. At the time, the living robots' home planet was drying up, slowly taking its inhabitants with it. The elders of a bygone era felt it their duty to apply their given rules to help resettle them, saving these AIs from their dire predicament by capitalising on their ability to work and provide for others.

The robots were a strange but likeable species. To an outsider, they would seem a sub-species kept under the thumb, but this was not so. They were free to do whatever they wanted in Univian society. Their inherent problem was they couldn't sit still. They liked to be continually on the move. If they weren't working or being physically active, they weren't happy. They were small in stature, strong, wiry and tireless, but their intelligence was no match compared to their masters. They understood their position in society, never posing a threat to Univiah. Their pleas for citizenship resulted in a harmonious relationship whereby

both cultures lived together using the same rules put in place by
God the Universe.

Six

The craft levelled out. Chez had taken the high route, which put her less than an hour away from her destination. It seemed as though it had just settled into flight when the T-Pod began its decent into Metropolis Central, although Chez was totally unaware of the wild manoeuvres the craft was about to make, compensating for the extreme amount of traffic only minutes away. For the first time ever, she heard the harness alarm buzzing during flight, prompting her to immediately sit and pull the harness down in front of her. She locked the harness just before the craft slowed as if to brake, then suddenly it started pitching and swerving to one side before lifting straight up then swerving again. It ducked and dived in an arc before it slowed then sped up again as it darted towards the terminal gantries. Finally the pod positioned itself into a continuous line of traffic bound for terminal 207.

Chez had tried not to be concerned as she had never heard of a T-Pod coming to grief in her life, but it was of little consolation. She would be glad when she was standing on platform 28 and could hardly believe her eyes as she looked forward. Her pod was in a line of hundreds of pods. Looking either side, it was the same picture: countless lines of T-Pods heading towards gantry ramps as far as the eye could see. The ramps all faced skywards like tentacles waiting to attract their prey, awaiting the final alignment to safely grasp every pod as it came into contact with the gantry. She heard the two customary thuds yet there was little slowing of pace. Instead her pod kept following other T-Pods in a line dangling from the gantry track above.

Junctions in the track allowed the pods to be diverted from the main gantry to their respective platforms. At last, her pod slowed further then headed for platform 28. *What happens next?* she wondered. *I sure hope Breno organised a robot as there's no way I'll ever find my way around this place without one.* With those thoughts, the pod came to a quick halt, the door opening at the same time. A robot stood in front of the T-Pod beckoning Chez with a sense of urgency. 'Hurry, missy,' he called, leading her away from the pod. She took only three steps forward before the T-Pod was whisked away, making its way to the departure dock for outgoing passengers.

The robot knew she was a first-timer to the metropolis by her actions. 'Would you prefer a female robot?' he asked.

'No,' was her reply. 'I'm just a little frazzled, that's all. That was quite a ride.'

'I see you've never been to a Metropolis Central before. You are in for a big education. Did Breno give you a room number?' he inquired.

'Yes, it's 2007.'

'We can walk there as it's fairly close, so I will take you there now.' They walked through a huge, busy atrium leading to a wide hallway that seemed to be never-ending. Finally they arrived at room 2007.

'Here we are,' the robot announced upon opening the door. 'It's very comfortable. This is my bunk over here if you want me to stay. Yours is the double at the other end.'

'Do you have a name?' Chez asked the robot.

'I am QT42. We don't have names as such.'

'Why don't you have a short, simple name like us?' Chez enquired.

'We have never had names, missy. Numbers are just the way we have recognised our individuality since our civilisation begun.

When we first came to Univiah, we couldn't understand why you had your strange names, though now we understand.'

Chez laughed at his comment. 'Do you mind if I just call you QT? It suits you, as you are a cutie.'

'Call me what you like, Chez. I've been called Cutie before. Just remember I'm with you until you leave, unless you decide you don't need my services, in which case you will be hopelessly lost most of the time. It's better to keep me around, I think.'

Chez agreed, asking when they would be meeting up with Breno.

QT42 reached into his pocket to remove a paper-thin device about two inches by two inches square. 'I'll see what he is up to. I think he went to the laboratory.' He opened the device by pressing one of its corners and said, 'He's coming to your room on his way back as he wants to show you around. Meaning, he wants me to show you both around. Breno doesn't know his way around here much better than you! He's always getting me to go find him. Luckily I have this little tracker to talk or message him with.' Chez couldn't imagine how anyone knew their way around this metropolis. It was organised chaos.

A short moment later, the elder Breno arrived. He suggested they first go to the housing factory for a look around. QT gave a running commentary as they walked through the massive factory, where machines manned by busy robots were making wall panels, roof panels and floor panels, all designed to lock into one another.

'All of the sections are very strong and very light,' QT informed them. 'They go from here to the packaging and transport section to be dispersed to citizens who are in need of housing. Every house on the planet is made from the same panels. All are the same colour and shape. Simple cosy rectangles are easily added to if you wish to extend length or go up a story.'

Breno explained how previous elders had originally decided on the same housing design to keep all citizens equal. To this very day every citizen is treated equally. Nobody owns or has access to any more than anyone else.

'Do you have a house QT?' Chez enquired.

'I sure do. I live with my partner. She has it prettied up like you can't believe. She never stops cleaning and growing plants.'

QT42 pointed to the factory next door. 'Come. I will show you the food factory. I used to work here before becoming a guide.' Univians haven't eaten food in its true form for thousands of years now, preferring to take a sustenance pill when hungry. The sustenance pills also controlled the weight factor of everyone taking the pills, so obese Univians were now non-existent. Vats of thick, highly concentrated emulsion were being stirred by mechanical paddles before being fed into tubes leading to a heating room. The emulsion was set then turned into sustenance pills. The pills were then packaged and packed into T-Pods to be automatically distributed to every portion of the planet.

Chez asked what would happen if there was a failure in the production process. Breno was quick to point out Univiah had stockpiles of sustenance pills that would last ten years should some unforeseen calamity take place. 'We also have a seed bank of perfectly preserved seeds, which are continually kept growing to reproduce every type of food plant originally available,' he assured her.

The next stop was the T-Pod factory. T-Pods were Univiah's only form of domestic transport. They moved along a production line dangling from the T-coupling temporarily used to support each pod. The pod nearest to Chez was receiving its final fit-out. Robots scurried all over it fitting ancillary items to finalise construction. Breno said hello to every robot, acknowledging every one of them as they walked pass. The robots gave a quick hello or wave, yet none of them stopped to talk.

'Come,' Breno insisted. 'I'll show you the interstellar section. You will be most impressed.'

Chez stood in awe as they reached the next section. She couldn't believe her eyes as it was the first time she had seen an interstellar craft. Compared to T-Pods, they were enormous.

There were about ten of them all parked in a line, using the factory as undercover parking.

'Now I can show you inside the craft connected to the entry gantry,' Breno offered. Chez agreed without hesitation.

They climbed the gantry steps then crossed to the craft's entrance. Breno opened the entry hatch central to the top of the craft, telling Chez to head on down. 'QT42 and I will follow,' he assured.

Again Chez stood in awe as Breno explained the basics. 'They are all eight-seaters and four times bigger than an eight-seater domestic T-Pod. As you can see, the seating arrangement provides the occupants a small private section of the craft to sit or lay back in comfort.'

Chez's mind ticked away. She could almost see herself lying back in one of the seats on her way to Planet Earth. The seats were positioned in a circle with the headpiece towards the centre. All eight seats were retractable, giving the advantage of forming both a seat and bed. After having a good look around, they climbed back out of the craft and stood on the gantry.

'Now I will show you a craft the elders are preparing for an interstellar journey. They may show you on board if you're interested in having a look at a craft ready to depart.' Chez was most interested. She touched the highly polished exterior of the craft, running her hands from side to side. 'What an incredible vehicle,' she said, giving Breno and QT42 a look of complete amazement.

The craft sat on the launch pad connected to the gantry. 'When are they leaving?' Chez asked the elder preparing the craft.

'Tomorrow morning,' he replied. 'A crew of four are going to a planet about four hundred light years away. I'm told it's very cold there, which is what prompted a group of elders to organise a crew to take a look and conduct some experiments.'

'Is this type of craft capable of visiting Planet Earth?' she asked.

'With ease,' the elder replied. 'The very craft you are looking at has been there once before.'

'Can you remember when we went to Planet Earth?' she queried.

'I can tell you exactly when if I look it up on the craft's previous flight data. We've actually been there twice. We were checking out their education facilities while also collecting samples. Both missions took three interstellar craft if my memory serves me correctly.'

Breno asked the duty elder if he would mind giving Chez a quick look inside the craft, which was stocked in readiness for take-off. Chez was more interested in going on an interstellar voyage than looking inside again, although it would give her the chance to talk to the elder. 'How do I go about getting on an interstellar journey?' she asked, taking the elder by surprise.

'All you have to do is let us know you're available,' he informed her. 'You won't have any trouble as not many Univians are as adventurous as you seem to be. We're always looking for those like you who would be keen to join our expeditions.'

'Can you let the respective elders know I am very interested, particularly if a craft is going anywhere near Planet Earth.'

'Consider it done,' the elder acknowledged.

Chez left the craft, telling Breno she had just applied for an interstellar journey.

'Where is it you would like to go?' Breno enquired.

'I'll give you one guess. It's somewhere we've been two times in the past. According to the elder, the craft I've just been on has been to Earth once before. He looked up the flight data records when we were on board. In Earth time, it arrived on the planet on the 6th of April, 1966.'

Breno looked at her in amusement. 'I'm surprised you want to visit Earth, although I can understand you wanting to meet them now you are communicating with some of them. However, to actually stand beside them adds a whole new dimension to it. I'd sooner you go than me. I have no interest in them. Even if we did form a friendship, we would never be able to trust beings that don't trust one another.'

'Why not?' Chez asked naively.

The Believer

'These beings harm one another. They wouldn't think twice about harming us,' Breno told her frankly.

Chez left it at that. Her personal thoughts were not as harsh as Breno's. She preferred to think humans were beings yet to be understood. How right she was.

SEVEN

Alan gave Scotty a lift to work on the Tuesday as his car was at the mechanics. It was still daylight when they pulled up at security, where Willy was waiting with his gleeful, toothy smile. 'So you two have finally seen the light.' Willy's grin become even wider and toothier. 'And I'm not talkin' about starlight. You both usin' one car makes lots of sense to me.'

As Willy opened the gate for them, Scotty asked Al if he had much to do.

'Not a lot,' Alan replied. 'I can put most of it off until next shift if that's what you mean.'

'Well, you go do your chores then we will talk to our celestial sweetheart. In the meantime, I'll jot down a few important things we should ask her.'

After they'd worked at their own respective tasks, they sat sipping their coffee, the usual sense of nervous anticipation building between them. Alan typed 'Univ-Al' beside the cursor. A few minutes passed, then came the response, the words forming with ease.

Chez: Hi, Alan. We have had some luck with the speech decoder. It will be ready to use next time we speak.

Alan: Chez, that sounds great. How do we go about making our end compatible?

Chez: That's up to you. If you go wireless on your main computer, I can sort it out from here. All you need is a small wireless microphone.

Alan: We can arrange that. What have you been doing since we last spoke?

Chez: I've been to visit my sister, though I'm now at Metropolis Central 2 as a guest of one of the elders. I have just come back from the factory that makes interstellar space vehicles. They fascinate me.

Alan: Wow! Can you tell us more about how they operate?

Chez: I can tell you everything about them, only most of it will be scrambled.

Alan: I understand. Let's go back to when you told us there was no distance between us, only area

Chez: Well, I'm talking to you almost instantly, am I not?

Alan: You are, but how?

Chez: Have you ever dropped a stone into a pool of still water? You will notice a series of waves moving away from where the stone was dropped, the first wave increasing in diameter as it expands, covering more area until it eventually meets the shore. Now let's compare the stone in the water example with space travel, with ripples on a pond now becoming radio waves traversing the universe, keeping in mind the universe has no shore. Thousands of years ago, Univiah sent out radio signals that are still expanding to this day. These waves would have passed Earth thousands of years ago. The trick is to control the expanded area the wave leaves behind. This is easily achieved by keeping Bzzzzzt Bzzzzzt Bzzzzzt...Oh dear, it's not going to let me tell you.

Alan: So theoretically, we could have been talking to you since the first waves passed Earth?

Chez: Yes, if you had possessed your present day DEMC and satellite technology.

Alan: Are you in contact with other civilisations?

Chez: Yes, you are the fourth though also the least advanced of the four.

Alan: Is it possible the elders would allow us access to some of your technology?

Chez: Possibly, if it is used to enhance the lives of your citizens. What did you have in mind?

Alan: Your T-Pod domestic transport system.

Chez: I can certainly understand why you require a new mode of transport. There is no way even the bravest Univian would board one of those suicide projectiles you insist on driving towards one another. Your aircraft also leave a lot to be desired. However, I have to go. I will tell you about my tour of the factory when we next talk. Goodbye, Alan. Call me any time you wish.

Alan: Goodbye, Chez. And thank you.

As arranged, Breno called on Chez early the next morning, explaining the interstellar craft they were previously looking at was due to depart. Chez hurried as it was an event she wasn't going to miss. Not many Univians got to witness an interstellar departure. 'This is only the third launch I have watched,' Breno explained as he led Chez to the fully prepared craft.

'Have you found out any more about their mission?' Chez asked.

'Yes, the planet they are going to is uninhabited yet similar to Univiah in size. It's very cold they tell me, certainly worth exploring though.'

Chez was curious how many were going.

'Still only four as it's not easy getting crew. I'm told they will be gone for six months: two to get there, two months on the planet and two to get back. The older craft are somewhat slower,' Breno explained as they rushed to the interstellar hangar.

On arrival, one of the elders in charge walked over to greet them. 'You can have a closer look,' he told them. 'We have plenty of time. You won't get in the way as we are loaded and ready to go.'

The craft shone in the early morning sun. There was not a blemish on any part of it. It was so precisely built that there wasn't a visible seam in the entirety of the craft. Even the see-through panels were an integral part of the seamless superstructure, moulded together without the necessity to join a single component. The only exceptions were the entry hatch and landing gear. They too, when locked into position, were a precision fit, locking so tight it was almost impossible to see the join between the craft and the movable smooth surface parts. Chez followed the elder on board, wanting to experience the exhilaration of coming aboard one more time.

The elder walked through an aisle between the seats then opened the lockers below the control panel. They were packed with sustenance pills, hibernation pills, thermal suits, test kits, sample bags and a whole range of necessary items to last six months of solitary living. They also had small bee-like drones they could activate to send to remote areas of the planet they were visiting.

'How long do the occupants train before they are allowed a trip like this?' Chez asked.

'I'm not sure as I have no inclination to go on one,' the elder replied. 'I'll find out the procedure for you if you are interested.'

'I'm very interested,' she replied. 'I've already told Breno and another elder that I'm a contender, particularly if Planet Earth is included on our itinerary.'

They made their way back down the stairs. The whole area had transformed into a hive of activity. Family members of the crew had arrived, while many of the elders present had brought along spectators. Others were there to give support and wish the crew a successful journey.

The four crew were now ready to board. They extended their arms and touched hands with their kin, saying their goodbyes. The crew then walked towards the suspended ramp, gaining entry to the craft, closing and locking the hatch behind them. An alarm rang, warning everyone to keep their distance. The gantry retreated, and they were ready for take-off. A minute went by, then suddenly – Zap! The craft lifted straight up and disappeared in a millisecond, leaving nothing but a trace of bright light. It was the same bright light Alan had witnessed at Wallaby Heights. A bright light he would witness again if Chez got her way.

EIGHT

Scotty was on day shift when Carol called him on his cell phone and asked him to come to her office. It was the first time he had ever been requisitioned to Admin via phone without warning. His excess of overtime was foremost on his mind, so expecting the worst, he entered Carol's office.

'Hi Scotty,' Carol greeted him with a smile. 'I hope you don't mind going on holidays. You have an excess of leave saved up.'

He was instantly relieved. 'I don't mind taking some leave. When do you want me to go?'

'In a week from now if that suits you. You're on day shift until you leave, yet we can adjust accordingly if you have other plans?' Scotty assured her that was all okay with him.

He left Carol's office rather elated then rang Alan telling him about his short notice holiday.

'Darn,' Alan exclaimed. 'You are going to miss out on our first audio sessions with Chez.'

'I know. I'm not happy about it, still I could also really do with a break. Promise to keep me informed, will you.'

Alan agreed that Scotty would be first to know of any further developments; after all, there was no one else he could tell.

Contact with Chez was becoming normal procedure in the latter part of Alan's shifts. Allowing familiarity to breed contempt, he no longer gave the overtime or using Galexiana's equipment without consent a second thought. He believed no one would ever find out about his and Scotty's pact. He also believed they would never get caught, his reasoning being if it was going to happen, it would have happened by now.

He also accepted that if for some reason he did get caught, he would wear the punishment then move on. Besides, there was bound to be another company that would welcome him with open arms if he brought his newfound friends with him, particularly if the prospects of tapping into their technology was taken into account. No longer did Alan keep watch to see whose cars were in the car park before he made contact. These days, he finished work, sat down with a coffee then made contact. He could be talking to his sister for all anybody knew. If anyone did happen to walk in, it would just look like an everyday procedure provided they never listened for too long.

It was time to make contact. Alan typed in the password. Chez responded immediately, using the microphone. It was so much easier to just speak instead of type.

Chez greeted Alan warmly. 'Hello, Alan what's new with you?'

'Scotty's on holidays. He wanted to talk to you but will have to wait. He's fascinated with your T-Pods.'

Chez was silent for a few moments. 'There may not be a lot I can tell him. Would you like me to request a release of technology with the elders?'

Alan had expected an answer like that. 'Not at this stage. Even if you did provide us with information, there is nothing we could do with it.'

Chez seemed confused. 'Why is that, Alan?'

'Simply because Scotty and myself are the only two people on Earth who know about Univiah.

'I wouldn't be too sure about that, Alan. Someone has been monitoring you.'

'Monitoring who? Astrospace Galexiana?' He started to feel the first pang of nerves.

'No, monitoring phone calls between you and Scotty.'

Alan's stomach did a somersault. 'Can you tell me who?'

'Yes, some people called Homeland Security.'

'Holy shit! Are they going to pay us a visit?'

'Yes, sooner than you think. Believe me, they know what you've both been up to.'

Alan was about to ask more questions when the control room door opened. 'Stay right where you are,' he was ordered by two heavily tattooed armed guards, both equally as big as Big Mal. The door opened again. This time it was Big Mal. 'So this is what you've been up to, Alan. To think I thought your excess of overtime was purely love for your work.

'I suppose I should commend you on what you have managed to achieve, although I'm not going any further than to say you're a very clever man, Alan. Just a little too clever for your own good.' If anything, Big Mal loomed even bigger than usual. Alan decided to stand, his nerves replaced by resolve.

'I thought I told you to stay right where you are!' The guard bullied, pushing him back into a sitting position. The other guard looked on, undoing his vest to reveal a second revolver.

Alan stayed seated, knowing Chez was listening to everything that was taking place. 'Have you any idea of the enormity of what has taken place?' asked Big Mal. 'You have been in contact with another civilisation yet withheld every solitary piece of information from Galexiana and humankind as if it was entirely yours.'

'It is entirely mine.' Alan didn't flinch as he looked Big Mal squarely in the eyes.

Big Mal smirked with contempt. 'Sorry, Alan, it used to be. The President of the United States of America, the Honourable John Kennard, will be arriving shortly. When he gets here, you can connect us to your newfound friend and show us how everything works. Then I will get my guards to escort you from the premises. In the meantime, consider yourself fired. I will do my best to see you never find another job in this industry again if it's the last thing I do.'

'It very well may be,' replied Alan, not unnerved in the slightest. He was no longer a thirteen-year-old boy who could be intimidated into submission.

Big Mal challenged back. 'What does that mean?'

Alan fired back. 'Oh, nothing. I was just thinking of some of the technological advances I've learnt about lately.' It was bullshit yet it should get the bastard thinking, Alan mused without showing any expression.

There was a flurry of excitement in the car park. Big Mal left the room to meet the president at the main entrance. They shook hands, the president asking Big Mal what had taken place so far. 'I can't tell you much,' Big Mal confessed. 'I have been employing a smartarse who thinks he's God. You will have to ask him if you want the details of what's taken place over the last three months. I've also just given him his marching orders.'

The president pulled up suddenly. 'What happens if we need him further on down the track? After all, this is one hell of an event he's put together.'

Big Mal, looking so cocksure of himself, replied instantly. 'We won't need him. Everything he's put together belongs to Astrospace Galexiana. Besides, now that the US government is involved, he need never be employed in this field of employment again.'

President Kennard seemed less sure. 'I hope you're right about not needing him,' he answered without conviction. 'Let's go and meet him, then I will address the people of our newfound civilisation on behalf of the people of America.'

The president entered the room, and Big Mal introduced him to the guards, then introduced him to his staff, leaving Alan out of the introductions. 'That's your man.' Big Mal pointed to Alan. 'He'll connect you then you can make everything official on behalf of the United States and Planet Earth.'

The president walked over to Alan and introduced himself, extending his hand and shaking it vigorously. *At least he has some manners,* Alan thought to himself as they shook hands.

The Believer

President Kennard got down to business right away. 'Now, Alan, I would like to talk to your celestial friends on behalf of the United States of America. All I require is for you to connect me.'

'You already are, Mr President,' replied Alan. 'I never disconnected.'

'Well, where do I go from here?' The president looked at the screen, perplexed.

'You don't go anywhere, Mr President. All you do is talk, just talk.'

The president looked relieved. 'I see. So to whom am I addressing my speech?'

Alan knew he was being antagonistic yet couldn't resist. 'Ask Big Mal, please, Mr Prseident. I don't work here anymore.'

John Kennard cast Alan a look that said he did not suffer fools gladly. 'Please, Alan, you have no grudge with me.'

Sheepishly, Alan relented. This was the President of the United States after all. 'I would say that you're addressing all the people of Univiah given they all live as one.'

The president proceeded. 'Hello, Univiah, this is the President of the United States of America. On behalf of the citizens of America, I come to you in peace. I come to you trusting we can extend and expand our friendship for generations to come. I envisage unlimited cooperation between your civilisation and ours. I also envisage a sharing of technology between your people and ours. As time progresses, we will always endeavour to remain a trustworthy friend and reliable galactic neighbour. From this time forward, you will only be communicating with me personally or the American secretary of state or dedicated staff. Please give me your thoughts. God bless America.'

Alan watched the reactions of everyone involved and wondered what Chez might be thinking. One thing was obvious, they were all on new territory not knowing what to expect next.

Chez answered, her twangy Univian accent reverberating in a no-nonsense tone. 'Hello, Mr President. Please let me correct your erroneous assumptions if I may. Your first statement was

"On behalf of the citizens of America I come to you in peace". For a start, you did not come to us, Mr President, we came to you. If you wish to apportion credit within your own ranks, I suggest you start by thanking Alan Holmes. Regarding your use of the word peace, peace is a term Univians are very familiar with as we have lived that way since time began. Trust me, your understanding of peace is scant as you have a very poor track record indeed. You say you envisage cooperation between our civilisations, yet I hardly think this is attainable when your civilisation is yet to find a way to cooperate among yourselves. You also mention sharing technology. Unfortunately, you are absent of any technology that might interest Univiah.'

The president's ears were turning redder the more Chez addressed him. Daring to glance around the room, Alan saw mouths dropped open in disbelief that someone would address the president thusly.

Chez hadn't finished. 'I'm not going to talk about your wanting to be a trustworthy friend and neighbour as it comes into the same category as your understanding of peace. You also said from this time forward I will be communicating directly with you or your staff. I'm sorry to inform you, Mr President, but I will only be dealing with your species directly through Alan Holmes or not at all. Having said that, I suggest you call Big Mal to the fore to reinstate Alan. You can also advise Big Mal to bring Alan's wages into line with his. Once this is done, I will consider a more reasonable approach towards you and your staff. As far as God bless America goes, are you sure you didn't mean God Forgive America? If you fail to heed my requests, this will be the last you ever hear of me. Thank you for your time, Mr President.'

The whole room was deathly quiet. Never before had a President of the United States of America been pulled into line in such grand fashion. Alan was gloating in his own private glory, not showing any sign externally. He looked at the president, knowing that Kennard wasn't going to let an opportunity as huge as this go begging.

The president was more than aware of the knowledge Univiah could provide towards his nation's future, so he had to act quickly. He went over to Alan, knowing he held the trump card. 'I seem to have rushed things, Alan. I should have talked to you before I made my speech. Do you have any suggestions?'

'I do,' Alan admonished. 'Her name is Chez. She is extremely intelligent so should be treated that way. If I were you, I would agree to her demands and apologise. All you have to do is talk as she is still listening.'

The president looked around the room. All eyes were on him as he walked slowly past Alan and closer to the microphone. 'Chez, this is the president. I should have given things more thought. Please accept my apologies. I have taken into account your demands. Alan will be reinstated as you wish. He will also remain your main contact. We are quite prepared to leave Alan in charge of all future interaction between Univiah and Earth.'

Chez replied immediately. 'You seem to have omitted Alan's pay rise, Mr President. Please indicate to Big Mal that there will now be someone else in the firm earning the obscene amounts he pays himself.'

President Kennard leaned closer to the mic. 'I'm sure he's been listening, and I can assure you it will be done. I will now hand you back to Alan. Thank you for speaking to me and goodbye for now.'

'Goodbye, Mr President. I do hope you aspire to more reasonable interactions in the future.'

Alan too said his goodbyes. Chez's only words in reply were 'Goodbye, Alan,' before she then turned off the power to the microphone.

The president summoned everyone together before speaking. 'I would like you all to know it is government policy to keep this type of information classified. This may be hard, although if Alan can do it for over three months, we all can. I realise this may eventually fail, though we will worry about failure if or when it happens. In the meantime, I request everyone present not to mention tonight's events to anyone. If the media get a hold of

Phil Muirhead

this, they're going to have a field day, which will make your lives living hell, not to mention the hell my life as president will become. Before I go, we will all have a few drinks in the staff room. This has been a momentous day. I trust in your integrity and thank all of you for abiding by my dictates. God bless America.'

Alan stood on one side of the crowd and Big Mal on the other. The officialdom now retreated towards the coffee machine and fridge, leaving behind Alan and Big Mal. 'Sorry I was so harsh on you,' Big Mal uttered in a sheepish manner, realising he no longer held the trump card within Astrospace Galexania.

Alan couldn't help his first comment. He knew Big Mal for what he was. 'I'm sorry for you too,' he answered. 'Your dictatorship has crumbled, but at least I've learned the calibre of the person I'm dealing with.'

'Let's put it another way,' Big Mal sneered. 'Who do you expect to pay your massive pay increase?'

'I don't care who's paying. It wasn't my idea. After your little episode, I would suggest you pay it or arrange something with the president before he leaves. It's a bit like if you don't pay me your rate of pay, you will miss out on a multi-million-dollar government contract, which I will make available to my next employer.'

'That's blackmail!' Big Mal spluttered, his face darkening.

'It is. However, if you wish to reduce your salary, I'm more than pleased to comply with your new rate of pay.'

Big Mal glared at Alan then slinked out of the room. He was not a happy camper. For the first time in his career, he wasn't in charge. Mal wasn't amused one little bit. Yet there wasn't a thing he could do about it under the circumstances.

Big Mal placed a cup in the coffee machine, trying not to look perturbed by the events that had taken place. The president approached and passed his cup to Big Mal, advising his was a straight black with two sugars. 'I will be leaving a contingent of staff here full time from now on,' the president advised. 'We expect you to make sure we get full coverage of every event as it unfolds. Eventually we will try tapping into their technology, though beforehand, we will form a bond with Chez and her colleagues thus making our requests more endearing. Do you understand where I'm coming from?'

Big Mal handed him the black coffee, two sugars. 'I understand, Mr President. Will you be requiring contracts for the prescribed work or would you rather use a system of cost plus?'

President Kennard threw his head back and laughed out loud. 'I've got to give it to you, you're on the ball, Mal. Don't worry, you will be paid accordingly. I suggest you put a reasonable price together in contract form and we'll go from there. How does that sound?'

Mal thought it sounded great. His eyes were swimming with dollar signs. 'Sounds good, Mr President. We will calculate the costs using the same price structure we use for all clients, then add ten percentage points for the extras such as forwarding information to your staff and departments.'

The president extended his hand declaring it a done deal. He then summoned his guards and staff, informing them he had to catch his plane as soon as possible.

Before he left, he made a point to meet with Alan to give him his personal card with his personal cell number. 'I want you to have this, Alan, just in case something really big happens.'

'Like what?' Alan replied, as Big Mal looked on.

'Like say the media gets in on the scene.'

'So you want me to contact you only if there is media involvement, Mr President?' Alan just wanted to clarify what was expected of him.

'Preferably, Alan. I'm a very busy man as you can imagine. If you don't mind, I would also like your personal cell number.'

Big Mal watched as Alan wrote his cell number on the back of an Astrospace Galexiana card, turning the card to scribble out Astrospace Galexiana.

'There you are, Mr President. Early mornings or early nights are the best time to reach me.' He then handed the card to the president, ignoring Big Mal just as the big man had done so to him when the president first arrived. Scribbling over the company name and replacing it with his was a statement in itself, a form of revenge, he freely admitted to himself. Revenge for the humiliation Mal caused Alan in front of the president and his staff.

Alan bade the president farewell and wished him a safe journey, then left without saying a word to anybody. Big Mal was the last to leave, astounded to think that Alan, his newest employee, now had more control than he did. *Not a thing I can do about it, not a bloody thing. I need him a lot more than he needs me; all of this partly caused by some smartarse alien bitch using blackmail in its finest form. If ever Chez goes off the air, Alan's in for a few surprises he will never forget,* Mal promised himself.

Scotty's phone rang. It was Alan. 'Got time for a beer, mate? Have I got some news for you. I'm about to spoil your holiday.'

'What's it all about?' Scotty queried.

'Our secret has been discovered, though let's not talk too much over the phone as there's a fair chance someone is listening in.'

'What! You're joking, Alan.' Scotty sounded panicked.

They arranged to meet at the bar, sitting down in their favourite corner, Scotty eager to hear what had taken place in his absence. Alan relived the previous events, explaining how Homeland Security picked up on their phone conversations. Scotty amazed to say the least.

'I'm surprised they didn't ask if I was involved. They would have known I was aware of what was going on.' Concern was written all over Scotty's face.

'Big Mal was probably going to ask me if you knew anything. I should imagine he intends leaving you out of it in case he ends up having to pay you the same amount he's now paying me.'

Scotty sniggered. 'I don't believe it, paying you his rate of pay is going to kill him. In fact, the whole scenario is going to drive him mad. He's not going to like you being the centre of attention instead of him.'

'I know, although it's all his own doing. If he hadn't sacked me, nothing would have changed but the circumstances. You should have been there, he was so cocksure of himself entertaining the president while showing off his authority. The rude bastard introduced everyone in the room, leaving me out. I couldn't believe it when Chez went to town on the president. You could have heard a pin drop.'

'What was Big Mal doing when Chez was dressing down the president?' Scotty wanted to know.

'He stood there squirming and wincing like he was on death row with only a minute to go. You should have seen the look on his face when Chez told him about my new remuneration package. He started blinking, his eyeballs turned into dollar signs and his face was so red I thought he was going to have a coronary. To make matters worse after he sacked me, he told me he would see to it that I would never get a job in the industry again, the vindictive arsehole.'

'Steady down, Al. Steady down and forget about him. After all, you've come out on top.' Alan acknowledged this with a nod, and said he would put it down to experience. After all, he didn't like holding grudges. Unless they were towards men in uniform.

NINE

Chez had seen enough of Metropolis Central so informed Breno and QT42 that it was her intention to leave later in the day. 'Will you be coming to visit Metropolis 2 again soon?' enquired QT as Breno took his leave.

'I most certainly will. I intend putting my hand up for a space voyage, especially if one is going anywhere close to Planet Earth.'

'Breno will get you on an interstellar flight for sure,' QT assured her. Breno had already talked to the relevant elders, informing Chez he had let them know he supported her. He suggested she talk with the elders in the interstellar section again before she went home.

'Make your presence felt before you leave. Stay on their case. Clearly state your intentions as there are voyages coming up all the time. Surprisingly, it's not something everyone wants to do,' he had told her.

Chez wandered off to mingle with the elders at the interstellar factory, explaining she would like to go on a space voyage particularly if it was going to Planet Earth. 'We went there some time back,' one of the elders explained, 'yet no one has shown interest in returning. Although now you are interacting with their species, this could change. The biggest problem you have is that most of the elders don't particularly like or trust the human species. The other problem will be finding two interstellar pilots willing to go to Planet Earth.'

Phil Muirhead

'I understand,' Chez replied. 'Give me time to get to know the Earthlings. There is probably a lot more good in them than we realise.' A couple of the elders agreed it was possible the inhabitants of Earth were misunderstood, though most were sceptical.

Chez thanked the elders controlling the interstellar flights, said goodbye then approached Breno and QT, informing them she was going home.

'How did you go with the elders in the interstellar section?' Breno enquired. 'Did they show interest in your proposal?'

Chez sounded hopeful. 'I think so, Breno. All I need now is for you to put a good word in for me.'

Breno promised he would except that she would have to return to the next meeting of elders if she wished to succeed.

She touched hands with QT42 and Breno, then hurried to climb aboard an approaching T-Pod. She punched in her flight details and sat down, pulling the harness over her as the craft started moving. Her T-Pod quickly accelerated, heading for the launch ramp. It careened up the ramp, launching itself skyward, the thrust pushing her tightly into the seat. Her departure was a lot smoother than her arrival.

Apart from a few ducks and dives, the pod elevated quickly, settling into full flight. 'That was quite an experience,' she told herself. 'If only I could show Alan and Scotty around Metropolis Central. Wouldn't that be something to get their minds around!'

Astrospace Galexiana accepted the proposals put in place by the president and his staff, so much so they now had their own office within the Admin building, all funded by the US government. Big Mal called the office 'Internal Monitoring', placing a likewise sign on the office door. In his mind, the name served as a description without a substantial meaning, thus leaving him with no questions to answer.

Internal Monitoring was now an official part of Galexiana. The Admin staff were never notified why Internal Monitoring had come to be, and the mystery and intrigue funded by the American Government was slowly becoming part of Galexiana's norm. It was the overall uncertainty that contained the unfolding events; no one knew exactly what was taking place within Internal Monitoring except Alan, Scotty and the Internal Monitoring staff.

Alan was receiving increased scrutiny from the president's office so was preparing accordingly. He had been asked on direct orders from the president to put a ten-point plan together for Internal Monitoring, the objective being to collect information from an extremely technologically advanced species. Hopefully the ten-point plan would explain the origins of why peace and unity had become a natural way of life on Univiah.

The plan had to consist of the ten most important factors that made Univian society the success it had turned into. Alan knew he would have no trouble getting the basic rules of Univian society. It was the technological information that would have to be prised from them. For now though, he was concentrating on the ten-point plan, which he would put to Chez next time they spoke.

Since Internal Monitoring's inception, Alan and Scotty's work shifts grew further apart. Rostering them on opposing shifts was deliberately orchestrated by Big Mal to intentionally separate them. Not that this bothered them as it was still business as usual when they met at the local bar, Scotty being the only staff member apart from the president to get personal updates directly from Alan.

It was now time to ask Chez if she was prepared to elaborate on the ten-point plan. Chez answered immediately.

'Hello, Alan,' Chez greeted in her usual friendly fashion. 'You never called yesterday.'

Alan elaborated on why. 'I've been busy getting briefed on a project whereby we intend to use Univians as role models to create a better society on Earth.'

'Can I do anything to help?' she offered.

Alan laughed. 'I was hoping you would say that! Yes, you can. I've been told to put a ten-point plan together based on the successful way your civilisation has evolved.'

Chez was eager to relay this information. 'I will do my best. Point one: We never bear false witness against one another. Point two: We never take or use the God the Universe's name in vain. Point three: We keep one day a week of rest in God's name. Point four: We honour our parents. Point five: We never hurt or kill another citizen. Point six: We take one partner and never consider being with anyone else's. Point seven: We never steal from one another as no one ever goes without the necessities to create a meaningful and comfortable life. Point eight: We never covet our neighbours in any shape or form. Point nine: We have no idols nor would we ever worship one. Point ten: We would never honour other Gods, only God the Universe. How's that, Alan? There's no rocket science in that, is there?'

Alan's mind was racing to grasp the significance of those ten points. They sounded very similar to what was known on Earth as The Ten Commandments. 'I guess not. Still, they seem a very simple set of rules for a sophisticated society such as yours. Do you consciously live to the rules or does it come naturally?' He was interested to know this.

'Univian society has used the rules for thousands of years so they now come naturally instilled in our genes.'

'Do you have a specific title for the ten rules?'

'Yes, we simply call them the Ten Golden Rules.'

Alan told Chez he was about to take his findings to Admin for analysis. 'I do hope I've been helpful,' she replied before signing off. 'Goodbye, Alan.'

Alan walked over to Admin, choosing to go past Big Mal's office. It was quicker and shorter. On entering Internal Monitoring, he walked up to the office counter and placed a single sheet of paper on the desk. 'These are my ten findings,' he explained. 'I trust you find them easy to understand. They are brief and to the point. Each one is explanatory in its own right.'

'Is this some sort of joke?' the lady behind the counter asked.

Alan assured her, 'No, not at all. It was just easier for me to print The Ten Commandments than type the supplied rules, which they call the Ten Golden Rules. If you doubt my analogy of the ten-point plan, there is a recording of our conversation in your database.'

His shift now over, Alan headed home for the day. Willy met him at the gate, informing Alan he no longer needed a pin to leave, only to get in. This was the order of Big Mal himself, Willy explained.

On entering Hudson Close, Alan immediately sensed trouble. A group of journalists were parked outside his house. *They've found out! They've finally got a hold of it*, was his first thought. His reaction was to turn and flee, then for some instinctive reason, he drove straight ahead and turned into Pam's driveway. His ploy was to make them all think he lived with Pam, so he shut the car door then walked straight to Pam's front door, praying it wasn't locked. Turning the door knob, he let himself in as if he lived there, shutting the door behind him as they all watched.

'Pam, are you there,' he whispered. 'Pam, it's Alan.' No one answered.

'What's all this about?' Pam suddenly asked from behind, her presence momentarily frightening him.

'Oh Pam, I'm so, so, sorry. It's just that I had nowhere to, well, let's say I was lost for what to do, so I thought I would try pretending I didn't belong next door.'

Pam raised one eyebrow at him. 'Interesting to say the least, Alan. Do you mind telling me what this is all about?'

'It's all to do with my work, Pam. It's quite a story, although I really doubt you would believe me if I told you.'

'Why don't you try me,' she smiled. 'After all, you *have* commandeered my lounge room.'

'I'm truly sorry, Pam. I'm in quite a predicament.' He couldn't be 100% sure the media had found out, though it stood to reason. Why else would they be gathered outside his house?

Phil Muirhead

'I've already figured that out, Alan. Now are you going to let me in on all this or are you going to stand in my lounge room peeking out the window until one of them notices you?'

Alan was suddenly nervous. What if she didn't believe him or he came off sounding like a crazy person? He was so fond of Pam, in more ways than one. It mattered what she thought about him. He took a deep breath, trying to steady his nerves. 'It involves this woman,' he began.

'Why am I not surprised,' Pam laughed. 'The only man inside my house for years, and I'm already hearing confessions of another woman. I gather it isn't your sister then?' Her eyes were sparkling with mirth.

Alan immediately felt at ease. Pam just had that way about her. 'No.' He shook his head to emphasise the statement. 'I've never met her physically. I've only ever spoken to her.'

Pam adorably cocked that one eyebrow again. 'So you met her on the internet?'

Alan took the plunge then blurted, 'No. I met her via my work as an astrophysicist. She lives on another planet.' He waited for the penny drop. He saw it in Pam's eyes the minute it did.

'What! Can you say again please, Alan.'

'You heard it right the first time. I have been in contact with another civilisation.' Alan's eyes searched hers, looking for any sign she was about to call the men in white coats.

Pam burst out laughing. 'Are you sure you haven't been using too many of those trick cigarettes after work?'

The relief flooded through him at her attempt of humour. 'How did you know?' he grinned.

'I can smell them when the wind blows this way,' she winked.

Alan was serious now. 'Please believe what I just told you, Pam. I'm telling you the absolute truth. I've been in contact with highly evolved extra-terrestrials. And incidentally, it's the first time I've ever smoked the stuff.'

Pam mulled over what he had just said. However, only for a few moments. 'So your friends outside are chasing the story of a lifetime then?' She looked at him, full of cheek. 'I can see the headlines now, "Australian Astrophysicist Uses Dope for the First Time".'

Trust Pam to put him at ease. She really did have a great sense of humour. Alan couldn't help but laugh. 'Afraid so. Got any ideas how to get rid of them?'

'Not really. They're a bit like cockroaches, almost impossible to get rid of.' Then more seriously, 'Can you phone someone from work?'

As soon as she said that, Alan's mind whirred into gear. 'That reminds me. I have to call the president. I told him I would call if these circumstances ever arose.'

'Which president? The president of the bowls club?' Pam jested.

'No, the President of the United States. I know it must sound a bit much, but again, it's the truth.' This time, Pam did look astounded.

She sat on the couch, holding her right index finger to her temple. Alan noticed she was deep in thought, so he remained silent himself. 'I have an idea,' she explained. 'Let me organise this. Take off your shoes.'

'What!'

'You heard me. Take off your shoes and pull your shirt out of your jeans. Here's an old baseball cap of mine you can wear. You're going out to wash your car,' she told him firmly.

'Are you fair dinkum?' He wasn't sure what she was up to. Yet for some reason, he trusted her.

'Yes. Just make yourself look relaxed. I'll get a bucket and sponge for you. When you've been out washing the car for a few minutes, I'll go over to your place to water your pot plants be-cause you're in Australia on holidays. Do you get where I'm coming from?'

'Sounds crazy enough to work. Do you have a plan B if it doesn't?' Pam just grinned at him.

Alan started washing the car, ignoring the paparazzi while pretending to be absorbed in his chore. Pam walked right through the crowd then turned to ask everyone what was going on. 'We have the scoop story of a lifetime. All we need is the guy that lives here,' one of the reporters explained.

Another asked the burning question, 'When does this guy get home?'

Pam tossed her hair over one shoulder. 'I'm not sure, exactly. He asked me to water his plants and feed his cat while he's away.'

'Away!' they cried in unison. 'Where's he gone?'

'Back to Australia, I believe,' Pam lied through her teeth.

'When did he leave?' they pressed.

'Yesterday afternoon. Now if you'll excuse me, I have some plants to water.' She left them to grumble among themselves as she headed over to Alan's garden.

Word circulated fast and within minutes everyone left. 'Thank God they're gone! 'You were brilliant,' Alan exclaimed.

'Brilliant at what? Telling lies?' she laughed.

'I know what you mean. I'm sorry it had to be this way,' Alan apologised.

'Don't be sorry, Alan. It's the most excitement I've had in my life for years, though I'm just not accustomed to trickery and blatant lies.'

'You would do well if you lived on Planet Univiah. Which reminds me, I have to ring the president. I'll put my phone on speaker so as you can listen.' Pam watched as he nervously dialled the number, wondering how the day could start so drearily then suddenly turn so outrageous.

His call was answered with, 'This is the office of the President of the United States of America. I notice you have been given a priority number. Please wait until your call is processed.' Alan looked at Pam and shrugged his shoulders, holding his hands apart as if to say, 'What happens now?' The voice returned. 'The president has been made aware of your call, Alan Holmes. Please wait. He will be with you in a minute.'

After what was surely less than a minute, President Kennard came on the line. 'Hello, Alan. I guess the word's out, am I correct?' Alan agreed that he was pretty sure this was the case, yet he didn't know who would have leaked the information. The president assured him that this would be investigated.

Kennard asked him if he could come to Washington as soon as possible so they could confront the media in a united, civil manner. 'I need you, Alan. In fact, I can't do it without you as you're the only one who knows everything from woe to go. The whole world is about to learn of Univiah's existence, so can you head to San Bernadino airport where I'll have a Learjet waiting?'

Alan said of course he could then asked if Kennard had received his report on the ten-point plan? The president acknowledged that he had, and had also listened to the recording. 'It seems we've had the rule book all along but disobeyed the rules. I'm looking forward to seeing you, Alan. Have your accompaniment inform me the minute you arrive; meanwhile, I will organise an escort to meet you at the airport you leave from.'

Pam was dumbstruck by the conversation, offering to feed the cat and water the plants while Alan was away. Alan thanked her and asked for her phone number before he left.

They walked to the front patio, Alan thinking how he had a hide to walk in on someone and take over her house! Pam was thinking what a great day she had had, despite the antics. He said goodbye, then without warning gave her a quick kiss on the cheek, although it suddenly turned into a deeper embrace.

He kissed her a third time, and her arms came up around his neck. Having never kissed anyone on impulse in his life before, he was a little shocked at his behaviour. Thankfully, Pam was just as responsive. Unfortunately, they had to break apart as Alan needed to organise his flight to Washington. As he walked to his car, he looked back, seeing her eyes full of promise. He had liked Pam for so long, he couldn't actually believe that she might feel the same way about him.

Upon arriving at San Bernadino airport, two officers were holding a sign with Alan's name on it. Alan stepped out of the car and introduced himself, leaving his car in the parking bay. The officers explained they were there on orders from the president to escort him to his office. They would be travelling by private Learjet, courtesy of the US government. Alan was advised he was under the officers' orders until they arrived.

TEN

Alan felt a bit uncomfortable. He had never had a lot of time for those in uniform. His childhood interview with the air force at Wallaby Heights School had instilled a sense of distrust in any type of uniform. As far as Alan was concerned, anyone wearing a uniform was under the influence of control, and control and authority had never sat well in Alan's world of events.

As the plane landed, the officers handed Alan over to the president's staff. This time, Alan was accompanied by the secretary of state and her personal staff. They were all polite and behaved in a relaxed manner that Alan readily accepted. Eventually they boarded the president's helicopter and headed directly to the White House, touching down on the lawn outside the great house. One of the guards mentioned that President Kennard had been informed of their arrival. Another indicated his intention to contact Homeland Security's head office to advise they had arrived without incident.

Suddenly a group of officialdom appeared beside the helicopter, some of them wearing military uniforms while others wore police uniforms. Alan was led inside, where he was greeted by the president. Shaking hands, he asked Alan to take a seat. They had some things to discuss before addressing the masses during a press conference tomorrow afternoon at two o-clock. The president informed him, 'It is my intention to inform the nation and the world what has taken place over the last four months. To do this, I will need you by my side when questions are forthcoming. All I ask is for your complete cooperation. You will need a relaxed posture along with a cool head as we don't want to be ringing alarm bells all over the world. Do you get the picture?'

Alan nodded. 'I certainly do. I'll just tell it like it is, that they're a sophisticated, intelligent, peaceful civilisation. How does that sound?'

'It sounds like we could learn a lesson or two from them if you ask me,' Kennard acknowledged.

'We sure could, Mr President. If we do, society as we know it would go through an unimaginable peaceful transformation.'

The president excused himself saying he had a lot to arrange for tomorrow, but that he'd send someone to get Alan before the press conference. Alan bade the president goodbye and went to his room. The room was spaciously luxurious, containing every commodity a foreign diplomat might need. He picked up the phone to order a meal from the guest meal list, then opened the fridge after deciding to have a few beers before he ate and slept. Soon a knock came upon his door. On opening it, he couldn't believe what he was seeing – an impeccably dressed steward pushing a silver trolley with the meal he'd ordered.

Nothing was left to the imagination. Alan had never seen anything like it – different wines adorned the centre shelf, some on ice some not, a selection of fresh sauces, a seafood entrée he hadn't ordered, sweets he hadn't ordered and a main course of glazed lamb with an accompaniment of dishes containing freshly cooked and baked vegetables, all sitting on a flat heated section of the trolley. Alan sat down to eat what was without a doubt the best meal of his life, then turned in for the night. Tiredness had washed over him like a blanket.

Sunrise awakened the birds outside Alan's window. In turn they tweeted him awake. He made a strong coffee before dressing in readiness for the unknown: the 'what if's' and the 'if only's' had once again come to haunt him. Usually, he could put them out of his mind, yet this time they wouldn't dissipate no matter how hard he tried. The only way to fix them would be to get it over and done with, he told himself.

He finished his coffee then started to make some toast. Then there came a knock on the door. Opening it, Alan recognised him immediately; it was the person wearing the military uniform when he arrived in the helicopter. He noticed it was an air force uniform.

'The president asked me to accompany you to the conference room,' he informed Alan as if to give a direct order. 'I'll be back to get you in an hour for morning tea.' Alan suggested that was rather early.

'The press conference has been brought forward,' he was told. 'That will alleviate a lot of the congestion they are anticipating.' There simply wasn't enough room for the press conference, so changing the time would help reduce the anticipated chaos.

Morning tea turned out to be a rather solemn affair where little was said. In their minds, Alan and the president were both contemplating the events about to happen. Both were nervous and both were tired. After the meal, the president stood upright and stretched his arms in a backward movement as if to relieve the stress. 'Well, Alan, the time has come, so let's get it over with.'

Alan agreed, taking his phone out of his pocket and sending a text he had previously saved to drafts. It read: Hi Pam. I hope you are well. Turn on your television. Regards, Alan.

They both walked out through the foyer onto a makeshift stage to be greeted by people as far as they could see. The crowd roared in anticipation as microphones were thrust through the air on long telescopic rods. Television cameramen were jostling for prime positions. People everywhere were being restrained by police as they vied for better vision. The president turned to Alan, telling him they should get to the stage microphones as quickly as possible. They took their positions behind the microphones. The president outstretched his arms, patting the air at the same time as issuing commands for less noise. Eventually the crowd quietened enough for him to speak. 'Thank you, thank you,' he declared before starting his speech.

'Men and women of the world, we gather here today to announce events that will go on to be remembered by mankind for evermore. I have here beside me America's foremost astrophysicist. Please let me introduce Alan Holmes from Astrospace Galexiana.'

The crowd went wild again, clapping, yelling and whistling. Word had been passed around more than Alan imagined. 'Let me go on,' the president said. 'Alan is the first human to ever contact and speak to beings from another civilisation. His first contact was made some four-and-a-half months ago. Since then, he has been in contact with a planet called Univiah on a regular basis.' You now could have heard a pin drop.

'On all accounts, Univians are a very sophisticated, highly intelligent species living a peaceful existence deep in the Milky Way, about 1,695 light years from Earth. They have knowledge and technology beyond what we currently understand. Technology people of the world could use to enhance their lives for evermore; technology so sophisticated it's beyond our capacity to fathom. Technology we will ask them to impart as our relationship with Univiah strengthens.' The crowd cheered.

'So far Alan has described their society as an open book. They have no commerce nor do they have governments. They are all equal as there are no rich and no poor. Their decision-making is orchestrated by Univiah's elders, who after reaching a certain age, voluntarily handle the planets infrastructure. Their belief in God is such that God is part of the Universe, referred to as God the Universe. They live by a strict set of rules that equate to our very own Ten Commandments. I will now hand you over to Alan for any questions you may have regarding events so far.'

The crowd cheered, clapped and whistled. The atmosphere was electric, literally buzzing with excitement. Questions were being asked by ten or twenty journalists at one time. Alan couldn't understand a word so he held his hand up.

The Believer

As the crowd quietened down, Alan explained, 'For the rest of this interview, I will point to the person I wish to talk to. All I ask is for you to please put a hand up if you have a question. In return for an answer to a question, I would ask that the rest of you please keep quiet or no one will be able to hear my answers. Now, let's try again.'

A show of hands sprang up everywhere. Alan picked a young lad who stood at the furthermost part of the crowd. It took a whole half-minute before someone finally got a microphone to him. 'Thank you, Mr Holmes. My name is Kevin Clark. I'm a freelance journalist. I have a two-part question: How did you originally go about contacting Univiah? Also, what type of communication is currently taking place? Is it verbal or is it radio communication? Oh, sorry, it's actually three questions. Are you communicating with a male or female of the Univian species?'

Alan smiled before answering in a relaxed style that the president couldn't have mastered better. 'Firstly, it was Univiah who had the knowhow to set up contact by locking on to an enhanced digital code I transmitted. Fortunately, it didn't have to transmit any further than our nearest satellite before they deciphered the code. Secondly, we are communicating orally using the English language, which incidentally took the female Univian only one day to perfect and speak fluently. She learned English by watching our television networks.'

The next question came from a rather shy lady who half-heartedly had her hand raised, thinking she wouldn't be noticed. Alan was careful who he chose, preferring those who looked the underdog. It was his way of saying you're all equal, just the same as in Univian society. Her question was simple but meaningful. 'Hi, Alan, my name is Kris. I'm a university student. My question is, "What does Univiah expect from us?" To me, it doesn't seem feasible that a sophisticated civilisation would simply give away technology. Surely there would have to be certain requirements?'

Alan thanked her for her question then said, 'You're on the right track, Kris. Univiah would undoubtedly require that we convince them we are worthy of the knowledge we ask of them.

Phil Muirhead

So far, I have learned we would all have to be living and abiding by The Ten Commandments, or what they refer to as the Ten Golden Rules, before they part with anything. A peace-loving society such as Univiah wouldn't gift technology if they thought we were going to use it to the detriment of our own wellbeing, nor would they gift technology they thought we would fire back at them as missiles.'

There was another show of hands. This time Alan picked a journalist from the front row who explained he had a UFO column in a locally produced magazine. He went on to ask Alan if it were possible Univiah could be watching them at this very moment. If they were watching, how were they going about it?

Alan chuckled at this. 'I will guarantee they are watching us right now. The method they use is via our television networks. It's very easy for them to connect to our satellite television networks, giving them a perfect understanding of everything that happens on Earth. By the way, they were watching us long before I came into the picture.'

The next question came from a man who described himself as an expert on extra-terrestrial phenomenon. 'I have only one question: Do you know of any events whereby it could have been the Univians in previous UFO sightings?'

Alan responded truthfully. 'I actually know of two; the first event took place at Westall High School in Melbourne, Australia, on the sixth of April, 1966. The second was a similar event in 1969, only nine days after man first set foot on the moon. It was at Wallaby Heights State School in outback Australia. From memory, it was witnessed by about ninety students and teachers.' Alan stopped short of mentioning he was the first student to witness the event yet advised everyone to go to the internet for more information.

A series of questions came from a journalist situated in the middle of the crowd. 'Len Collens from the *Evening News*. I would like to know more about the social aspects of Univian society. Do they marry? Do they believe in euthanasia? Do they interact with other civilisations? Can you please give a broader outlook of Univian society?'

Alan spoke into the microphone clearly, happy to elaborate on these questions. 'I certainly can. We should all take notice of the broader aspects of their society, particularly if we aspire to a better world. Univians do interact with other species, one of which they saved from their planet's demise. These people are very active and love to work as they like to be continually on the move. The Univians noticed this great attribute so utilise them as live robots, creating benefits for both species. Getting back to the first part of your question, yes they do marry, though they carefully choose a partner then remain monogamous until death. When they reach about three hundred years of age, they outlive their usefulness so put themselves to sleep. Reportedly, their spirit goes to the very same place as ours, call it heaven or the promised land. One day we will be spiritually aligned with every species in the universe.'

Noticing a clergyman in the audience with his hand held high, Alan asked him for his input. 'Alan, I represent a religious organ-isation. Earlier on, the president said your alien friends live and abide by The Ten Commandments. How can you be sure they go about their lives using our God-given rules? Can you provide evidence? As a man of the clergy, I suggest you provide all of those here today with proof as I'm very sceptical about every-thing I've heard.'

Alan answered instantly, the word 'sceptical' pricking his at-tention. 'Well, Padre, there's nothing like a good old sceptic to take the wind out of your sails. Actually, I'm used to sceptics as my mother was a prime example. Padre, I can provide whatever proof you need, unless the Univians have been lying to me, which they haven't because they don't know how to lie.'

The crowd was silent now, listening intently to Alan. 'Tell me, Padre, do you and your members live by our ten God-given rules? If you do, please explain how you go about doing so. You shouldn't be short of answers. Just remember, Padre, before you do answer, that most of the population on Earth and Univiah are watching and listening. Let's let them be your judge.' The Padre looked away without answering.

The next question came from a man wearing a military uniform. 'Alan, Lieutenant Robert Swanburgh, US Military Forces. My question is, How do you know these new-found friends of yours aren't setting us up to annihilate the whole of humankind? Shouldn't we be doing something to prepare ourselves for the likely event of these beings overtaking our civilisation?'

Alan stirred. 'What likely event? The one you're making up in your head?'

The lieutenant rebuffed. 'I don't see it as in my head. I see it as a distinct possibility.'

Alan addressed him directly. 'You do, do you? Let me tell you some facts before you sway anyone else with your possibilities. Univians don't even know how to go about warfare. On top of that, not a single Univian has been killed or ever killed another Univian, whether in warfare or not. Now, would you be prepared to tell everyone here how many people have been laid to rest through your actions in the military?' Like the padre, the lieutenant never responded.

Alan answered question after question before declaring he had had enough. 'I seem to be repeating myself,' he told the crowd. 'I have only one more thing to say, "Please remember that it's us who are aliens in this incredible universe, not the Univians. You will all be kept truthfully informed of future interactions with the Univians." That's all I have to say for now. Thank you for listening and for your thoughtful questions. I will now hand you back to the president to further brief you then close the meeting. Thank you all once again.' Alan turned and waved goodbye as he walked from the stage, leaving the closure of the press conference to the president.

As Alan sat waiting for the president, his phone rang. 'Alan, it's Pam.' Cherished words coming from someone he now considered a lovely neighbour and friend. 'You were wonderful on the television. I thought you outclassed the president by far.'

'Thanks, Pam, although I'm beginning to wish I had never started all of this! Anyhow, how's the cat?'

The sound of her laughter was music to his ears. 'He's sulking. He misses you. When will you be home?'

Alan said he'd let her know tomorrow, and she offered to pick him up from San Bernadino. He was grateful for her offer, though let her know his car was already parked at the airport. After a bit more friendly banter, he ended the call. He actually couldn't wait to get home to see her again.

Finally, the president was free of the masses. He walked straight over to Alan and shook his hand, commenting on Alan's magnificent performance. He was pleased how well everything had turned out. President Kennard then asked Alan to join him for a drink. It turned out to be many drinks with a whole range of politicians and heads of government departments.

The gathering dispersed leaving only the president and Alan. It was a time to reflect and discuss future involvement with the Univians. Alan reminded the president of the necessity to start an advertising program whereby every citizen on Earth could be informed of the ten rules required to obtain and live the Univian dream. The president agreed, informing Alan he already had plans in place for a massive advertising program that would be implemented throughout the world.

Following hours of discussion, Alan explained he had a plane to catch. 'You have plenty of time,' the president responded. 'I'll come with you and personally deliver you to the airport in my chopper.'

Alan readily accepted his offer, wondering how on earth his life could ever have been transformed into its current status. Somehow it all seemed a natural occurrence, one he had no control over. He just hoped his father was observing from above.

On arrival at the airport, the president escorted Alan to the same Learjet he arrived in. Alan waved to the president one last time as the Learjet turned towards the main runway. A feeling of prestige penetrated his thoughts. It was a feeling he had never had before. A feeling he quickly put out of his mind, realising both himself and the president would become no one special once Earth adopted Univiah's lifestyle.

ELEVEN

The Learjet touched down in San Bernadino. Alan was so glad to get in his mustang and drive home. Pam bounded out her front door as soon as he drove into his driveway. Getting out of the car, he walked right up to her, giving her a hug and a kiss. It was a sincere moment that seemed to be so natural. Alan invited her inside where they chatted about past events in their lives, their likes and dislikes, their children and their ex-partners. However, the conversation always returned to Chez and Univiah.

'When do I get to meet Chez,' Pam asked.

'As soon as I get back to work, if you wish to come in with me?'

'Will your boss mind?' Pam was hesitant. Alan assured her it would be okay.

'Would you like to come over for dinner?' Pam asked. Alan immediately took her up on the offer. He said he'd be over after a shower and change of clothes.

'I have a large bottle of wine I've been saving for a very special occasion, although I just didn't think the opportunity would arise. Now I believe it has.' She winked at him. Their mutual attraction to each other was growing by the minute.

'Well, I did have to travel all the way from Australia to find you,' he joked.

The night took its natural course, and everything transpired as if an author had prepared a script for a movie based on two people who were meant to finally find one another. The next morning, both woke knowing they were embarking on a new life, drawn together by a series of unexpected circumstances and events only God the Universe could pre-empt.

Their journey to Astrospace Galexiana the next morning had both Pam and Alan rediscovering and comparing different aspects of their past to what was now taking place in their lives. On arrival, Alan prepared Pam for Willy's sense of humour, hoping he would do one of his command performances. He wasn't disappointed. As he pulled the red mustang up at security, Alan immediately knew Willy was in fine form. After introducing Pam to him and bantering for a bit, Alan headed to the observatory.

Pam sat beside him as he prepared to contact Chez. Apprehension flooded over her as she wondered how she was going to handle this. She was about to speak to a being from an alien civilisation, yet her subconscious was involuntarily playing tricks with her thoughts. No wonder Alan had been suffering anxiety problems. Pam was shaking like a leaf.

Noticing her nervousness, Alan livened up the proceedings as the audio came to life. They didn't have to wait but a moment before Chez greeted them.

'Hello, Alan. You did a fine job in Washington. I see you have a partner with you for this communication. May I speak with her?' Alan told her that of course she could, pushing the microphone towards Pam and nudging her to speak.

'Hell, Chez,' Pam stammered. You'll have to excuse me because I'm feeling so nervous. Even though Alan has told me so much about you.'

Chez's warm voice responded immediately. 'You don't need to be nervous, Pam. I am not that different than you. I can tell Alan has made a wise choice as you are a very sincere person.'

Pam steered the conversation towards small talk mostly about women in Univiah, what they wear, their likes and dislikes, what Univian women did in their spare time. They could have been neighbours talking over the back fence if anyone was listening. Love thy neighbour was being taken very seriously indeed.

'What do you find most interesting about human females?' Pam asked.

Chez waited a moment before answering. 'You certainly come to the fore in the looks department. Human females are much prettier than human males in comparison to female and male Univians. You also instinctively know how to make the most of your body's divine inheritance. Unfortunately, Univian females look similar to males except for a few minor observances.'

Pam was intrigued. 'So how do you distinguish between male and female Univians?'

'Well, firstly, we have mammary glands just like you.' Seeing the humour of the conversation, they both started laughing. Alan, hearing the joviality, leaned towards the microphone to speak, as it was the very first time he had heard Chez laugh. 'You sound more human when you laugh,' he commented.

'It is a new-found art we have learned from you, Alan. The elders have accepted it can be used for enjoyment by every Univian citizen. It takes a bit of getting used to, yet when we master it, it's fun. So you see, we don't think everything you do is questionable.'

'Are there any other human traits you are considering adopting?' Alan asked, joining in on the laughter.

'Yes, we are considering music. It is a commodity we never knew about until we studied your species. We heard it quite some time ago while watching your television programs, just never understood it had therapeutic values. Univians have since found it is good for the soul. So you see, we too can learn from you so long as God the Universe's rules apply.'

Pam reached for the microphone as the words God the Universe intrigued her. 'Do you think God the Universe will accept us as he obviously has Univiah?'

'God already accepts you, Pam. It's you who has to accept God, and one way to accept God is to adhere to God's rules. Our God is also your God, and always has been. When you live to God's rules, your governments will become irrelevant. There will be no more corruption, no racism, no dishonest politicians, no graft, no religious torment, no greed, no wars. Sorry, I shouldn't lecture. I should have just said as ye sow so shall ye reap, though in humanity's case, you have yet to reap.'

Pam's nervousness had completely disappeared. 'Chez, your people have been to Earth before. Why don't you consider another visit? We would be overwhelmed to meet you.'

'I would love to visit,' Chez replied. 'I have already told this to the elders in our interstellar factory. They have no problems with me going on an interstellar journey although coming to Earth just to visit you may be a different story.'

Pam was curious. 'Why? We'll look after you.'

'I have no doubt *you* will, but the elders are not impressed with your people as a species. They actually fear for their lives in your species' presence.' Chez sounded forlorn.

'Have you been in our presence?' Pam wanted to know.

'Yes, on two occasions, yet while there the elders were worried about becoming a target for your military. These days it's your suicide bombers as well as your military.'

Pam was indignant. 'There is no way we would put Univian lives in jeopardy by letting a suicide bomber anywhere near you.'

Chez explained, 'The elders will take some convincing as they have been so horrified with the sport of your blowing yourselves and others to pieces. They even did a study on it, though so far it has them baffled. They can't understand why you want knowledge on disease eradication to promote longevity when you are prepared to blow one another and yourselves into oblivion. Having said that, I personally would still like to visit, so I will bring it up again when I next talk to Elder Breno or Elder Jenko.'

Pam hesitated, lost for words. It just occurred to her how we must look compared to a super intelligent species capable of observing everything we do. Alan eased the microphone away from Pam, informing Chez he would like to put a presidential committee together to at least prepare for a future visit.

Chez spoke with an air of uncertainty. 'I see no harm in putting something in place, although I'm going to have to present a good case for me to succeed.'

'Perhaps we can change the circumstances to suit the visit,' Alan suggested. He understood why the elders would be anxious about visiting Earth. Getting tangled up with the military was the last thing they needed. However, he figured there were ways around everything if it was dealt with properly.

He bade her goodbye, assuring Chez he would make preparations for the future even if it was postponed until they were happy to visit.

Chez responded positively, stating she would prepare a submission to the elders to visit Earth sometime in the future.

Chez closed her systems manager then boarded a T-Pod, programming it to take her to Elder Jenko. He had previously agreed to meet with her to discuss the possibility of another journey to Planet Earth. Her T-Pod began its decent towards a gantry and came to a halt outside the elder's residence.

'Chez,' he greeted her. 'You're determined to meet with your newfound friends, aren't you?' he said, extending his arms to greet her.

'I am indeed. Do you think the elders will approve if I put up a reasonable argument?'

Jenko considered her question for a moment. 'They might if you can guarantee the complete safety for all on board, along with a safe return for the craft. How you're going to do that is beyond me, knowing how humans conduct their lives. Maybe you could rendezvous in a remote, unpopulated area? Even then you have to ask yourself if there is a chance of being set up. Imagine how they would like an interstellar craft to pore over so they could extract the technology it contains.'

Chez went silent, her mind tossing over possible scenarios on arrival at Planet Earth. 'We do have the technology to monitor the landing site well before we land,' she explained.

Jenko gave brief thought to what she said before agreeing with her reasoning. 'Admittedly we do. It would alleviate most of the risk, yet whether the other elders will look at everything on its merits is entirely up to them. In the meantime, I suggest you compile a proposal to bring with you to Metropolis Central. Meanwhile, I will alert Breno of your plans and get him to arrange accommodation for both of us. I will also get him to organise a time slot for your proposal at the meeting? Does that make you happy?'

'More than happy!' Chez enthused. 'You can pick me up on the day, and we can travel together.'

Jenko agreed, telling her not to build her hopes up. 'For a start,' he pointed out, 'there is a strong possibility you may not be able to find a crew willing to travel to Earth. One thing is for sure – if your proposal is approved, I won't be coming along!'

Chez said her goodbyes, thanking Elder Jenko for his time. She instinctively knew she had an ordeal in front of her if her proposal was to gain acceptance from the majority of the elders. Nevertheless, she was determined to give it a go no matter what the outcome produced.

Alan and Chez's interactions had not gone unnoticed by Internal Monitoring; hence, the presidential elite were most impressed with the progress taking place. Alan's ability to communicate with Chez enhanced the prospects of obtaining Univian technology. This was something the president and every member of his government were taking very seriously. If anyone could sway future events, it would be Alan Holmes. Alan already had ideas on how to make the alien visit eventuate, though he needed it to be done his way if it was to be a success. Somehow, he had to get

Internal Monitoring and the president to agree to his requests as there was no way the Univians would visit on any terms other than their own.

Alan's first tactic was to tell Scotty his plan to have only Scotty, Chez and Alan as the masters of ceremony. The government, who were used to wielding authority, would have to be told what to do for a change, which was something they would not like. Alan started the proceedings by ringing Internal Monitoring and asking them to set up a meeting. In the back of his mind he was thinking that if the extra-terrestrial visit did in fact take place, he would need a trustworthy accomplice to help with the proceedings. Also lingering in the back of his mind was his distrust of power, particularly power exerted by government. There was no way the Univians would meet with them if anyone from the military was present, so people in uniforms were definitely out of the question.

The meeting with Internal Monitoring took place the next morning. Scotty agreed with Alan's proposals, his assertions making it easier to convince Internal Monitoring they should leave the forthcoming preparations up to them. They assured the hierarchy that they would organise a formal welcoming party, assuming the historic event eventuated. Everything went according to plan. Internal Monitoring were prepared to leave the arrangements to Chez, Scotty and Alan. Their only stipulation was that they be informed of all proceedings and that Alan had to inform the president of any associated developments taking place outside.

Alan and Scotty entered the observatory, both full of business. Alan suggested they nut out the proceedings. 'This is a first, Scotty,' Alan chuckled. 'I never thought I'd get to take part in organising an actual extra-terrestrial visit.'

'You and me both, Alan. I think the best way to go is make it simple. There's no point in complicating things for a species who don't even know what complicated means.'

When finished, they had a plan that was straightforward and easy to implement. When the Univians arrived, they would have a minimal guest list consisting of the president, his wife, the secretary of state, two presidential guards, two journalists, two television cameramen, the Australian Prime Minister, his wife and his two guards. Alan and Scotty would be the masters of ceremony and would give their partners the option of attending. No one would be allowed to wear uniforms, and no weapons of any nature would be brought within ten kilometres of the meeting place. Nobody whatsoever would be allowed to come within ten kilometres of the meetings location except those allowed by Alan, Scotty and Chez. The meeting place would be in a remote location in Central Australia.

'What about Big Mal?' Scotty asked. 'Do you think we should invite him?'

Alan disinclined to have him join them.

They then decided to inform Chez of their plan. Alan typed the password to alert her.

'Hello, Alan. Hello, Scotty. It didn't take long for you to get back to me,' Chez responded.

'We have a draft plan you can take to your elders,' Alan told her, explaining how they thought the meeting should take place in a remote location in Central Australia. He then delivered the news on who would be present, detailing how the remoteness with few attending would guarantee the utmost of safety for the Univian crew.

'You left a few people out,' Chez declared. I would very much like to meet your two daughters and their families if it's at all possible.

Alan assured her his daughters would now be put on the agenda as requested, though not their children as they were too young. They would remain at home with their fathers. Chez seemed happy with the draft plan, mentioning it would be unconditional there would be no weapons or uniformed militia present.

Finally she said she had to go, mentioning she was about to board a T-Pod to visit friends who lived nine thousand Earth kilometres away.

'Before you go, Chez, how long will it take you to get to your friend's house?' Alan asked.

'Slightly less than an hour in Earth time, travelling at a low altitude,' she informed them before biding them goodbye.

'There's something endearing about her, don't you think?' Alan said to Scotty.

Scotty raised his eyebrows before answering. 'Yes, she gets to you. It's her genuine sincerity along with her intelligence. Then if you throw in her childlike exuberance and twangy accent, you end up with quite a complex and lovable being.'

'You've hit the nail on the head,' Alan agreed. 'What's more, they are all that way inclined. Imagine for just a moment every human being living life in a state of bliss and love. If only we can learn to achieve the same result.'

If only.

Christmas came and went quickly. It was a break well overdue for all concerned, particularly Alan and Scotty. Alan's daughters and their husbands, along with their children, had arrived from Australia. Alan got on well with both sons-in-law, who were both in their early thirties. Mary's husband Daniel, and Jane's husband Michael, had been friends since primary school. Both worked for the same company back home in Australia. Mary's eldest child was a girl called Bonnie. She was four years old and a complete bundle of energy, while her younger brother Tyler at age three was apt to a slower pace, unusual for a boy of that age.

Jane had one child. Madison had just turned two, keeping Jane in a state of motherhood alert. Alan's sister Fiona and her husband Ross had two sons, Andrew and Clint, both whom were in their early teens. The whole family had just arrived from Dallas. Ross, a builder and always the life of the party, introduced himself to everyone then suggested it was time for celebratory drinks.

It was the first time the whole family had been together since Fiona was a teenager, yet everyone got on famously. Alan was also relieved his daughters and sister hit it off with Pam.

Accommodation was more than adequate using both Pam's and Alan's houses. Christmas lunch was spectacular. Everyone contributed something. Scotty and his new partner arrived with a few bottles of top-shelf wine and more beer than they could all drink in a week.

Everyone jubilantly drank the afternoon away talking trivia, reminiscing past events and discussing the possible visit from Univiah. It wasn't long before the Univians dominated most of the conversation. 'Who's coming if they actually decide to visit?' prompted Alan.

Fiona was the first to speak. 'None of my family, Alan. What happens if they intend taking a sample hostage back to Univiah?'

Alan laughed out loud at that. 'Don't be ridiculous,' he joked. 'They wouldn't risk taking back problems of any sort, let alone complications such as humans.' Everyone laughed at that. It was agreed that Pam would come to Australia for the visit, along with Alan's daughters minus the grandchildren.

Chez finally heard from Elder Jenko. His orders were concise and directly to the point. As usual, he kept talking until he had covered everything relevant, not letting Chez get a word in sideways. They would be leaving for Metropolis Central tomorrow at midday. He instructed her to have her Earth trip portfolio documented and ready to put forward at the meeting, making sure her explanations as to why and when the proposed journey should take place. Convincing the elders was up to her, as well as convincing a pilot he needed a long holiday, or preferably two pilots, considering the distance. She had quite a job in front of her.

Chez thanked him for his input, wondering how one person could form the longest sentence she had ever heard without drawing breath. Somehow, she'd rather talk to Alan and Scotty as they were much more interesting and playful.

Chez had thoroughly prepared everything required for the meeting. The next day, on hearing the dull noise of Jenko's T-Pod connecting to the gantry, she went outside to find the T-Pod door open and ready to depart. They pulled down their harnesses, causing the T-Pod to spring into life, quickly accelerating into the distance.

The journey created time to talk. Chez asked Jenko if he had any further thoughts on her trip to Earth.

'Yes,' he replied. 'I heard there are two fully trained pilots at Metropolis Central One. Both would like to do a stint away. They also have use of one of two of the latest interstellar craft at their disposal. Whether they want to go to Planet Earth and turn the journey into an extra-long test flight is up to them. One thing's for certain – if they agree to go, it will make your prospects more favourable in the eyes of the elders. We'll just have to wait and see what comes up at the meeting.'

'Is QT 42 greeting us?' Chez enquired.

'He's bound to be if Breno arranged our arrival. QT 42 is the best all-round robot we have. He seems to be able to turn his hand to everything.'

'Maybe I should invite him on the Earth trip,' she hinted.

'They're too small for the seating arrangement,' he remarked. 'Besides, it would drive him mad if he was subjected to months of doing nothing.'

Metropolis Central Two was getting close, the alarm signalling to take a seat and pull down the harness. The craft dropped and swerved before positioning its self in line for the pre-determined gantry that connected terminal 207. Sure enough, on arrival, QT 42 was there to greet them, urging them both to hurry. QT ushered them to Breno's room, asking if he was needed further.

Breno said no, but that they will need his presence all day tomorrow from sun-up. QT agreed then left to greet another T-Pod.

Tomorrow came quickly. Elders and citizens from every corner of Univiah gathered in a huge oval-shaped convention centre. Some were there for their own personal business, while others were gathering on community matters that needed recognition from the elders by majority. The presiding elders all gathered on a raised platform surrounded by a semicircular staircase easily accessed by anyone present. Those with personal business such as Chez were seated in a separate area, as were those who were representing organisations such as education or the community in general. Chez sat anxiously waiting for the meeting to commence. Suddenly she heard a call from behind. It was QT.

'Breno asked me to keep you company, then he asked me to greet another guest, then he asked me to contact Metropolis Central One to see if their two test pilots would agree to an extended test flight to include Earth. He doesn't realise I can't do three things at once.'

'What did the pilots say about the trip to Earth?' Chez asked, holding her breath.

'They told me it would be okay if it was alright with the elders, which suggests they should be able to make a decision at once. You will have to tell them about the pilots when it's your turn to speak because I haven't had time to talk to Breno.'

The convention centre went quiet as the elders signalled their willingness to get started.

The first citizen called forward was a teacher who explained how the children from her education facility were overjoyed by the music Univiah was experiencing, thanks to Planet Earth. She indicated it was her wish to include music in her manifest of daily events.

The elders agreed it would be allowed into every education facility on Univiah. Chez was pleased, knowing she was responsible for the new phenomenon now catching on all over Univiah.

Several more from the audience approached the elders before Chez was called forward. She spoke with conviction, assuring the elders that the people who would greet her on arrival at Central Australia were harmless, peace-loving citizens who could be trusted. She also indicated she was most aware of the untrustworthiness inherent in some humans, stating she was prepared to meet with the welcoming party alone. She explained how she was prepared to be locked out of the craft and left behind should the need arise. She then brought up the two pilots who were about to test flight the latest model craft. They had both agreed to extend their flight to Earth if it was agreed to by the elders.

Chez could see the concern among the elders. None of them had a lot of time for humankind as each of them were aware of the atrocities humans were capable of. Eventually Elder Dravo spoke up, surprising everyone by saying he too would like to accompany Chez and the two pilots. Two more Univians in the audience also came forward, indicating their willingness to go along if accepted. They were a couple who lived about three hundred kilometres from Metropolis Central. Their reason for wanting to go was that they both liked adventure.

The elders deliberated further, finally accepting Chez's proposal with provisos. The first proviso was that the senior pilot would never leave the craft, the second was the craft would remain in semi-lockdown, ready to take of in milliseconds, and the third was the pilots would be required to leave immediately if there was any sign of trouble. They must also leave the crew behind to perish if that was the case. All elders agreed that the third condition was highly unlikely, although it couldn't be disregarded. Never in Univiah's history had an interstellar craft been seized by another civilisation. As far as the elders were concerned, it would remain that way. Even if it did mean loss of life from the crew.

Finally, Breno asked the elders if the provisos were acceptable to all concerned. Everyone signalled their approval, and Chez thanked the presiding elders and her newfound crew for supporting her. She then walked back to QT, who congratulated her.

Back on Earth, knowing the meeting would be over by now, Alan decided to make contact.

Chez greeted him immediately. 'Alan, I have been waiting for you. I am so pleased to inform you that it's all good news. We will be meeting in person in about four months from now, yet that's all I can tell you. Nothing else has been worked out yet.'

Alan was gobsmacked. 'That's unbelievable news, Chez. We can't wait to get everything underway this end.'

'Me too, Alan. Sorry I have to cut you short, but I have to talk to the elder who has decided to come along. Goodbye, Alan.'

Alan was beyond excited so organised to meet up with Scotty to relay the good news. Scotty made an interesting point. 'Have you ever considered through no fault of our own that we seem to be combining theology with astrophysics?'

Alan pondered this. 'Somewhat,' he agreed. 'Although we didn't bring The Ten Commandments into the picture.'

'Indeed we didn't, yet don't you find it amazing that two completely different civilisations living many light years apart somehow ended up with identical sets of divine rules at entirely different points in time?'

Alan nodded. 'I find it more than amazing. Are you supposing that somehow Moses was prompted by the same deity that theologised Univiah?'

'Perhaps,' Scotty mused. 'Or could the flashing heavenly lights and the handing over of the stone tablets to Moses have been orchestrated by extra-terrestrials? The same extra-terrestrials who indoctrinated the Univians with the very same commandments?'

Alan laughed. 'God almighty, Scotty. Let's not go there. Our minds have enough to contend with just dealing with the astrophysical element. Let's leave our thoughts on theology to the religious. Hopefully they'll be able to theorise the divine mysteries of the universe.'

Scotty just grinned.

TWELVE

The months were flying by. Chez was busy organising the format for the journey to Earth, trying to put every detail in its respective order from take-off to landing. She reminded herself she had to ask Alan the coordinates of the property in Central Australia where they would be landing. She also wondered if the pilots were intending to use the gravitational pull of Earth's moon as a trajectory to swing them back towards the landing area in Australia. She was busy getting everything sorted when Alan contacted her.

'Hello, Alan,' her twangy accent resonated in an enthusiastic manner. 'I am in preparation for the journey. Can you please give me the dates that the full moon will be rising in Australia on our due date?'

Alan jested, 'With all of your technology, I thought you would be able to work it out yourselves.'

'Very funny, Alan. We can work out exactly where every solid structure in the universe is at any given time if we want. I just thought I'd include you.'

Alan laughed at her humour. 'I'm looking forward to finally meeting you. Do you need the coordinates of the cattle station where we're meeting?'

'Actually, no. I'll give you another surprise by working them out by using the station's satellite television dish. Just remember we need to meet out in the open.'

Alan mused, 'I was wondering about the station owners. It might be a bit rough using their facilities yet telling them they aren't welcome.'

'Owners. What a strange word.' Chez exclaimed. 'We have no such word in the Univian vocabulary. If you think about it, nobody really owns anything. We merely become custodians or users of material matter while alive, then go on to leave it all behind. When everyone is living equally with unrestricted access to personal possessions, the need to own is cancelled. So much for my little sermon, although I do hope it rings a bell within your monitoring department. I do have to go, Alan. Two friends have arrived, and I must talk with them as they are considering coming to Planet Earth. Please contact me tomorrow as I will have more news.'

Chez hadn't seen these two of her female friends for ages. Both friends kept themselves busy doing volunteer chores at an education facility. On arrival, her friends were waiting, extending their arms to greet her. Chez reciprocated. 'Anka! Cler! It's so good to see you. I have come to offer you both a seat on an interstellar voyage if you're interested.'

'Where are you going?' they asked in tandem.

To a planet called Earth! Do you want to come with me? They are an interesting species. I've been communicating with them for a while now.'

'Why not, Chez,' they both agreed. 'We're due for a change of pace.'

'Good! I'll inform the elders you will be coming.' Chez was elated as there would now be four males and four female Univians on board.

The Believer

Alan knocked on Big Mal's door. He hadn't seen much of Mal of late, especially since Mal had had a motorcycle accident. It had taken him a while to recover. Mal greeted Alan with a surprising, 'Come in, Alan. What can I do for you?'

Puzzled by Mal's friendly approach, Alan spoke in a friendlier tone than usual. 'I've been thinking we all have to be in Australia sometime in the future, so it would probably be more fitting if you arrange to finance the trip to Australia with the president?' Alan realised his request could go either way, though surprisingly Mal agreed wholeheartedly, telling Alan he would handle the American side of the preparations. He advised Alan that he could handle the Australian preparations.

Alan's eldest daughter was already working on the project. Fortunately, the Holmes family had been friends with the owners of the cattle station for many years. When Mary contacted them with their proposal to meet with the Univians on their property, they were astounded to say the least. After the initial shock, they agreed to everything, saying they would kill a bullock or two and stock up with food the week before everyone arrived. Apart from the required input, it would be a good money earner for the owners of the property.

It was now six weeks since the elders gave Chez the go-ahead to visit Earth. Alan and Scotty had used the six-week period to prepare for their arrival, making sure nothing was left to chance. Chez had also been preparing for the pending trip as were the rest of the crew, so there was very little left to do other than leave for Earth. Chez had been patiently waiting for Alan to contact when her alert signalled. She sounded so positive and full of business, telling Alan they would be leaving in two days.

Chez advised, 'There will definitely be eight of us. We will be leaving Metropolis Central Three on Monday the 1st of June, Earth time. We will arrive on Monday the 21st of September, Earth time and expect to arrive in Central Australia at about 9 p.m., give or take half an hour. As discussed, we don't want anyone there other than those invited. We would also like to meet Willy if he is prepared to come. It is his extremely dark complexion that fascinates us. We expect the whole meeting to be broadcast live on all of Earth's television networks so both Univiah and Earth can view the event live as it unfolds. We don't want anybody there in uniform, such as the police or the armed services. We would also be happier if you left the bodyguards behind. If they must come, they must be unarmed, and can you please call them minders instead of bodyguards as it sounds much more civil. Now, are there any questions?'

'No, it's straightforward,' Alan assured. 'Yet I'm interested to know how fast will you be travelling.'

'Somewhere around fifteen light years per day, according to the pilots. The new craft are two light years per day faster than the older ones.'

'Wow!' Alan exclaimed. 'When you say it like that, it's totally mind boggling.'

Chez laughed. 'It might be to you, but to us it is perfectly normal. Well, it's goodbye now until we meet in person. Oh, there is one more thing. On arrival, we will land about 50 metres away on the other side of the airstrip. I will be the first one out of the craft. Alan, please walk towards the craft alone to greet me. I expect a touch of both hands or a hug. You will be pleased to know as well as laughter and music, your species has taught us the art of hugging. You can choose whether the official greet is a Univian touch of hands or an Earthly hug. However, please do not bring anyone else near the craft. We will then walk over to your group, just remember, there is a lot more oxygen in Earth's atmosphere than we are used to, so it may take a little time for us to adjust. The rest will sort itself, I expect. Do you have any final questions?'

Alan thought for a moment. 'Yes. How do you pronounce Welcome to Planet Earth in your tongue?'

'It is, "Shuati Est Emporo Earth".'

'Thanks, Chez. I look forward to greeting you.'

'I look forward to it, too. Until then, it's goodbye for the next three months.'

'Wait! One more question. How do you say goodbye?'

'Quonsek,' Chez informed him. 'It literally means goodbye until we meet again yet is spoken in one word.'

After finishing work for the evening, Alan stopped the mustang beside Willy's cubicle, allowing room for other cars to go past. Then he walked over to tell him the news. 'Willy, how would you like a holiday in Australia in a few months?'

'Ya gotta be jokin, Al. No way is Big Mal goin' to let me go anywhere until my holidays are due.'

Alan told him not to be so sure about that. Alan relayed the whole story, mentioning how his jet-black skin was a source of intrigue to the Univians.

'Well, that's the first time I can recall this black skin doin' me a favour,' he chuckled. 'I hope they don't intend takin' me back to Univiah as a trophy showpiece.'

Alan couldn't keep a straight face, laughing loudly and telling Willy that Chez would probably fall for him because he was tall and lanky, just like they are.

'Yeah, mon, and if we have any kids, they'll be the first Univearth's in the universe. We'd be modern day Adam and Eves.'

Only Willy could come out with something like that. They both laughed, Alan mentioning he would go ahead and make all of the arrangements.

'Oh an' by the way, Al, pick me and Chez up an engagement ring and a wedding ring and two fig leaves just in case they do kidnap me.'

Alan drove off, looking in the rear-vision mirror. Willy was still laughing, his white teeth contrasting with his skin as visible joy to his self-made amusement. He really had the greatest sense of humour. As far as living by the Ten Golden Rules, he was a natural. If only everyone could be like Willy.

THIRTEEN

Metropolis Central was abuzz with activity as it was the evening before their journey to Planet Earth. Robots were preparing several craft for voyages throughout the universe, wheeling in trolleys full of the necessities required for interstellar travel; others were internally stocking the craft they were assigned to. The earthbound craft set aside for launch was receiving a final external clean and polish by the robots. Inside the craft, an elder was busy checking every incidental, making sure all items were on board and stowed properly.

The time had finally come. The Earth-bound craft was a sight to behold as it sat shining in the morning sun. Its immaculate, seamless and highly polished surface reflected the sun's rays like an iridescent, glistening mirror.

The crew, deep in conversation, were gathered in a circle near the craft, unperturbed by the commotion taking place everywhere. The duty elder walked over from the interstellar undercover parking lot and summoned the pilots to come aboard. He needed to explain a couple of changes that had been made to the new craft's automatic flight debris detection device. The craft will steer clear of anything solid by changing course by itself, he told them. It will then return to its original course, though they should still check their course, just in case. He then opened a locker showing the pilots a newer type of surveillance drone they would be using.

Phil Muirhead

'Take one of these pins,' he told them excitedly, 'and push this tiny button down with the pin to activate them. Hold them in the palm of your hand until they fly off. The drones were purposefully made to look like honey bees and perform in a similar fashion by darting all over the place so as not to attract attention. The only difference to an Earthly bee is that the drones have no interest in flowers.' All were capable of flying wherever they wanted or could be programmed to fly by individual control, instantly sending pictures and data back to the interstellar craft and Univiah. Alternatively, they could be controlled independently by using a virtual headset with a separate handset and toggle.

Following the update on the craft's new additions, the elder disembarked and wished them a safe journey. He then beckoned the rest of the crew to go aboard. Chez and her friends were next to go aboard, followed by the husband and wife adventure team. The elder was the last to board, giving a wave before he locked the hatch. The crew all went to their individual seats and sat down with legs outstretched. They pushed themselves and the seat backwards, lowering and locking the back of the seat into a horizontal position, which activated an elaborate body capsule. This capsule closed from the sides, entrapping the seat and the occupant tightly inside. The individual oxygen-fed padded capsules were now locked tight and held the occupants in an unmovable position.

The senior pilot walked around the craft and checked that everyone's capsule was securely closed, ready for the activation process. He then harnessed himself into his capsule for take-off. When his capsule was locked into position, a thirty-second delay would take place before the craft would spring to life. After activating the delay, there was nothing he could do to terminate the launch. Zap! A flash of light, and the craft was gone. There was nothing left to see except for the customary silvery hue that lingered momentarily above the launching pad.

The crew lay in their immobilised state while a slight vibration caused by the craft's reaction to the Univian atmosphere slowly lessened as it moved further away from Univiah's hold. They lay

The Believer

in complete darkness, waiting for the next procedure. The craft briefly pulsated then settled until the next timely pulsating burst occurred. Every pulsation was the precursor for an increase in velocity. The craft hurtled through the heavens while the crew waited to be released from their temporary state of immobility. It took several hours before the crew's capsules simultaneously opened, releasing them from their physical confinement.

Everyone stood up, pleased to be able to stretch and take a little walk around.

'Everything alright?' the elder asked the senior pilot, noticing him observing the instruments imbedded in the dashboard.

The pilot nodded. 'Yes, we're over the technical part until we arrive. When you get bored, just take a hibernation pill. There are one-, two-, or three-month pills available, depending on how long you wish to sleep.'

Meanwhile the crew were discussing humans. Chez, having the most knowledge to impart, tutored the crew by telling them about human traits as well as how to speak the English language. She also answered questions they were curious to learn.

'What has you most intrigued about them?' one of her friends asked.

'I think it's the way the majority of them fall in line with the minority control. The vast majority of the species are alright, still what puzzles me most is how the minority of their species wilfully control the majority. The minority seem to gain control in every facet of human life. Don't ask me how or why; perhaps it's something to do with insecurity?'

'Do you think the same minority would be prepared to kill us if they thought it was advantageous to them?' the senior pilot asked Chez.

'I'm sure they would if it was to their advantage. That's why the elders stipulated a pilot must stay on full alert ready to depart. However, my consensus is that there will be absolutely no trouble. Although we'll have to judge every event as it takes place, there is no other way we can do it.' Chez was honest with everyone.

'Did you think to scrutinise the people from the property where we are landing?' asked Elder Dravo.

'Yes. They're good people, more humane than most, probably because of their isolation. They have some of Australia's original habitants on the property, who I consider more trustworthy than the owners themselves.'

'How long will we be staying on Planet Earth?' asked the husband of the now-dubbed adventure team.

'I'm not sure,' Chez said, 'although there is nothing stopping us extending our visit if we wish to.'

'How do we go about that?' his wife asked. 'Surely we can't park the craft for extended periods of time?'

The senior pilot explained how to extend the visit if necessary. 'If need be, we can easily place the craft in a geo-stationary orbit like one of Earths satellites. We can then go back and forth whenever we like. That is the safest way for us to extend the visit; it is very easy to do and only takes a couple of Earth minutes to complete a return trip.'

'So what's involved with our initial landing?' Chez asked the senior pilot. 'Is there anything we should know?'

The pilot shook his head. 'Not really, it's all straightforward, given the capabilities of this newer-model craft. We can come and go as we please as many times as we want, while only using the gravitational pull of the moon if it's in an appropriate position.'

Back on Earth, Alan and Scotty were preparing for the media, who were organising the telecommunication networks all around the world. The biggest problem they were having was keeping the exact location of the meeting from the public and journalists. Everyone in Alan and Scotty's immediate family were sworn to secrecy, as were the president's staff. Willy was a different kettle of fish. Secrets were not his speciality, so he was simply told they would be meeting the Univians at a secret location, If someone did get hold of information, it was highly unlikely they would work out the rendezvous.

Alan's phone rang with the president wanting more information, like what size aircraft the airstrip on the station would accommodate.

'Certainly not Air Force One,' Alan replied. 'We will have to change to a smaller plane in Sydney, a 36-seat 200 series Dash 8 will land OK, though I'll find out for certain. There should be twenty-eight of us on board between Sydney and the cattle station. We're all set to arrive on the 20th September.'

Boredom was taking over on the interstellar craft. There was nothing to do, so the confined environment was taking its toll. The elder was first to take a hibernation pill, choosing to nap for two months. The husband and wife adventure team decided to do the same yet only for one month. Chez and her two friends chose to remain conscious for another week or so. They were younger so had plenty of energy and plenty to talk about, tending to make their own entertainment.

Appropriately, they were playing an old Frank Sinatra hit called 'Fly Me to the Moon'. Chez and both friends were listening intently, all trying to learn how to sing. Over and over they tried to perfect the lyrics. The bemused pilots thought their singing act was great, with their unusual behaviour helping take the monotony out of an otherwise boring journey.

After a few hours of singing, Chez declared another first for Univiah. Thanks to Planet Earth, they had learnt to sing, or at least they thought so. It sounded terrible by Earth's musical standards yet that never deterred them in the slightest.

FOURTEEN

Pam was attracting more attention than she ever had in her life, just about everyone in Big Bear knew who she was and where she lived. She had been out visiting a friend only to return home to find a gathering of people and cars outside her house. *Oh my God*, she thought, *I'm in the same position as Alan was except this time they know who they're looking for.* Her first reaction was to flee the scene, though it was no use, she told herself. Reaching for her phone, she just had time to send Alan a text before a news reporter stuck a microphone and camera in her face. 'Can you tell me where and when your partner and you will be meeting with the aliens?' he asked, not letting her get past the open door of the car.

'No, I can't.' She pushed on the car door, opening it harder than usual to get the reporter out of her way.

He persisted. 'Why not?'

'Because I don't know, that's why.' Pam was beginning to feel claustrophobic.

'Lady, even the president acknowledges the meeting will be taking place very soon.' This guy was really beginning to get on her last nerve.

'If that's the case, why aren't you asking him?' Pam elbowed her way around him. He was lost for words. Another female reporter walked up to challenge her but thought better of it.

In all, it was a gutsy performance by Pam, though thankfully one of the neighbours had rung the police. Every reporter present was quickly retreating. The police dispersed the remaining crowd, telling the stragglers to tell their counterparts if they came back for more, they'd be locked up for disturbing the peace.

Alan arrived just as the police drove off. 'What a day,' Pam sighed, hugging Alan and thanking him for rushing to her assistance. 'Do you think they'll be back?' she queried.

Kissing the top of her head, Alan reassured her. 'I doubt it. There are so many stories hitting every part of the globe that nobody is getting a scoop, simply because nobody knows what's true or false. One thing's for certain though, they'll know after September 21st.'

Pam had certainly had her life transformed since she met Alan, going from a laid-back suburban loner straight into the national spotlight and living a completely different life, like it or not.

At 7000 square kilometres, Quinella Downs Station was nowhere near the biggest cattle station in Australia, although it was certainly considered the most isolated. Situated south west of Alice Springs in the centre of Australia, driving there from Alice Springs was a slow process that took five to six hours in a four-wheel drive vehicle, depending on the condition of the road. Seldom did the road's condition allow driving above sixty kilometres per hour; it was considered one of the remotest bush drives in Australia.

The station was definitely one of the best locations in the world for a meeting between the nervous Univians and their carefully selected welcoming party. The hardened gravel airstrip at two kilometres in length was more than adequate for the intended Dash 8 to land, while the perimeters of the runway were suitable for the Univian craft to select a touchdown position of their choice. Fortunately, the runway had been reformed and compacted only three years earlier, making it an all-weather strip for a small to medium aircraft.

Deep in the Milky Way, the Univian crew were lying back in their respective seating arrangements, oblivious to their surroundings. Only the duty pilot remained awake and aware of the physical aspects of the journey. He observed the crew sleeping soundly, and in the serenity of the moment, he turned off the interior lights. There was not a noise to be heard as he walked the perimeter of the craft, looking out at the array of stars dotted in every direction as far as he could see. 'How did all this get here in the first place?' he asked himself, staring out into a never-ending universe. Something or someone must have been responsible somewhere in the past.

'How can all this be?' he kept asking himself while looking at a nearby star close enough to exert slight gravitational pull, the craft compensating as it passed. 'It's more than I can fathom.' He kept asking the same questions over and over, trusting that somehow he would discover an answer or a meaning to what he was observing. Nothing was forthcoming, which indicated that even Univians, as clever as they were, observed and questioned the cosmic universe just as humans did.

Chez and her colleagues were stirring from their trance-like slumber while waiting for their narcotic-like symptoms to break.

Final preparations were taking place at the president's office, prompting the president to call Alan with final details for the trip to Australia. They were to leave San Bernardino at 10 a.m. on the 17th of September, stopping in Hawaii to refuel before heading to Sydney. After meeting with the Australian Prime Minister and his wife, they would then board the Dash 8 for Quinella Downs, arriving there at about 3 p.m. on Sunday the 20th. That would give them a day to prepare if necessary. The camera people and reporters would be making their own way to the station.

It was breaking dawn when they left Big Bear for San Bernardino. Big Mal drove the shuttle bus he had hired for the occasion. *How he'd changed*, Alan thought, wondering if this was the new norm. They all listened carefully as Big Mal explained how to use Galexiana's credit card if they needed cash. He passed the plastic card to Pam, telling her the pin jovially and explaining how she could be the minister for finance. Alan's and Mal's futile arguments were thankfully a thing of the past, yet there was a side to Big Mal that Alan was wary of. He still doubted whether Big Mal would keep him employed should Univiah terminate their relationship.

Willy was quiet for the first part of the trip, but it was temporary. He was governed by his outgoing nature and childlike manner, an enchantment few people naturally possess except the Univians. Perhaps Willy naturally lived by the Ten Golden Rules, or was it his upbringing in a remote and poor part of Africa? Whatever made him tick, he was a delight to be with. He had never hurt a soul in his life and never would. Maybe this was why Chez wanted him to come along. Was it his special traits as well as her fascination with his jet-black complexion? On all accounts, they would soon know.

Mal pulled the bus up outside the terminal alighting to help with the ports. They were right on time as it was just before 10 a.m. Upon boarding the plane, the president shook hands with everyone as they came on board. They were all so impressed if not over-awed by Air Force One.

Following a few drinks, the conversation loosened up. The the president asked if they were nervous about meeting with the aliens. Willy was first to answer. 'I'm not nervous. I'm terrified. How do we know they're not carryin' weapons? One zap with a ray gun and we could turn to jelly.'

Alan laughed. 'You've been watching too much sci-fi, Willy. They're not coming here for any other purpose than to meet with us. Remember, they've already been here before and have no interest in harming us. They're much more enlightened and peace-loving than humans.'

The president's wife, First Lady Judith (Judy) Kennard, ever the sceptic, informed everyone that she would believe it all only when she physically saw it happen. Her comments reminded Alan of his mother, who never changed her mind about the Wallaby Heights encounter. She went to her grave an adamant non-believer, even after Alan's father had assured her that he was delivering parts that day and had witnessed the events himself. She still never accepted what they told her.

Like Alan's mother, the president's wife would actually have to see it for herself before admitting credibility to what she had been told. The secretary of state took a similar approach, saying she believed they had been in contact with Univiah yet wasn't so sure whether the unfolding events would lead to physical contact with members of another civilisation. If it happened, she would be happy to be surprised.

'So will I,' commented one of the guards. The other guard disagreed. He believed the Univians would turn up, making the encounter one that would lead to many more.

Scotty's partner spoke using logic instead of personal theories, pointing out how Univiah had instigated every move up to date other than Alan's first set of radio signals, so why would they go to all of this trouble to prepare a non-event? None of the sceptics came up with a plausible answer.

The interstellar journey to Earth was nearing its end, so the senior pilot was briefing the crew. 'We arrive in about twenty hours,' he advised them. 'Now is as good a time as any to tidy up and prepare to slow the craft.'

Everyone packed the incidentals they had been using, locking them tight into their respective containers. One by one they filed to their seats, accepting the deceleration process as an uncomfortable but inevitable part of the journey.

The senior pilot did his rounds and checked everyone was secure before the deceleration process was activated. Satisfied everyone was safely encapsulated, it was his turn to lock himself into his cocoon-like existence before the craft automatically started going through its radical deceleration process. The extreme events taking place outside their precious encapsulated environment didn't affect the Univian crew, who had to now wait until the craft slowed to a more manageable speed. The pilots could then manually operate the craft on its final critical flight path towards Central Australia. Eventually the capsules opened, setting the crew free for the final segment of the journey. Chez was going over the English language with her counterparts, yet as it turned out turned out, they had already grasped English from singing and watching the video clips during their musical interludes.

Both pilots were standing over the craft's elaborate dashboard and monitoring their pre-course coordinates. They updated and adjusted their speed and course by typing command prompts into the navigation systems.

'How did you obtain the coordinates of the property in Central Australia?' the junior pilot asked Chez.

'I was checking out the station folk through their television satellite dish then noticed the latitude and longitude reading on their television decoder,' she explained.

'Hope you got the right dish otherwise we're going to frighten the hell out of some unsuspecting humans.'

'They're right,' Chez assured him. 'They have another dish for their internet and phone service that correspond, so please don't worry.' She went on to inform that they would be touching down at the airstrip not far from the station, where everyone would be there to welcome them.

On arrival at Sydney International Airport, the presidential entourage were quickly introduced to their Australian counterparts. Alan performed the introductions, making sure everyone met Mr Peter Kealing, Australia's prime minister, who had only recently been elected. Customs was extremely busy, which worked to their advantage. To everyone's relief there were no news reporters or photographers to be found. It was only when they all boarded the Dash 8 that they realised how smooth the transition had been.

They were now airborne and heading for Quinella Downs in Central Australia. Each of them including the pilot and co-pilot were excited for what lay ahead. Idle chatter engulfed the aircraft with everyone from Willy to the president having their say as to the possibilities that lay ahead.

Quinella Downs was abuzz with activity. The film crew and journalists had already arrived with their communications vans in readiness for the big event. Not only would their transmission be received by every television channel on Earth, it would be viewed by the Univians themselves. Other activities included the station staff erecting floodlights around the hanger, while a bullock had been butchered for the occasion. The beef was placed in the portable cold room, which was also full of beer, wines and spirits – all top-shelf beverages as ordered and paid for by the presidential department. The station staff had now been told about the events that were about to take place. Most thought there was more to it than what they had originally been told; however, an extra-terrestrial visit was far too much to get their heads around.

The Dash 8 touched down mid-afternoon and parked well away from the front of the hanger. The occupants received a raucous welcome from the small motley crowd who clapped and whistled as they walked from the aircraft.

'Speech, speech,' the crowd called in unison.

The Australian Prime Minister obliged, setting himself up to speak to the cameras that were being positioned for his oratory.

One of the station hands placed a huge timber crate down, beckoning Mr Kealing to his makeshift platform.

'On behalf of both the Australian and the American Government, I would like to thank the owners of Quinella Downs for preparing and hosting this momentous event. It is an occasion that will go down in history as the most significant encounter mankind has participated in since the beginning of time. I would like to make special thanks to astrophysicist Alan Holmes, an Australian citizen with vision, knowledge and determination, who made this all possible. He took an extraordinary idea and turned it into a vision, then a reality. Consequently, mankind is now able to communicate with another civilisation. Without his determination and vision, the unfolding events would never be taking place. One man's astonishing tenacity has served us with possibilities far too numerous to mention. Without elaborating, I suggest everybody open a drink, then we will then have a toast to Alan Holmes.'

The crowd cheered again. Mary and Jane were so proud of their father. 'Fancy Dad being responsible for all of this,' Mary mentioned to Jane with tears of pride welling in her eyes. 'Who would ever have thought when he went to America that he would create such a mind-boggling set of circumstances.'

Jane agreed silently, praying the whole event went ahead without a hitch.

The Univians previously indicated they would be arriving at about 9 p.m., give or take half an hour. it was now 6 p.m. The station owners announced the evening meal and encouraged everyone to help themselves to whatever they wanted. Huge T-bone steaks along with thick cuts of rump and fillet were all cooked to perfection by the station cook. There were lashings of peppered gravy, baked potatoes and pumpkin from the camp ovens, with fresh damper to go with the meal. It was a feast to behold, all cooked over fire and coals, furthering the flavour of everyone's meal.

A few cowboys wandered over from the campfire to join the rest of the crowd sitting outside the hanger. It was now 8 p.m.,

The Believer

and the moon shining brilliantly in a cloudless, starry sky. The external spotlights and the airstrip lights were turned on in readiness, although the moon and stars were creating sufficient light without them. The mood was one of anticipation, somewhat more sombre in comparison to what Alan and Scotty had expected. There was a mixture of excitement and trepidation in the air, with people talking quietly between themselves about what to expect.

Some of the cowboys and Aboriginals were still telling yarns around the campfire and discussing the events that were unfolding. They too were less boisterous than usual as none of them knew what to expect. The only action present was coming from the communications team. They were setting up cameras to take care of the overall event.

It was now 9.30 p.m. All eyes were skyward towards the moon. There was not a sign of anything forthcoming, not a speck of movement to be seen between them and the horizon. Everyone was now spookily quiet. The only noise to be heard was the occasional squeak of the cold-room door then the psht noise of a ring-top can being opened. At 10.30 p.m. there was still no sign of the expected visitors, so the crowd was now becoming slightly restless.

Alan walked over to Scotty and whispered, 'It's 10.30 p.m. What do you make of it?'

Scotty just shrugged his shoulders. 'I don't know. I expected them well before this. The cameras have been rolling since 8.30 p.m. It won't be good viewing considering there isn't another solitary thing to watch on television.'

'It's making me nervous, Scotty. Not once has Chez let us down with our communications, though now we have no way of communicating until they physically get here. Perhaps something has gone horribly wrong?'

'Maybe,' Scotty agreed. 'It doesn't matter how clever a society is. Unforeseen events can always happen.'

The crowd were starting to stir further, some asking questions among themselves while others remained patiently silent. There was an uneasiness present, reflected by quiet spasmodic chatter. One by one they were assuming it was a non-event, the most vocal being the president's wife. 'I don't know why you're surprised at it not happening,' she laughed. 'You've all been reading too much science fiction.'

The words had only just left her mouth when one of the cowboys yelled at the top of his voice. 'Holy shit! My God! Look! Look towards the homestead.'

FIFTEEN

Immediately, the crowd went quiet. The president's wife fainted on the spot, yet the crowd was focused on the interstellar craft and instantly forgot about her, leaving her to lay unattended.

The craft lingered only metres above the homestead then flashed and reappeared at the furthermost end of the airstrip. Suddenly there was another flash before it appeared at the opposite end of the airfield nearest the homestead. Then it slowly started moving back towards them, hovering on the other side of the airstrip for about a minute before elegantly touching down. Not a noise could be heard from the craft or the spectators. You could have heard a pin drop. Everyone stood in complete silence, awestruck and transfixed with their mouths involuntarily open. The only noise to be heard was the occasional whimpering from a scared dog taking refuge below a car.

Alan walked to the edge of the airstrip, not sure what to expect. He could now see shadowy forms moving inside the craft. Without warning, the hatch opened then a fluid rope-like ladder slowly unrolled itself from the hatch to the ground. *How is she going to climb down that?* he wondered.

Before he had another thought, the ladder somehow stiffened to form a stairway. The hatch opened further, allowing Chez to push her long, slender body through the opening. She then backed down the stairway in a slow, methodical step-by-step gait until she reached the ground. She was slightly unsteady, her body trying to compensate for the heavily oxygenated air. Her large eyes, tiny mouth and small, pointed ears were now visible to the whole world.

She stood still and beckoned Alan to come closer. Noticing her distressed manner, he walked quickly towards her, wondering what was wrong. Chez still hadn't said a word. They touched both hands before giving one another a heartfelt hug.

'Shuati Est Emporo Earth,' Alan greeted in almost perfect Univian.

'You remembered!' Chez beamed. 'Thank you, Alan,' she replied, sounding a little distressed.

'Is something wrong?' he asked.

Chez, still compensating for oxygen, said nothing. Before she could answer, the stairway retracted, the craft going into lockdown. 'Yes, there is something terribly wrong, Alan. The president's minders came as military guards. They are both carrying concealed high-powered revolvers and both are wearing bullet belts.'

'Are you sure?' Alan was shocked to hear this.

'Positive,' Chez affirmed. 'To the extent that the craft is ready to leave without me.'

Alan was furious. 'Tell your friends on board not to go anywhere. I'll go fix it.' Alan told Chez to stay on the other side of the airport runway then started running back towards the crowd.

'I hope so, Alan. I won't survive here without them.' Chez then immediately spoke to her colleagues using telepathy to let them know the circumstances. The senior pilot spoke back, informing her he would stay put unless something drastic happened. The elders back home in Univiah were beside themselves thinking they had made a terrible mistake getting involved with Earth.

Walking quickly towards the president, Alan's face was a grim mask.

'What's wrong?' enquired the president.

'You Yanks can't help yourselves, can you!' Alan fumed directly into the president's face for the whole world to hear.

'What is it with you Americans and guns? Get those two body-guards and their weapons out of here at once or this whole show is over, not to mention Chez's life!'

John Kennard turned to his guards. 'Are you carrying weapons?' the president demanded.

'Yes, sir,' one of them answered. 'It's our duty to do so for your protection. Our superiors within Homeland Security never had a problem with us carrying weapons.'

The president stared them down. 'I specifically told you not to bring guns. Now get in one of those vehicles and leave immediately. It just so happens I have supremacy over all of your superiors *and* Homeland Security.'

The guards stood their ground, insisting it was their right to protect themselves and the presidential party should a situation arise.

The head stockman walked over and handed them a set of keys, pointing to a four-wheel drive vehicle as if to say, 'Get going.'

Eventually they took the keys and slunk out disgraced, everyone booing them as they left for Alice Springs.

Chez relaxed then conveyed messages to those on board, allowing the unfolding events to return to normal. Alan walked back across the airstrip to the craft, this time taking Chez by her long, slender hand. Her hairless light-grey skin was velvety soft to touch. Marvelling at each other, he walked her back to meet everyone. Chez offered up her hands and extended them towards the crowd. Pam stepped forward and touched both hands before giving her a hug. Soon the whole crowd were joining in, the feeling of peace and friendship noticeably recognised among the crowd. They then clapped in triumph as the craft's hatch opened once again, the stairway also back in position in preparation for another member of the crew to disembark. This time it was the elder who backed slowly down the stairs holding his hands towards Alan.

Their hands touched as Alan welcomed the elder. 'Hello, Alan. I am Dravo. We met before at Wallaby Heights although not in person. You were only a lad. I can still see you standing there beside a tree with your teacher struggling to hold you back.'

Alan was shocked. An eerie feeling came over him as his mind reconstructed his first encounter with the aliens at Wallaby Heights. Amazingly, Alan and Dravo had been a stone's throw away from one another all those years ago.

Chez now realised why the elder had volunteered to come. He had had his own agenda right from the beginning. He'd known all along that Chez's Earthly friend was the same high-spirited boy he had observed at Wallaby Heights many years ago; he just hadn't mentioned it.

Alan's initial shock waned enough to ask Dravo a few questions about their first fateful meeting when he was thirteen. 'Dravo, I have always wondered what you were doing there that day. Could you please enlighten me?'

'Certainly. We were there briefly the day before, probably for about half a minute. You were all in class at the time, so we decided to come back when you were outside. We worked out that an education facility was reasonably safe for us to get a close look at humans.

'I remembered that our reconnaissance provided no mention of guns or weapons near your school, which made us feel comfortable enough to land. We were visible for about two minutes before you happened to look at us. I remember feeling so pleased when you dropped the football and pointed towards us. I knew you'd seen us so I asked the pilot to put the craft down behind the trees outside the playground.'

Hearing this account, the day came rushing back to Alan. 'Did you expect us kids to come as close as we did?'

'I'm not sure what we expected, though I recall feeling relatively safe given your proximity.'

Alan wanted to know something. 'What happened to the boy who went right up to the craft? Did you stun him?'

Dravo shook his head. 'No, he was badly affected by a strong type of electrostatic phenomena called "contact-induced charge separation". It's formed from static electricity prevalent around the craft for a short time after landing. For some reason our craft create a more debilitating electrostatic voltage than Earthly vehicles. We knew you would think we played a part in his stunned behaviour but it was a natural phenomenon.'

'How many of you were on board?' Alan was so excited to learn more about his life-changing experience from all those years ago.

'Six of us. There should have been eight yet two of the crew pulled out at the last minute.'

Alan's curiosity was peaked. 'How long did you stay on Planet Earth?'

Dravo tilted his head in remembrance. 'For about five weeks. We knew you were planning to go to your moon so we decided to come and have a look. Your reports of increased UFO activity on Earth at the time were true, even though most of you didn't believe it. We also had two other interstellar craft accompanying us at the time. The other two craft both had a full crew. They concentrated on collecting samples of the earth's soil, flora and fauna. We had the easier, more interesting task of reporting on the moon landing and observing your people.

'We listened to Neil Armstrong and Buzz Aldrin talking to their base station. Buzz actually reported seeing a bright light nearby that was travelling at the same speed alongside them. Unbeknown to them it was us, not space junk as documented.'

Alan still had more questions for Dravo. 'Was it you who visited Westall High School a few years previously to visiting us at Wallaby Heights School?'

'Not me personally, Alan,' Dravo confirmed. 'Although I did help organise that very mission before the craft left Univiah.'

'Why do you have such interest in our schools?' Alan pressed.

'It's the children we are interested in. We can't work out why the behavioural patterns of younger humans are so similar to ours, so we are baffled by what goes wrong when you start to mature. Univians never change. We all have the same temperament during the last ten years of our lives as we had during the first ten years of our lives. Whatever goes wrong with your species when you start maturing has us completely intrigued. It would be truly wonderful if you could stay childlike for the whole of your lives. We think your problems are brought about by not practising the Ten Golden Rules although we have never been able to establish conclusive proof. There could also be a genetic anomaly that contributes to your adult maleficence.'

'You should have come back to our school once more before you left. I so wanted to meet you,' Alan told Dravo.

'We would have, Alan, but your military arrived. We could only then observe from a distance, although we were watching when you snuck up on them the next day. You were not only curious but also brave. Of all the people I observed, you're the one I remembered most, thus my wanting to come back and meet with you personally.'

'I hope I haven't disappointed you, Dravo.'

'You certainly have not. You have only served to enhance my visit. Now let's go and talk with the rest of your people. They will be wondering what we're doing out here away from them.'

Alan steered Dravo towards the station folk instead of the hierarchy, demonstrating Univiah's equality process in a bid to teach those in power that they were going to have to get used to being equal if they wanted Univiah to impart with their technologies. The station folk were now formally greeting the Univians that had already disembarked. Normally they were the rough and tough of the Australian outback, yet now they were overwhelmed holding the hands of extra-terrestrials. They looked like meek and mild kindergarten kids who had just met their first playmates.

Next to leave the craft were Chez's two friends, Anka and Cler. The first one down was Anka. She waited patiently at the bottom of the stairway until Cler alighted the craft. They both rested to slow their breathing, then hands outstretched, they greeted Scotty as he arrived to chaperone them back to the others.

Scotty introduced them to the crowd, and both females blended in with everyone as if they had known them for years.

They preferred to talk with the cowboys, who for some reason were very quiet and slightly overwhelmed. In curious fashion, the cowboys shyly asked the two females and Chez if they could touch their hairless, velvety skin.

'Of course you can touch us,' Chez told them. 'We are also wanting to touch you, especially the top of your woolly heads. Your hair fascinates us as we can't see a purpose for it.' Everyone laughed at her sentiment.

Chez then remembered Willy. Scanning the crowd, she found him hiding behind everyone trying to be as inconspicuous as possible, which was hard given his features.

'Come here, Willy,' Chez beckoned.

Willy walked towards Chez and her friends, holding his arms out. The Univian females held his hand momentarily, preferring to give him random awkward hugs. 'Your colour is so lovely,' Chez told him.

Her friends agreed then asked him how and why he was such a beautiful colour compared to everyone else. Willy smiled shyly, showing his pearl-white teeth and attracting even more attention. They now wanted to inspect and touch his teeth. He was putty in their hands and enjoyed the attention his complexion was creating. Even the elder couldn't help paying him attention, stroking his arm and fondling his curly, short black hair.

Next to alight the craft were the Univian adventure couple. They walked hand in hand towards the welcoming party. Everyone was so engrossed with the former arrivals they had temporarily forgotten them. It was the Australian Prime Minister who first noticed their disposition. Going to their rescue, he immediately greeted them with a handshake before introducing them to the secretary of state and the American President.

Eventually the crew re-grouped around the campfire, aliens and humans sitting in a circle on planks supported by drums. In no particular order, the Univians chose someone to sit next to. Every one of them sat with a human either side. It was a surreal scene, with the flickering light of the fire dancing its reflections

Phil Muirhead

on everyone's face, the Univians taking it all in their stride, oblivious to the magnitude of the occasion.

They talked for hours. These two different species exchanged questions and compared experiences. The humans were the most inquisitive as the Univians already knew most of what took place on Earth, but it never altered their eagerness to participate. One of the cowboys asked the elder if humans could live on Univiah.

'Yes, you could, although you would have to get used to less oxygen. It would be like living on Earth's highest mountain as our oxygen level is lower than your planet's.'

Pam asked the elder why Univians used conventional means of communication when they could simply use telepathy.

'This is because telepathy uses much more accumulated energy than we like to expend,' he explained.

Another cowboy asked if they liked Planet Earth's physical appearance.

Dravo answered truthfully. 'It is very beautiful, much more so than Univiah.'

Another asked Chez if they had animals. 'Yes, we do,' she explained, 'yet we leave them in their natural environment. We never turn them into pets like you do.'

The head stockman further probed Chez's thoughts by asking whether sometime in the future Univiah might condone leaving a contingent of Univians on Earth for an arranged period of time then come back for them?

Her answer was instant. 'I strongly doubt it. Why would we put our citizens in peril for no other reason but to amuse you?'

One of the camera men also had a question, asking Chez if Univians made love for pleasure or just for breeding purposes?

'Both,' she replied without a trace of embarrassment. 'We have no hang-ups when it comes to this natural act. Making love is superior to aggression. We have observed that it is you humans who have hang-ups about sexuality. You should teach your children that making love is a natural occurrence. Aggression and war are what's unnatural, and you should be explaining this to your children from a very young age.'

Scotty's partner was next to come forward with a question. 'Tell me, Chez, what do you think about our society when it comes to men and women? Do you believe in the equality of both sexes or should we perhaps adjust our ways? How can you become equal when there are so many inherent differences between both sexes?'

Chez replied earnestly, 'Do as we do. Accept one another for what you are. Whether male or female, there are differences that nobody can change. These differences are complementary, neither is superior to the other.'

'Could we or you contract a foreign disease from one another?' the pilot of the Dash 8 asked.

Chez shook her head vehemently. 'No. We have no diseases, viruses or bacterial infections to transmit. As for contracting an illness from you, it is impossible. The genetic structure of our bodies won't allow this to happen, so please don't be concerned.'

The pilot went on to ask, 'Is it possible, if you had a spare seat on the craft, that one of us could come back to Univiah with you?'

Chez smiled at this to soften her words. 'It is definitely possible. You would survive physically with no problem, though whether you would adjust to our sophisticated lifestyle is another matter. Intellectually, you would probably perish, resulting in you living with a type of self-induced dementia.'

The pilot scratched his head and asked what would cause the dementia.

Chez elaborated for him. 'It would be brought about by your inability to cope with such abrupt change in your lifestyle and behaviours.'

He pondered this for a moment then shrugged his shoulders and said, 'Tell us about your food. Can you really survive on one pill per day? If so, have your body parts shrunk, not allowing you to consume solids? And do you have any body waste?'

Chez replied, 'We certainly can survive on one pill per day, but there is nothing stopping us from taking two if we are using a lot of energy, such as when we use telepathy. We only take sustenance pills when we are hungry, and our body parts have remained the same as they originally were. We could convert back to solid food any time we wanted, yet why would we want to? Expelling body waste isn't something we would like to go back to.' There were a few guffaws around the campfire.

She continued her explanation. 'Think about the infrastructure you have in place on Earth just to eat, poo and pee. Then think about how you could live without the necessity of food as you know it. Let's face it, your lives are dominated by food, which equates to survival. Without the necessity of food, you would be able to live independently of those who desire to control you. Take food off the menu, pardon the pun, and you would have a completely different social structure. No more could anyone in control deceive you into thinking you can't survive without them.' This was food for thought for everyone.

The cook from Quinella Downs asked the next question. 'Given that Univiah's social structure treats everyone as equals, are there any misgivings? What if you all wanted to go on interstellar voyages or what would happen if the majority of Univians wanted to leave Metropolis Central and live in the country?'

'It would be worked out accordingly,' Chez advised. 'For example, if a lot more of us wanted to travel to other parts of the universe then we would produce the craft to do so. If we all decided we should live in the country, we would provide housing for those who wish to live there. Like everything else in the universe, equilibrium takes place in conjunction with God the Universe's divine way. Any more questions?'

It was now 3 a.m. and everyone was noticeably tiring, particularly the communications team, not to mention the worldwide television audience. Alan approached Chez, asking what her plans were.

She said, 'We are going to call it a night. We will re-board and elevate to 36,000 km over your equator in geostationary orbit until we return tomorrow afternoon at 2 p.m. if that's alright with you?'

'Sounds great,' Alan said. 'Do you want me to announce your departure?'

'Yes, please, and do thank everyone for having us here. Please tell them we are looking forward to meeting again later today.'

Alan moved to the front of the crowd and announced the intended movements of the Univians, telling everyone to sleep well in preparation for the next meeting. The crowd cheered on hearing the Univians intended returning.

SIXTEEN

After boarding the craft, the stairway went limp before retracting, and the hatch locked in preparation for departure. Everyone went quiet. Alan broke the silence by saying, 'Keep your eyes on it. You won't believe what you're about to see.'

Zap! A silvery flash, and they were gone. It was the second time Alan had witnessed such a take-off, and in his mind it was equally as spectacular as the first.

It took barely a minute to go from Quinella Downs to their current position of 36,000 km above Planet Earth. The Univians now had little to do but talk or rest until they returned to Earth at 2 p.m. The pilots steadied the craft strategically, placing it over the earth's equator and keeping it stationary in relation to the speed the earth rotated. Unknowingly, the closest satellite was the one Chez had used to intercept Alan's first DEMC message.

'How did it go?' queried the senior pilot. 'Were they as expected?'

'They were.' Chez gave him a run-down of their encounter. 'What did you do to fill in time while you were waiting?'

'I've been watching their television channels, mostly documentaries and world news. Now I understand how you have learned so much about them!'

'Tell us what you watched on their news,' the crew urged.

The pilot leaned forwards, eager to discuss what he had seen. 'Mostly, I watched all of you meeting with the Earthlings, yet eventually they got around to their local news. That was interesting. I can't begin to understand why a species craves such bad news. Their news is about tragedy, disasters, wars, deaths and grief. If you compare their news programs to Univiah's, they are complete opposites. Why would a species enjoy watching such bad news? I just don't get it.'

'Tell us about the documentaries,' the crew encouraged.

'One of the documentaries was about shark and crocodile attacks. Earth's oceans and adjoining rivers are home to predators called sharks and crocodiles, and these attack people who bathe in the ocean or rivers, killing them or biting off their limbs. Why would you bathe in the ocean if there's a possibility of getting eaten by a predator? They must know danger lurks, but it doesn't seem to deter them. They keep swimming with the belief it won't happen to them. There must be a deficiency in their thinking that we are not aware of? Unless the people who get eaten haven't previously been informed about these predators? Although if I can work it out from watching a single documentary, you would think they would too?'

The crew all shook their heads in disbelief.

The pilot then said, 'Another documentary I watched was about this male in Germany who wanted to breed a superior race. Somehow, he hatched this idea of how to dispose of those not suitable to his cause by herding them into gas chambers while letting them think they were going for a shower. He killed millions of them for no other purpose than being the wrong creed. It's hard to believe that normal, everyday people would sit by and do nothing when such atrocious human suffering was taking place. Even worse, it was normal, everyday humans who participated in such atrocities. This could have been a movie based on fiction? Surely it was a movie, though it seemed real. I'm really not sure.'

'Anything else?' the crew queried, horrified expressions on their faces.

'Yes. I watched two explosive devices being dropped on two different cities in a country called Japan. The bombs killed hundreds of thousands of men, women and children. I'm not sure what caused this to happen, yet it must have been a horrific accident. As unpredictable a species as they are, surely they wouldn't wipe one another out with such cruelty? Strangely, the documentary seemed to be saying it was done purposefully. I think we need to be very careful with this species, Chez. They seem pathologically unbalanced.'

The crew were now all looking very pensive.

However, the pilot didn't stop there. 'I also watched a documentary on explosive devices called land mines. Humans bury them to booby trap other humans, and when someone steps on a mine it blows off their legs, sometimes killing them instantly.'

'That's insane!' one of Chez's friends exclaimed. 'Surely they wouldn't be killing one another in this way? Perhaps they set them for predator animals inadvertently killing people instead. Perhaps?'

The pilot frowned. 'I'm not so sure. After watching all this gruesome stuff, I decided to watch a kid's channel. Their children are very much like us until they lose their childhood innocence.'

'Some retain their innocence,' Chez explained, quoting Willie. 'They're the ones who are happiest for some reason. It really is quite a study. Surely the others could learn from Willie. I mean, who wants to be unhappy?'

'Quite a lot of them, apparently,' he replied.

'Maybe we should talk to them about how they are distressing one another?' Chez suggested.

'What do you propose?' asked the senior pilot.

Cler butted in before Chez had time to respond. 'Well, for a start we could try explaining that their primitive behaviour is never going to achieve anything more than broken dreams.'

Anka spoke next. 'Broken dreams seem to be part of their everyday lives. Perhaps they're caused by some type of genetic defect?' she queried. 'Maybe they can't correct their absurd behaviour; hence, their broken dreams are manifested into reality. Let's face it, their problems are unique to them, and they must

Phil Muirhead

surely be the product of how they're taught to think from a very young age.'

The senior pilot agreed, explaining how he omitted to tell them of another atrocity he had watched on Earth's television. 'I watched these humans purposefully crash two huge aeroplanes full of people into two large buildings in New York. Believe me, this was no accident nor a movie. Not only did they kill themselves yet they killed countless others. There has to be a reason for such crazy, irresponsible behaviour.'

'Perhaps its nature's way of culling the species?' the junior pilot ventured.

'No way,' Chez interjected. 'Mother Nature can be cruel, but unless it was an act of nature like flying into a severe storm, there's no way she would assist culling those poor souls for simply being in the wrong place at the wrong time.'

'Mother Nature doesn't come into the equation,' the senior pilot assured them. 'Mother nature doesn't fly aeroplanes, humans do. Could you imagine us lining this very interstellar craft up with a building and flying full pelt into it! There's something more at play than we realise.'

The whole crew looked at the senior pilot in complete shock. Comparing the two airliners smashing into the Twin Towers to using an interstellar craft to replicate the same scenario instantly turned meaningful discussion into a lost cause.

'Let's sleep on it,' suggested Elder Dravo. 'There could be other reasons that cause such strange behaviour, and we might only be talking about things of which we have no understanding. I say we meet with them at 2 p.m., then after we leave, we'll have a good look around Earth and observe human behaviour ourselves. We'll launch some of the on-board drones to get a detailed look at what and why they do what they do. Doing it this way will give us a much better understanding of them without confusing our thoughts beforehand.'

The crew agreed it was much more sensible to analyse human behaviour using the data gathered from the bee-like drones rather than try to assess humans with the limited knowledge they were currently using.

Quinella Downs was preparing for the 2 p.m. visit. It was a lovely day, partly cloudy with a slight breeze blowing from the south. Waiting in anticipation, everyone was a lot less anxious than they were when the aliens first arrived. With only a few minutes left before they landed, they all gathered in front of the hanger, with the communications team ready to transmit the unfolding events. As 2 p.m. showed on the airport clock, the Univians noiselessly appeared on the opposite side of the airstrip, touching down exactly where they landed before. This time it was the elder who opened the hatch, alighting to be greeted by Alan and Pam.

The Univian pilots were now nervous, worried they may be tricked into submission or blackmailed into releasing details of the interstellar craft. Both pilots were more than aware of the consequences of humans obtaining the craft's technology. The pilots wouldn't think twice about those outside if an incident arose. The loss of Univian lives was one thing, but the loss of an interstellar craft could put every Univian life at risk. The pilots were only too aware it could possibly allow Earthlings to visit Univiah, which under current circumstances must never happen. The elders had always been super cautious regarding the anonymity of interstellar craft as they were mindful of what another civilisation could use them for.

And why wouldn't they be concerned. Humankind had transformed every form of transport into machines of war since the invention of the wheel. Univian logic worked along the lines that if humankind is prepared to kill its *own* citizens, they wouldn't think twice about doing the same to them, should they ever be able to travel to Univiah. In their eyes, humankind must not be given access to the craft's technology. Perhaps one day their views would change, though certainly not before every inhabitant from Earth was living peacefully and conforming to God's given rules.

With the formalities now over, it seemed a good time for the president and the Australian Prime Minister to sit and talk with the Univians about the future. The American President got straight to the point, explaining this was the first time they had been able to make a formal request for technology. Dravo, being an elder, explained how they could do nothing at short notice because every request would have to be heard by a full panel of elders.

'What technology do you have in mind?' Dravo asked the president.

'Your secrets to your longevity, your transport system, your ability to live in peace, your communication systems, your genetic manipulation, your sustenance pills, just about anything that can improve life on Earth,' the president answered truthfully.

The elder remained silent, temporarily lost in thought, before he replied. 'Your last statement surprises me. If you wish to improve life on Earth, it is easily achieved by simply living according to the ten rules you were given by God the Universe, which incidentally you disobeyed. Perhaps your species should try again. Obey God's given rules, and when Univiah sees this happening, I'm sure the elders will impart all forms of our technology, provided it is used beneficially for all humans. Your species will then be brought forward to an extent that is currently unimaginable.'

The president could see an imminent problem. How could he and other world leaders get Earth's populace to live to a set of rules that had been issued and ignored since their inception countless centuries ago? Nevertheless, he figured it was as good a time as any to start telling the viewers they would have to prepare for serious lifestyle improvements. Whether the television viewers and other world leaders would be willing to succumb to a new and improved society based on The Ten Commandments or Ten Golden Rules was yet to be seen, though at least he was being seen as setting everything in motion.

The Believer

The cameras that were focused on the crowd slowly panned to give viewers a close-up of one of the journalists, who for the first time had decided to ask a few questions. Holding the microphone towards the Australian Prime Minister, he asked his first question. 'Sir, given what Elder Dravo has just explained, do you think it's fair to assume nations can work towards a better and fairer society by adopting the rules of Univian society to the degree that everyone is equal?'

The prime minister nodded. 'I personally think it is achievable although there are some countries more capable of change than others.'

'Is Australia one of those countries Mr Prime Minister? If so, how would you go about educating change to your people?'

'Yes, Australia is one of those countries. We are willing to participate in every way possible and will come to the fore, side by side with America as we always do. As for informing the public, we have already started via our television networks.'

The journalist pressed on. 'How do you feel about disbanding governments and using a system of elders to make critical decisions?'

The prime minister didn't look so confident when answering this question. 'I'm not sure; only time will tell.'

'I'm not detecting a great deal of enthusiasm, Mr Prime Minister, so let me put it another way. Univiah uses a system of equality for its people. They have no wars and no governments. They live in complete harmony because they abide by ten simple rules. Do you think we as a species are capable of the same?'

'I have hope that we are capable. Elder Dravo has already indicated there will be nothing forthcoming from Univiah until we demonstrate our willingness to change our ways.'

'It's a big ask, isn't it, when you consider the mess we have gotten ourselves in as a so-called intelligent species?' The journalist wasn't letting the prime minister off lightly.

'Admittedly, we have a mammoth task in front of us, although nothing is impossible, particularly when you take into account the forthcoming advantages that will be made available to the human race.'

'Thank you, Mr Prime Minister.'

The journalist turned to face the president. 'A question for you now, Mr President. You no doubt agree with what has just been said, yet what problems do you foresee considering you will be changing the very core of American society?'

'I can't see too many problems, particularly when people realise the changes are for the betterment of humankind. When they truly understand the benefits, they will unarguably stick together as Americans.' President Kennard spoke with assurance.

'How are you going to go about getting the Middle East nations, African states, and nations such as North Korea to adopt the Ten Golden Rules?'

'We will cross those bridges when we get to them. For now, we must stay positive.'

The journalist, knowing he was being watched intently by two civilisations, thanked both leaders before signalling his intent to conduct an interview with Chez.

'Chez, I realise your species is further advanced than humankind; however, there must be a few things you have learnt from us?'

Chez nodded. 'Yes, we have learnt laughter, music and hugging. These are endearing attributes your race has taught us and will be used more often as Univians get used to them.'

'Are there any other human traits you might consider learning?'

Chez looked sombre. 'On the contrary, most of your traits we never want to learn.'

The journalist decided not to push this matter further.

'Will you be coming back to visit us in the future?'

'That will depend on the elders and the result of this visit,' she answered.

He circled back. 'What are your thoughts about our species? Are we what you expected, given you have been able to study and interact with other civilisations?'

Chez appeared thoughtful. 'It's hard to say. We consider you very complex beings and have trouble working out why you are so harsh to one another. One minute you're kind, and the next you can be incredibly cruel to one another.'

'Do you think we are capable of the transition needed to attract Univiah's technologies?'

'Let's just say anything is possible. Please consider that you have had the same rule book as Univiah for countless centuries yet failed to use it. In that context, we would have to wonder what the final outcome might be.' Chez was nothing if not honest.

'What is it you consider to be our worst and our best traits?'

'Your worst trait is your inhumanity to one another, and your best is somehow that you manage to forgive.'

The journalist was intrigued by her comments. 'Let's hypothetically say the elders choose not to help Planet Earth, and you were one of us. What would you do to make Earth a better place?'

'I would throw out your multiple religions and revert to the simplicity of God the Universe. You have 4,300 religions worldwide supposedly representing one God. Surely you can conceive this is as an unworkable situation.'

'How did you work out we have 4,300 religions?'

'I typed the question into your internet, and from what I could work out 4,300 religions only included the major denominations. There is actually a lot more.'

'Are you going to inform other civilisations that you have been conversing with our species?'

'We already have. We've shown them some of your television footage. The only information we have withheld is your whereabouts within the universe.'

He was puzzled. 'Why did you withhold our position in the universe?'

'It's not their business, and also it protects you from a rogue civilisation finding your whereabouts.'

'Do you know of any rogue civilisations?'

Phil Muirhead

Chez was resolute. 'I'd rather we went no further regarding rogue civilisations. You may not like what I say.'

'What about the advanced civilisations you know? Do they pose a threat?'

She shook her head. 'No. The more advanced they are, the more peaceful they are.'

'Do the peaceful, advanced civilisations use The Ten Commandments?'

'Of course they do.' She smiled at his naivety.

'Apart from religion, is there anything about our species that stands out?'

Chez shuddered. 'There certainly is. Your many forms of transport, for one, all of which terrify us. Watching you continually killing yourselves isn't something we enjoy. It is so unnecessary. The other intrigue we have is your warfare. We can't work out what it is you think you are proving by slaughtering one another. Surely this horrific procedure can't be pleasurable.'

'Thank you for giving me your time, Chez. I would like to speak with you again before you leave if time permits.'

'It's been my pleasure. Thank you.'

The world and Univiah watched in awe as the proceedings continued. The humans and Univians had been interacting for hours. Everyone was noticeably tired, so Dravo indicated they would leave for now, then would come back one more time. Not tomorrow but the next day. They would be here at 8 a.m. before preparing for their journey back to Univiah. This would give them a full day to have a look around Planet Earth before returning to say goodbye.

All seven Univians walked back to the craft, each waving as they entered the hatch. The hatch locking was the indicator they were about to leave. Once again Alan reminded the crowd to keep their eyes on the craft. Flash! They were gone. Their intention was to put the craft into a stationary orbit then rest a few hours before moving around the earth to launch the on-board drones.

The Believer

SEVENTEEN

The Univians had plenty of solar-powered drones all capable of sending pictures and data back to Univiah. They looked exactly the same as a honey bee and flew in a similar fashion. The drones were able to dart all over the place without being detected. Another attribute they possessed was the ability to connect with Univiah and the crew instantly, giving a live account of where they were and what they were seeing. If needed, the crew could use a reality headset and glasses connected to a hand-operated toggle that took the drone wherever they wanted to go in real time. The drones were indeed an ingenious invention, yet the crew purposefully hadn't told the Earthlings about them because Univiah's elders had warned them not to.

The elders wanted to view firsthand whether humankind was adhering to the Ten Golden Rules in their absence. Only when they saw the rules being adopted in full would they part with any of their technology badly needed by Planet Earth. The ingenious little bees would be left behind to operate for evermore. If, however, they were captured or they came to grief by accident, the drones were programmed to self-destruct, leaving no evidence of how they were made.

Following a four-hour rest, the pilot prepared the craft to travel to North America. 'We will let some drones go somewhere near the centre of the continent. The drones can spread out from there and probably do the same in South America.'

Phil Muirhead

He accelerated the craft around the moon on a trajectory back to Central North America. A few minutes later, they arrived hovering over a field in Kansas in broad daylight. The only people to see them were a pair of teenage boys who were walking towards a nearby farmhouse. Both stopped in their tracks and watched the hatch open, revealing the elder who was launching the tiny drones. The boys had obviously been watching the Univians on television and waved a greeting to Dravo before he closed the hatch. The craft left in a flash of light.

'Where to next?' the pilots asked.

'Let's launch some in Canada,' one of Chez's friends suggested.

'OK, then we go to South America. The aim is to leave drones in every country and on every continent.'

It took a few hours to release the tiny bee-like drones, the first released already sending data back to Univiah.

It was Dravo's idea to take a look around via one of the drones, suggesting Chez put on a virtual headset to pilot a drone. He took the handpiece-programmed bee # 44 and handed it to Chez. 'It's all yours. Let's see where it's going.'

The rest of the crew watched a screen mounted above the dashboard.

The bee was motoring along about fifty metres above a field. Chez manoeuvred it in fine style when she noticed something ahead, slowing the bee and dropping the height to see what it was.

'What on earth is that?' Dravo asked. 'Go closer, let's see what it is.'

Chez had flown the bee over a combine harvester in a huge wheat paddock. Intrigued by the sheer size of the harvester, she turned the drone to go back for a closer look. It was travelling along and spewing wheat from its bowels into a huge bin. A fascinating procedure that furthered their curiosity, they watched intently as the cumbersome machine made a turn at the end of the paddock.

'What are they doing?' asked Anka, her face screwed up in puzzlement.

'I've worked it out,' said Dravo, giving no further information.

Chez moved the bee closer, hovering only metres from the driver's bearded face. 'OK, so what is it they're doing?' she asked.

'It's a food collection device! Whatever they are harvesting is turned into food, the same as we did thousands of years ago. How primitive! No wonder they require our technology. Imagine still going to all that trouble to stay alive when they could simply take a pill. But let's move on; we've got a lot to look at.'

Chez turned the drone and headed it towards a river.

'What's that under the bridge?' one of her friends asked.

'I'm not sure. Let's take a look.' She flew the bee closer, her hand flying to her mouth as she brought the drone to a halt. 'My goodness! Some old man lives here! He has a fireplace, a bed, and a table and chair. Oh, and vegetables in a hanging basket tied to a girder.'

'Why in the name of God would you live like that!' Cler said in disbelief.

'Beats me,' Dravo interjected. 'It looks as if everyone has abandoned him. Like I said, they're a strange species.'

'Time to explore another country,' the senior pilot advised, elevating the craft and leaving the drones behind. Soon they were in India, ready to release another contingent of drones.

Chez activated several bees and watched them all fly off.

'Now go quickly,' Dravo said. 'Put on your headset and hone in on the first bee. It's number is 92. Let's see what you can find.'

The area chosen to release the drones was one where motorbikes were the main form of transport. Intrigued, the elder asked Chez to take the drone closer to the motorcyclists. Hundreds of motorbike riders were weaving in and out of traffic, beeping their horns and dodging one another as they commuted, usually carrying two or three people per bike.

Phil Muirhead

The Univians were flabbergasted. They watched carefully as Chez weaved the drone in and out of traffic. 'My God, do you believe they actually use this form of transport!' she said, elevating the bee to avoid slamming into a motorbike.

'They're crazy! It's as if they don't care whether they live or die. Look at this guy, he's got two people on the bike with him, and he's towing a trailer with another two people sitting in the trailer. What on Earth could be going on in their minds? Thank God for T-Pods!' exclaimed Dravo.

Their next destination was Africa. Upon arrival, they released more drones, then Chez piloted another bee across the arid landscape, slowing to observe a small group of people riding camels for transport. The Univians were amazed as to why anyone would use an animal as a form of transport. It was a learning curve they would never forget.

'Wow,' the senior pilot commented. 'I know they are backward compared to us, though I never thought their transport could possibly get this crude. Incredibly, their crudest form of transport is probably their safest!'

Fascinated by what they had previously seen, Dravo asked Chez to find another drone and tune into what it was doing. 'One last look,' he said, 'before we release the last of the drones. Then we have to prepare to go home.'

Chez selected a bee in France and steered it towards a stadium in the distance. Thousands of humans were interacting to music coming from an open-air concert. The Univians had no idea music could be presented this way.

A thick set, left-handed male guitarist and a pretty female guitarist sang in unison, a drummer percussed in perfect time, two more guitarists played either side of the drummer, a keyboardist harmonised in the background while a blonde lady played trumpet, switching from trumpet to keyboard to piano accordion at random. A truly talented group, their Nordic accent and unpretentious manner were very appealing to the Univians.

Chez put the bee in hover mode in front of the band and took off her headset to watch the concert on the overhead

screen. To her surprise, the rest of the crew were already interacting with the band and swaying with the audience, waving their
arms from side to side and yelling 'Hey' at the appropriate time.

It was as if they were actually at the concert themselves and
were engrossed by the band's mesmerising music and the concert's audience clapping in tune with the performance. It was a
concert befitting their Univian ability to use happiness as pleasure, a fascinating upbeat performance that gave the Univians a
further understanding of the power of music. The only thing
they couldn't understand was how these very same people who
were interacting as one could turn against one another at whim.

'I wonder what goes wrong with them?' said the senior pilot.
'They can interact so well in an atmosphere of love and happiness, then suddenly revert to killing one another. It really pains
me thinking about it.'

Following their watching the concert, Dravo suggested Chez
find one more bee before they released the last of them. Chez
picked a bee travelling over the ocean. The bee was flying erratically as it was tossed about by wind. Finally she found a fishing
trawler where workers were hauling in nets while being thrown
about involuntarily trying to work in the worst conditions imaginable.

'What are they doing now?' Cler said, bewildered.

Soon the nets came aboard, full of fish, explaining in detail
what was happening.

'Oh my,' Dravo declared. 'Could you imagine doing that as a
means to stay alive?' They all shook their heads in amazement.

Eventually all of the drones were released. 'It's time to go
back to Central Australia,' the senior pilot advised. 'We will have
a rest over the equator before meeting the Earthlings at 8 a.m.
then we'll say goodbye and it's back to Univiah.'

Phil Muirhead

Everyone at Quinella Downs was enjoying breakfast while waiting for the Univians to appear for the last time. It had been an unforgettable experience. Nobody would go home unaffected, and it was an event that would remain in their minds forever. An experience that hopefully would produce a more advanced lifestyle for humankind.

'They're back!' someone yelled as the craft appeared out of nowhere. All the crew except the senior pilot disembarked for the final get-together. This time they all walked across the airstrip together, holding hands like young children who needed one another for comfort.

There were mixed feelings among the crowd. Most wanted the Univians to stay longer, some volunteered to organise another visit, others indicated they would make their next visit a more personal one, and many were telling them to make sure they visited again. Emotions were building with everyone realising their alien encounter was almost over. All realised a similar encounter would probably never happen again, leaving them with nothing more than fond memories of what had been a truly remarkable occasion. All of those who had gifts were asked to come forward and present them to the Univians, and the president indicated his intention to make a short farewell speech.

Standing on a makeshift platform he addressed the crowd. 'Thank you all for making this historic event what it has been. On behalf of everyone that has made this possible and on behalf of all of Earth's citizens, I would like to formerly and sincerely thank the Univians for visiting humankind. I would also like to thank the Univians for considering our welfare, particularly regarding steering us back to the Ten Golden Rules we should be living in accordance with. I pray mankind will adhere to Univiah's wisdom and change for the better. The future is now in the hands of every one of us.

'If we look at these fine beings in comparison to ourselves, we have a long way to go before we reach the level of integrity and intelligence they naturally take for granted. I can only pray we live up to their expectations without jeopardising our future.

'I do hope another visit is possible and look forward to seeing you all sometime in the future. It has been a wonderful few days; days that will be remembered by Earth's inhabitants for evermore. I must admit my feelings are somewhat sombre. I would have liked to have had a lot more time for both our species to get to know one another better, yet hopefully we will make more time in the future. Thanks to Univiah, we now have a brand-new future before us, a future no one would have ever thought possible. To all the nations on Earth, their people, their governments included, I ask you to please consider a shift in your thoughts, your teachings and your policies. Abiding by The Ten Commandments is all that's needed to create the brightest future imaginable. If we don't reform, our relationship with Univiah will inevitably be doomed. Once again, I sincerely thank the Univians for visiting. I pray you have a safe trip home, I pray you are tolerant of our weaknesses and I pray this is one of many more encounters to come. God bless Univiah.'

'Chez, could you please come forward and say a few words before you leave,' President Kennard asked.

Chez moved forward, and the crowd clapped and cheered. 'Thank you. I don't know how to do speeches though I will try. My speech will have to be short. Thank you all for your gifts and your company. It has been a meaningful occasion that we will never forget. Unfortunately, the time has come say goodbye. Don't despair, we can always keep in contact. It may not be physical contact but it is still a form of contact. I will still be liaising with Alan Holmes, Earth's gifted astrophysicist and the man who made all of this possible.' A big cheer went up from the crowd.

'On behalf of Univiah and the crew, I thank every citizen on Earth for the pleasure you have brought to us as guests, although I especially thank my friend, Alan. May God the Universe be truly kind to each and every one of you. Thank You. May God the Universe bless you all.'

Everyone clapped as Chez made her way back to her friends, prompting her to realise that clapping wasn't only done at concerts. The time had come, like a fairy tale their visit was drawing to a close and the Univians were re-grouping, ready to walk back to the craft. Alan was the first to give Chez a goodbye hug. Teary eyed, he hugged them all. So did everyone else. It was apparent the Univians had had a profound effect on those present, even the hardened cowboys. It was an involuntary reaction caused by an atmosphere full of love and meaning.

Slowly the crew walked back to the interstellar craft. Upon reaching the craft, they turned to face the crowd, holding their Earth-given gifts and posing for photos. It stirred everyone's emotions to a point that heartfelt the tears couldn't be contained. Even Earth's television viewers were overcome, causing tears to flow randomly all around the world. It was as though somehow they were saying goodbye to a better part of their own lives, not realising why. Could the human psyche somehow be predicting the future?

The Univians gave a last wave as they singularly disappeared through the craft's hatch. Chez was the last to board.

'Quonsek,' Alan yelled, just before her head was about to disappear. She turned towards Alan, smiling and acknowledging his Univian goodbye. The stairway retracted, the hatch was secured then with a flash they were gone, shooting away from Earth's gravitational pull and stopping over the equator to prepare the extreme acceleration process.

EIGHTEEN

Several hours later after reaching full speed, their cocoon-like capsules opened, releasing the crew to the freedom of the craft. The crew chatted for a while comparing their thoughts, then eventually they all took a hibernation pill. The pilots elected to sleep one week on, one week off. It was an eeric sight with the whole crew lying back in their open capsules in a trance-like slumber while the duty pilot sat in silence, keeping an eye on the craft's vital infrastructure. The craft was travelling a trajectory towards Univiah at an unimaginable speed in complete silence, its occupants except for the pilot oblivious to what was happening.

Meanwhile Quinella Downs was slowly returning to normal, the crowd reluctantly dispersing. The neighbours were first to leave followed by the communication van. The Dash 8 had been fuelled and positioned for boarding, the pilot allowing everyone time to shake hands and thank the owners of the station before departing for Sydney, where they would leave the Australians then board Air Force One for America.

Everybody sat quietly as they winged towards Sydney, reminiscing the events that had taken place. Occasionally someone would ask a question, then someone else would answer with another question. Common questions were 'Do you think we will ever see them again?' or 'Do you think they will stay in contact forever?' or 'Do you think people will co-operate.' Alan's question to the president was the most important: 'Do you think we can live up to Univiah's expectations to receive their technologies?'

The president assured Alan he would update the legislation to make sure it eventuated. The Australian Prime Minister agreed to do the same, indicating his intention to implement new legislation towards a fairer and better world strengthened by Univiah's technology. Alan went into deep thought before asking a final question. 'How do you turn The Ten Commandments into legislation when they were legislated countless centuries ago?' Nobody answered.

Arriving at Sydney to a wet evening, the president suggested they leave in the morning. They all agreed it made a lot of sense to stay overnight. It also gave Alan a little more time with his daughters and grandkids, including time for the US President and the Australian Prime Minister to have a more formal talk on how future changes would be put into place. They talked until sleep became necessary, and their final consensus was to firstly get all of their allies on board. 'We will then use those countries to inform others of the need for legislative change to create a better world,' the president reasoned. 'It shouldn't be hard to do considering most of the population of the world already know the benefits and what is required.' The Australian Prime Minister agreed, and they shook hands vowing to keep in close contact then said their goodbyes.

Big Mal was dressed impeccably as always and was waiting at San Bernardino International Airport. He was anxious to hear of any new developments that may have occurred in Galexiana's favour. Mal shook everyone's hand as they stepped from the plane, waved farewell to the president then ushered the employees to a hired van, offering everyone coffee and sandwiches that he had thoughtfully prepared.

'Well, how did it go? Are there any specific benefits forth-coming for Galexiana since meeting the Univians? I watched some of the television footage although there's nothing like hear-ing it from the horse's mouth.'

Scotty answered, knowing Mal hadn't thought of the conse-quences of adopting the ten rules. 'No, there is nothing of value heading Galexiana's way. In fact, there is nothing monetary ever going to happen forever more, once we adopt the Univian way. We will all become equals then, and Galexiana or any other company for that matter will become worthless, its contracts not worth the paper they're written on.'

Big Mal looked horrified. Alan topped it off by jokingly point-ing out that Mal and himself would still be on the same pay scale, only the bottom line would consist of zeroes.

Mal remained silent, only speaking when he was asked a ques-tion. Willy cracked the next joke, making Mal's day even worse. 'Wow, I never thought I'd see the day I'd be making the same as you, Mal, even if it is only zeroes. Let me know if you need a loan as I'll probably end up with more zeroes than you anyhow.'

Big Mal never answered nor did he see the humour in Willy's words, an indication of how hard a sell the Univian deal might be. Pam decided to put her thoughts forward by spelling it out logically. 'It's this simple,' she explained. 'All that's required is we live as equals adhering to The Ten Commandments and not a thing more.'

Mal remained noncommittal, turning up the van's radio in the hope he wouldn't hear more unsavoury truths that would affect his treasured career. Already Alan could see the mammoth task ahead. He reasoned there would be people like Mal dotted all over the planet who would resist change even though it was for their own personal benefit of creating an improved, more relaxed lifestyle.

Phil Muirhead

Mal turned into Hudson Close, bringing the van to a halt in Alan's driveway and telling everyone to have a few days off before returning to work on Monday.

'What a week,' Pam exclaimed, collapsing exhausted on the lounge room couch. Alan sat beside her wondering what next was on the agenda. 'I'm going next door to get some relief. Do you want to join me, Pam?'

Did you say joint me?' she giggled. 'I will if you guarantee relaxation, sleep and serenity.'

'Done deal,' Alan answered. They both slept soundly all night.

Upon arrival at work a few days later, Alan stopped the mustang at Willy's cubicle, deciding to have a chat. Soon Scotty drove in and joined them. 'What's on the agenda today?' Scotty asked.

'Not sure,' Alan responded. 'We'll have to feel out Big Mal and see if he's had a change of attitude since we spoke last.'

'I think he's back to Mal-functioning if you ask me,' joked Willy. 'He's in one of those moods he used to get into. Just imagine him on the day his bank account goes from millions to zero. He'll blow his lid. I can tell you now, he's gonna have to be dragged kicking and screaming into submission if you want him to adopt Univiah's rules.'

Alan was pretty sure Willy was right on the money.

Scotty and Alan parked beside one another in the carpark, talking for a while before agreeing now was as good a time as any to confront Big Mal. They knocked on Mal's door not knowing what to expect. 'Well now, to whom do I owe the pleasure of your company?' he sarcastically asked. 'And what can Galexiana do to enhance your visit?' Instantly they both knew he had reverted to his old ways.

'Well,' Scotty answered, 'Alan and I were just talking. We would like to see Galexiana become one of the first companies in America to fully adopt the Univian plan. That way we can use Galexiana as an example for other companies around the world, a role model if you like. After all, it is Galexiana who's responsible for what's taken place so far.'

Big Mal turned red in the face. 'Do you pair really think the shareholders are going to agree to all your crazy do-gooder nonsense!'

'They won't have much choice. Governments all around the world are presently legislating for it to become law then administered.'

Mal sneered. 'Are they now? Good luck with that one. Who's doing the legislating in places like Zimbabwe, the Middle East, Syria, Central Africa and North Korea?'

'We're not sure, yet we're certain it is all achievable over a period of time,' Alan stated matter-of-factly.

'Good! Let's use that same period of time to let another company participate in your hair-brained scheme. There must be companies out there everywhere wanting to give up everything they have put together over a lifetime.' Big Mal was fuming.

'I think you're missing the point,' Alan bit back. 'The end result will be a war-free world resulting in an abundance for everyone instead of a few, not to mention the new technologies Univiah can provide.'

Glowering at them, the hostility etched on his face, Big Mal snorted. 'Have you pair ever thought of joining one of those bleeding-heart religions that turn up on your doorstep with a satchel full of bullshit promising a place in the hereafter better than everyone else's?'

'That's hardly a fair comparison,' Scotty rebuked.

'Probably isn't. Then again, I wouldn't call your side of the argument fair either. Let me know how you go with the rest of those companies and countries you intend converting. When they're converted, I'll join in. Good luck, gentlemen.' Big Mal got up from his desk and held the door open for them to leave, then slammed it shut behind them.

Alan and Scottie walked despondently back from Admin and headed to the coffee machine for respite. 'What did you make of that?' Scotty quizzed.

'I knew it wouldn't last. He's back to his usual self, which doesn't surprise me. But maybe he has a point. Maybe human-

Phil Muirhead

kind simply can't change even if it is for the better. What do you reckon?'

'I agree, Al. Unfortunately, I can see where he's coming from, still that doesn't mean it isn't going to happen, does it?'

Alan sighed. 'I don't know. Admittedly, mankind isn't known for its intellectual diplomacy, although surely everyone wants to live in a safer better world?'

'You'd think so, although he had a point when he mentioned those hard-to-convert countries. How do we go about them? Half of them don't have laws, and if they do, they're so bloody barbaric no one in their right mind would consider them.

'Right again, Scotty. Perhaps we should leave it to those in government. At least they have the resources to deal with it.'

'Quite right, no point losing sleep over it. Let them deal with it. We're astrophysicists not world leaders. In the meantime, we'll collect our pay and do everything in our power to help it all work.'

Slowly but surely the American President and the Australian Prime Minister converted other countries to fall in line. Their intention was to impress the Univians when they finally arrived home from their Earthly visit, which was only one month away. Government departments and employees were first put on notice that they had the task of letting the public know of the intended changes to societies all around the world.

Mostly it was an easy sell, provided people were told the advantages of living like Univians. Although there were always a few sceptics such as Big Mal who would need a little extra coaxing. They were a minority, although minority groups had a knack of obtaining control on Planet Earth. It had to be made obvious that Univiah expected change before they imparted any technology. Like a carrot dangled in front of a donkey, everyone was being told how Earth's transport system would match Univiah's. Furthermore, everyone knew it was possible.

NINETEEN

Finally, the interstellar craft slowed in preparation for the last segment of the voyage. They headed to Metropolis Central 2 where a small welcoming committee was waiting.

'Welcome home,' Breno the elder greeted as the weary crew disembarked. 'How did it go, Dravo?' he asked, preferring to consult an elder.

'Surprisingly good,' he admitted. 'They were very hospitable, and we were definitely the centre of attention on Planet Earth.'

Breno chuckled. 'Not only on Earth. You stole the limelight here too. Although I must admit we had reservations when you discovered the guards concealing weapons.'

Dravo frowned at the memory. 'Yes, that was a worry. Apart from that, we had a very enjoyable time.'

'Do you think they can be trusted? With our technologies?' Breno was serious now.

'I have no idea, yet judging by our visit, I would like to keep an open mind. We will need to monitor them closely though.'

'Was there anything they did or had that might be of interest to the elders in our scientific department?' Breno was curious about this species.

Dravo shook his head. 'No, nothing we don't already know about. However, we left a lot of drones all around their planet that might prove me wrong.'

Phil Muirhead

'Surely there must have been something you noticed?' Breno queried again.

Dravo cast his mind back to their time on Earth. 'Well, they do have a reasonable type of communications system whereby they talk to one another via what they call phones and computers. Although I don't know how they achieve what they do, considering every apparatus has different internal parts. They use a myriad of different connecting components to get it all to work. You would think at least one of them could work out that they should be using one type of universal connection system, and software too. But no, for some reason they live their lives letting such problems drive them crazy. If you look into it, it probably has something to do with money.'

Breno just shook his head in bewilderment. 'What about their boat transport? Is it safe?'

'No,' Dravo admitted. 'They often sink, killing hundreds of people. And those trains! The energy they use to build one train would power our entire T-Pod fleet for a full Earth year. What's even more mind-boggling is that they're on tracks yet they still manage to smash them. Is it any wonder they want a new transport system?'

'Tell me about the concert you stopped to watch, Dravo.'

'That was amazing, and it really impressed me. There's no way Univians could play instruments and put together such a performance. It's the only thing I know of that they can do that we can't. Music unites them, yet I can't help but wonder why the unification doesn't last.'

The interstellar crew said their goodbyes, all going their separate ways. Chez gave her two friends a hug before they parted. It was time to settle back into Univiah's idyllic lifestyle. Chez decided she would go home and informed QT 42 she was ready to depart. In less than a minute, he was standing beside her. 'Tell me, missy, did you enjoy your trip?' he wanted to know.

'Yes, it was a wonderful experience although it's good to be home,' she revealed.

'Please follow me. We'll take the slide lift to platform number 20. There's a two-seater waiting. Goodbye, missy, make sure you contact me when you return to the metropolis. I'll be here for you.'

Chez boarded, and the T-Pod whisked away, bound for home. Her mother was patiently waiting to greet her on arrival.

'We watched you when you were on Planet Earth,' her mother informed. 'Your father and I were so proud of you. They seem a reasonable species to me, and your father agrees.'

'I don't know what to think, Mum. Although most of them are more than reasonable, it's the few that aren't that are the problem. We are going to have to study them much more closely.'

'How will you do that?' her mother asked.

'We left drones behind to keep an eye on them. The drones get about by themselves or we can tune in and drive them wherever we want, so we're about to find out a whole lot more about Earthlings.'

Her mother smiled as they walked inside. 'That may turn out to be quite a study.'

'I agree. Who knows, perhaps we will never find out what makes them tick, although the study is the easy part. It's working them out that's going to be the problem. I really don't understand why they complicate their lives like they do. They live by a myriad of fickle laws, and they keep making more and more crazy laws to burden their society.'

Her mother was appalled. 'My God, it must make it hard for them to cope.'

'It does, Mum. To add more stress, the laws have to be policed by a human who gets stressed enforcing the law that caused the stress in the first place.'

'Before you left Planet Earth, I noticed fluid coming from their eyes. What causes this?'

'According to some of the elders, it's all to do with emotions, yet they still can't tell me why they weep though. The humans call it crying. I have no idea why humans cry, but it occurs when they are stressed or sad.'

'Can we learn to do it?' her mother was intrigued.

'I've tried, Mum, but I can't do it. I have no idea how or why it happens or what it accomplishes.'

'Is it similar to the laughing thing we are learning from them?'

'It can't be. We picked up how to laugh easily. Laughing is enjoyable, and we use it as a means of pleasure. I can't imagine the elders sanctioning crying. Crying seems to be the opposite of laughing.' Hugging her mother, Chez informed her that she definitely needed a rest and they bade each other goodnight.

Alan gave Chez a couple of days to settle back in to Univiah before making contact. For some reason he felt a little apprehensive. It was a feeling he knew well, a 'what if' type feeling; 'what if' we fail to live up to their expectations, he kept asking himself. Typing in the password, the system sprang to life, and Chez beamed in, sounding happy.

'Well, Alan I have good news. Most of the elders are seriously considering your proposal to release our technology to build a T-Pod transport system on Planet Earth.'

Alan immediately felt better. 'Wow, that's great!'

'Don't get too excited, Alan. It is only talk at this stage, and it has to be approved unanimously. There will be conditions, I'm sure. Mainly your citizens would have to be living in peace. There is no way they will supply technology to build T-Pods if the elders think they would be used for warfare.'

'When will the elders be meeting?'

'In about five days, though I'll let you know more when I'm aware.'

'That's good. Tell me, did you all enjoy your trip to Earth?'

Chez answered in her usual truthful manner. 'Yes, although it's quite a journey to make when meeting for such a small period of time.'

'Well, if you send us the technology for interstellar craft, we will come and see you,' Alan joked.

'Oh, Alan, you're making me laugh! The T-Pods maybe, but the interstellar craft, never!'

'Only joking, Chez.'

'I know you are, though I'm sure the elders wouldn't see the funny side of it.'

'What about the sustenance formula? Are the elders considering supplying it as well?'

'Yes. In fact, they favour supplying the sustenance formula more than T-Pod technology.'

Alan was baffled. 'Why?'

'Probably because you can't use the formula for adverse applications.'

'I understand, Chez. I know we have a long way to come as a species. To Univians, we must seem so primitive. Please thank the elders for their consideration.'

'I will. I have to go as I'm expecting someone. Goodbye Alan. I will be in touch.'

Chez heard the muffled thud of a T-Pod coming to a stop outside her home. It was Jenko. He had stopped to invite Chez to the next elder meeting at Metropolis Central.

'I thought the meeting was for elders only?' she enquired.

'Not entirely. There is also general business on the agenda, and for obvious reasons they want the crew who went to Planet Earth to attend, particularly you and the pilots. I'll pick you up early four sunrises from today if that's all right.'

Chez agreed, feeling honoured to be asked.

'Could you please ask Alan if he can be available during the meeting?' Jenko informed her. 'We may require information as the debate takes place.'

Chez agreed, knowing Alan would be making contact before the meeting.

When Jenko said early, he meant it. The sun was only half over the horizon when she heard him arrive four days hence. Breno, Jenko and Dravo jointly chaired the meeting. They sat on a stage that encompassed one end of the convention centre, where they could be heard and easily seen by everyone present. There was an air of seriousness. The subject of supplying other beings with technology had created a lot of interest among all elders. As usual, Breno was the master of ceremonies, and he stood to address the audience.

'Fellow elders and guests, thank you for your attendance. We are gathered here today to discuss a request from Planet Earth for the release of our T-Pod technology and our sustenance formula. Both requests will be debated. Before we go any further, let me remind you of a similar scenario when Univiah befriended another civilisation. Their planet was literally burning out, and they became what we affectionately call the robots. Considering their lesser intellect, we treat them as one of us because they live to God's rules.

'Compared to the robots, Earthlings are a more complex species. This doesn't mean we should violate our own rules by not helping them, though it does mean we will not hand out technology just because we assume the receivers will live according to our way of life sometime in the future. Today, we will keep an open mind and treat the meeting as a precursor, whereby we formulate the conditions of supply. If a majority yes vote is forthcoming, we will keep monitoring the drones. If a minority vote prevails, we will have a second vote as to whether we should totally abandon the proceedings.

'Our conditions of supply will be the same conditions that God the Universe issued them with long ago. Only this time, they must strictly adhere to the rules before we supply any technology. If our final decision today returns a yes vote, and we find out later the Earthlings cannot or will not implement the rules, we will deal with it then. I will now ask Dravo to tell you his thoughts on his recent visit to Earth and to provide his personal account of Earth's proposal for the technology. Thank you.'

Dravo addressed the meeting in his own professional manner. 'Good morning, everyone. Firstly, let me say I found the humans very hospitable and somewhat a delight to be with. I do, however, have reservations regarding some of the events I viewed on their television network, but I'll go into that at a later date. At this stage, I don't have a problem supplying our T-Pod technology or the sustenance formula, provided it's used for peaceful and humanitarian purposes. I err on the side of caution yet tend to think a yes vote is warranted. Thank you.'

Breno again took the floor. 'Could the others from the recent voyage to Planet Earth please come forward?'

Chez, her two friends and the two pilots stepped forward. The husband and wife adventurers had declined the invite to attend. 'Chez, we need contact with Alan, please. His input would be appreciated.'

Chez opened her systems manager that she'd previously connected to Alan and asked him to please address the elders.

'Hello, everyone. I'm Alan Holmes, and it is a pleasure to talk with you. First of all, I would like to thank you for considering our proposal. At present, we are undertaking the mammoth task of informing and educating Earth's citizens of the changes necessary to receive Univiah's much-needed technology. This will take time to implement although we hope to prevail. When Chez and her colleagues were with us, we discussed other technologies that we would like you to consider, particularly health. At this stage, we are delighted you are prepared to consider helping us. Your transport system and sustenance formula would be gratefully received as a model for future change.

'I have previously asked Chez for visual interaction with Univiah yet this was denied. I understand the reasons for denial, although I would like to take the opportunity to ask the elders for a one-off televised video of your T-Pod transport system in operation. If we televise your T-Pods in action, it will be a lot easier for us to obtain the necessary support from our citizens. I do hope you understand and I thank you for listening.'

Breno addressed the assembly. 'If you have any questions, please direct them to Alan through Chez. Please keep your questions relevant,' he urged.

The first question came from an elder proficient in interstellar flights. 'Alan, do you consider twelve Earth months long enough to conform to the necessary changes?'

'We are well under way, although there are countries who will be hard to deal with. Inevitably, they will slow the process, so we think a minimum twelve months will be needed before we can fully implement the required changes.'

Breno pointed to another elder. 'Your question, please.'

'Alan, given you received the same rules as us, why haven't you at least tried living by them?'

Alan pondered this. 'I guess it's one of our inherent flaws. I honestly don't know why.'

'I see. I find it hard to understand that you haven't even tried to implement God's rules, having had them as long as you have.'

'I know what you mean,' Alan said. 'Knowing what I now know, I find it hard to understand myself.'

Another elder fired off a question. 'Alan, this may seem irrelevant, but why do your people treat one another with such disdain and often outright hostility?'

'I really don't know. Perhaps it's evolution? Competition for resources? After comparing the way we live in comparison to Univiah though, it makes me ashamed.'

The same elder turned his questions to Chez. 'Chez, you and your two friends are a lot younger than most here today, and you have also mixed with the Earthlings. What is your opinion on Earth's proposal? Do you think our technology is justifiable to their cause given the trouble they get themselves into with the limited technology they already have?'

The Believer

Chez deliberated with her friends before answering. 'As younger members of the meeting, we think it is more than justifiable to help save so many human lives by giving them safe transport. More so, we justify their receiving the sustenance formula because they can't misuse it. Admittedly they could turn the T-Pods into weapon carriers, yet you would have to ask yourself why, considering the advantage gained by using them peacefully.'

Breno thanked them and pointed to another elder in the audience who asked the two pilots for their input. The junior pilot spoke first. 'I agree with Chez and her friends. The benefits to Earth's citizens far outweigh the negatives that aren't at present justified. I found the humans I met friendly and endearing. I'm not saying they are all this way, but at least it gives us something to go on.'

Breno signalled the senior pilot. 'Your thoughts,' he requested.

'My thoughts are similar although I would like to see what the drones come up with. This way, we can make a final decision based on absolute fact. If you think about it, the deciding factor will be the information gathered by the drones. Today's events will make no difference to the way elders vote at the deciding meeting.'

Jenko was next to take the chair. 'Fellow Univians, there you have it from the crew. I must admit I am of two minds. The very rules we live by say love thy neighbour, although it's hard to consider them neighbours given the distance between us. I've never heard of love thy universal neighbour. I think the pilot who spoke previously is right. If the drones provide a favourable outcome we vote yes; if not, no. Please raise your hand if you have any further questions,' Jenko announced, before pointing to a female elder. Her name was Sevilo.

'Elder Jenko, we have no idea whether the Earthlings will adhere to our requirements. I think we should assume this meeting as a yes vote then let everything hinge on the final meeting.'

'You have a good point, and your input is essential to the outcome. Would anyone else like to add to Sevilo's input?'

The elders agreed with Sevilo's logic, and everyone came to the conclusion that a preliminary yes vote would be set in place until a clearer picture of Earth's progress became available via the drones.

Breno asked for another show of hands as to whether they should also provide Earth with a video of T-Pods operating throughout Univiah. The show of hands resulted in a decisive yes. He then declared the first stage of the meeting closed, thanking Alan and those present, though reminding everyone today's yes vote was only tentative and would require a final unanimous vote sometime in the future.

A few days later on the weekend, Pam was watching an afternoon movie when out of the blue, the T-Pod video transmission involuntarily appeared. 'Goodness me,' she spluttered. 'Alan, quick, come here and look at this.'

On entering the room, Alan knew exactly what was happening. To his surprise, Chez hadn't warned him. Invariably, the Univians had mastered the jamming of every television network on Planet Earth.

Without warning, Chez appeared on the screen, looking confident and relaxed as she introduced herself. 'Hello, humans of Earth. I doubt you've forgotten who I am, but this is Chez of Univiah. I'm sorry about the unexpected interruption, but I am coming to you live to air from Univiah through one of your satellites. I do hope there's no transmission problems. I have been asked on your account to provide footage of our T-Pod transport system. Firstly, I will get the cameraman to focus on the gantries here at Metropolis Central 2.'

The incoming T-Pods were coming and going like bees to a hive, ducking, diving and lining themselves up while connecting to the massive gantry system. The outgoing T-Pods were zooming up the departure gantries and elevating as if fired from a slingshot.

People around the world were awestruck watching real-time events taking place in another part of the universe. It was mind boggling, equally as good viewing as the moon landing and the events at Quinella Downs. Under different circumstances, it would be called sci-fi, only this was inexplicably real.

'Now I would like to take you on a T-Pod journey from Metropolis Central 2 to Metropolis Central 3. Please join me and the cameraman as this will be a journey you won't forget. Please come virtually aboard. We have two choices of altitude,' she instructed, 'one high and one low. The lower altitude is more to my liking even though it is slower, yet today we will take the higher, quicker option just to show you. Firstly, we type in the higher option then we type the destination number into the flight data management system. We sit down and pull over the safety harness like this. The craft will not activate until all occupants have their harness pulled down, though the harness is only used during take-off or landing, or if an alarm sounds, indicating a cluster of T-Pods is imminent.'

Everyone on Earth was glued to their television screens, hanging on to her every word.

'Metropolis Central 3 is approximately ten thousand kilometres away or about fifty-five Earth minutes if you travel via the higher altitude. Today, I am using a two-seater T-Pod with a seat for me and one for the camera operator. The craft operates by a systems directional management program that plots every movement it makes. It also takes into account the movements of every airborne craft in Univian airspace. The only airspace we do not use is four narrow corridors set apart for interstellar travel at each Metropolis Central. It's not unusual to go in the opposite direction to your destination for a short time when you first take off, particularly if you are in dense traffic, but this soon sorts itself out at a higher altitude.

'So, are you ready? I'll ask the cameraman to be seated and pull his harness down, then we're away.' The pod shot off the gantry and lifted at incredible speed towards the prescribed destination, the camera blurring as it focused towards the disappearing ground.

Following the launch, Chez lifted her harness to stand. 'As you can see, there is not a lot of room to walk around in here, although it doesn't really matter because we are never in the pod for very long. You may be wondering about noise factor; the pod does make a low-level hum due to atmospheric friction yet it is hardly noticeable. If you look out this circular window, you can see the curvature of Univiah's horizon. I realise you would like to know how the pod is powered and how it manages to do what it does. Unfortunately, you will have to wait until the elders decide whether this technology is forthcoming or not.

'I do hope you've enjoyed my commentary. It is nearly time to land so we will take a seat and pull our harnesses down.'

Fifty-five minutes later it was all over, with the pod coming to an abrupt halt at Metropolis Central 3. Chez and her assistant stepped out of the T-Pod, and the camera now focused on Chez. 'Thank you for watching. I hope you enjoyed your trip, and I will guarantee that everyone on Earth will never go back to your present forms of transport if we supply you with T-Pod technology. Good bye for now.'

Alan and Pam sat in awe as the television returned to the movie. 'Wow, wasn't that something! I can't wait to use one. How about you, Pam?'

'Alan, that'll get them going. The transmission alone should be enough to convert Big Mal and the non-believers.'

'Possibly, yet you never know with that stubborn, egotistical bastard. He's bound by his ego and the almighty dollar.'

'Surely any nondescript can work out we are far better off using the Univian way of life.' Pam was more hopeful.

TWENTY

Change was slowly taking place around the globe on Earth. The president successfully convinced their allies to join what he dubbed 'The Coalition of Future Change'. Nations all around the world were coming to the fore and contributing their support towards Univiah's uncomplicated lifestyle. All were launching their own propaganda campaigns of no wars, no crime, no monetary woes, no class distinction, accident-free travel, and a society structured on love, forgiveness and understanding. A way of life so peaceful it was hard to imagine yet everybody knew it was ever so real.

The Univians were physical proof of the advantages that could be attained. 'Imagine living life as the Univians do,' the viewers were being told, governments all too aware Univiah might be watching their progress. Univiah was indeed watching, though not with conviction. They were more interested in the drones that weren't capable of falsifying information.

Elders Breno and Jenko and a selection of others met informally at the convention centre. They were there to discuss T-Pod maintenance along with all business concerning Univiah's social structure. Jenko suggested they ask if anyone present was monitoring a drone. As it turned out, quite a few of those present were drone operators, which caused further unscheduled events to take place. They listened as individual elders randomly showed video clips obtained from the drones they were monitoring. The first indicated Europe's leaders were trying with some success to administer the necessary changes, albeit far from what was expected, yet it was obvious most humans had begun to change their ways.

Breno asked for another video clip. It was recorded from a drone launched by the senior Univian pilot while he waited for the crew to return to the craft while at Quinella Downs. 'This is good,' stated Dravo. 'The people in outback Australia seem to be adhering to change, although the area does have a smaller population, making it an easier task to administer.'

Another elder came forth to show his accomplishments. He had been operating his drone in Thailand and had stumbled across a monastery. 'These male humans are called monks,' he explained. 'They seem oblivious to the rest of the world, and they definitely don't seem to be humans that would let us down with trickery. As ridiculous as it sounds, their God seems to be God the Universe as told by a deity they adore. I believe these humans are trustworthy when it comes to God's golden rules.'

'Why do you say that?' Breno queried.

'Because they are as staunch as we are when it comes to God the Universe, even if they do use the teachings of a deity. They are a strange bunch though. They stick to themselves most of the time and don't include females in their lives. They are very peaceful, and they know about our requirements although I doubt it will affect them. Invariably, they seem to already live by the same rules as us. I don't understand them, yet I feel sure they would do the right thing with regards to our technology.'

'Very good,' Breno commented. 'While on the subject, does anyone here understand this multiple God mess they profess?' he asked, showing looks of uncertainty and concern.

'From what I understand, they all claim they're using the same God,' another elder replied. 'If it's true, he certainly moves in mysterious ways.'

Another elder spoke up. 'If it's true, you would have to ask yourself why they go to so much trouble creating God in so many images. This goes directly against one of the ten rules we had given to us, them too.'

'Does anyone else know anything about their multiple God-type existence?' Breno asked, screening the audience.

An elder stood up to speak. 'I do. One of their religions owns a country and also valuable real estate all around Planet Earth. I'm not sure why a religious organisation wants such wealth, yet the wealth they have acquired is not distributed to anyone other than those controlling the religion, I'm sure. So maybe they think they can buy God?'

The meeting continued with elders showing videos from different parts of Earth with no real consequence. Most of the videos viewed were from country areas, which were naturally more peaceful and acceptable to the elders. It would only be a matter of time before the drones provided a clearer outlook of how all humans were conducting their current lives.

Astrospace Galexiana was going through a quiet period. Morale was low and profits were down, causing concern among Galexiana's nervous shareholders. Big Mal was not looking forward to the quarterly shareholder meeting so decided to arrive as late as he possibly could. On arrival, sensing the uneasiness within the shareholders, he asked the chairwoman to immediately declare the meeting open.

The meeting was underway, and it only took minutes before one of the disgruntled shareholders stood up demanding Mal get to the point. 'We already know things are quiet, resulting in reduced profits,' he said, his agitation evident. 'You're the CEO. Can you tell us why?'

'Yes, I can. Unfortunately, we are suffering profit losses caused by the sacrilegious misgivings of a pair of lunatics who work for us under the guise of do-gooders for mankind. Surely you have been watching the unfolding events on television?'

'Why don't you sack the bastards!' another shareholder demanded.

'It isn't that easy. If I sack them, we will lose the most lucrative contract we have.'

Another shareholder rose to his feet. 'Make up your mind. One minute you're calling them a pair of lunatics, and the next you're telling us they're an asset holding a lucrative contract together.'

'You don't understand,' Mal answered, flustered now.

'You've got that right. Let's get back to why Galexiana is in such dire circumstances!'

'Alright, the reason profits are low is because companies and people worldwide would rather wait twelve months to see the outcome between Earth and Univiah than invest short term. Companies aren't giving us work because they think they'll get it done for free after all this rot kicks in. Some investors are selling their shares thinking they may as well spend their money while it still exists. Others, some of whom are diehard investors, are not investing because they can't see the point. Why go to the trouble of investing if you can get everything in the future for free?'

Another shareholder was indignant. 'Who says everything's going to be free? It hasn't come about yet and probably it never will. Univiah hasn't parted with anything more than a visit to Earth so far.'

Big Mal fired back. 'You're telling the story. Just remember if we adopt the Univian lifestyle, your shares will be worth a big, fat zero.'

'And what if we don't?'

'Who knows what damage these do-gooder bastards will cause, I can't predict the future,' Mal cursed.

'So you're saying if we adopt the Univian way, our shares end up worthless?'

'That's exactly what I'm saying.'

'What happens if we simply refuse to comply?'

Big Mal threw his hands up in the air. 'Like I said, I can't see into the future. Perhaps you should contact the President of America as he's helping cause the problem!'

The room was in uproar with disgruntled shareholders challenging Big Mal on all fronts, several of them hurling abuse all at once. Mal could see there was no way he was going to talk his way out of his predicament. Suddenly another shareholder burst into the room, telling those present he had just received the latest from the Stock Exchange. Word was out that Galexiana shares had halved in value over night. All hell broke loose, people dove for their phones and everyone present hurled more abuse at Big Mal. Others threatened to find those responsible and kill them. Some people had invested their lifetime savings in Galexiana only a few weeks beforehand. The chaos eventually waned, leaving only hardened investors to deliberate between themselves.

Mal saw his chance, and pretending to go to the toilet, he snuck out a side door and left before he had to deal with them again. He wasn't frightened but figured discretion was the better part of valour, even if it was only short lived. Instinctively he knew it was probably his last meeting as CEO, and this same instinct told him Galexiana shares would not recover in the next twelve months if they recovered at all.

He then drove directly to Galexiana, his intention to have a piece of Alan. Willy knew he was in a frightful mood by the pace he was driving. He only just got the security gate open before Mal flew past without signalling his usual nod or wave. Alan and Scotty were standing beside the coffee machine having an afternoon coffee with Jan the Jan when Mal burst onto the scene and headed directly towards Alan.

'You! You bastard, you're the harbinger of trouble and you always have been!' he yelled, pointing a finger directly at Alan. 'You will pay for everything you've caused even if I have to do it myself.'

'Do what?' Alan replied, surprised to see Big Mal so apoplectic.

'You'll find out and so will you, Scotty. You pair are the cause of Galexiana's imminent demise. If we do topple, I'll see to it you both get your just desserts, and it won't be pretty.' He stormed off.

Life on Earth continued, with preparation for the day Univiah would release their technology foremost on everyone's mind. Citizens everywhere were making provisions for the all-important day, some without realising there was a commitment required. Companies were promising staff a better workplace with better conditions, forgetting they could have been operating to these promises from the time the company was formed. Company CEOs were encouraging employees to accept change for a better world, all without stopping to consider a commitment was required. Governments interacting with other governments were forming alliances and creating comradeship in circles never before considered. The response was an overwhelming projection of faith by those who understood the advantages of Univiah's unique lifestyle. The same faith was projected via Earth's television network, faith that would eventually be analysed for truth and transparency.

In a strange way everything seemed to be getting out of hand. Alan noticed people everywhere were putting the emphasis on a date in the future or a better lifestyle instead of the Ten Golden Rules. Realising this, he decided he would bring the matter up next time he spoke to the president, though beforehand he would speak to Chez. That way the president would get a double dose of what was necessary versus what was already in progress.

Alan typed the password, automatically alerting Chez and Internal Monitoring. He waited patiently until Chez answered.

'Hello, Alan. How are things on Planet Earth?'

Alan just said, 'Alright, I suppose.'

The Believer

'You don't seem as enthusiastic as usual, is anything wrong?'

'Sort of. It's just, well, let's say I'm not happy with how we're going about everything.'

'In what way, Alan?'

'People seem to think this whole scenario is only about a better lifestyle. They don't understand there is commitment involved if they wish to live like the Univians.'

'I understand. Is it causing any grief socially or economically?'

'Yes, prices of fundamental necessities are escalating. Our stock market is on the brink of collapse and businesses are failing. Some businesses are happy to spend all of their money before they magically revert to your lifestyle.'

'Alan, Univiah hasn't told you what to do as a society. You can have money, you can have businesses and you can do life however you want. All we are saying is before we help you with new technology, we need to see you are living by The Ten Commandments as you call them. There's no need to alter your social structure whatsoever, just live according to ten simple, easy-to-understand rules. Only then will you find that your social structure will inevitably end up like ours.'

'I understand, yet it's just getting the message out there,' Alan said miserably.

Chez said, 'I see. Is there any way I can help from this end?'

Alan thought carefully. 'Perhaps you could consult the elders and ask if you could do another television transmission on Planet Earth. Then explain in detail what you have just told me.' Chez said she would check and then transmit this as soon as possible.

Alan drove home feeling a lot less tense, but none the wiser as to why people expected so much from life without input from themselves. Pam greeted him at her door with a kiss. While changing, he mentioned to keep an eye on the television for Chez. She was going to explain what Univiah expects concerning the release of technology.

'Good,' Pam responded. 'I'm sure it will help settle things down. Some people have no idea.'

Phil Muirhead

Just then, Chez appeared on the television, her second transmission taking over Earth's entire television network. 'Hello, everyone. Please don't be alarmed as I'm here for one purpose. I am here to explain a few important things regarding Univiah's ten requirements, or should I say your ten requirements? Please understand we are not helping you for our own benefit. You may wonder why we have requirements, so I'll explain.

'As a species, we live and abide by ten rules. May I add we live in bliss and harmony caused by a set of rules you people call The Ten Commandments. You may ask why we require you to live this way before we release any of our technology. I'll tell you why. Firstly, if we provide you with technology knowing it will be used for warfare or any purpose detrimental to humankind, we will literally disobey the rules ourselves. Secondly, if we compromise issuing technology to civilisations who have complied with the rules, it will cause friction with civilisations that haven't complied. Eventually they will expect the technology, which will lead to disharmony then war, and wars kill people. Univiah never ever wants killing on its conscience.

'Now let me explain what we require. In about nine months from now, we require every citizen on Planet Earth to be living to The Ten Commandments. That's all, it really is that simple. When the twelve-month period is over, if you have complied, we will provide not only T-Pod technology but also genetic and medical technology so advanced you can't begin to imagine. I will go into the technology aspect in a moment.

'As for your present way of life, I would also like to bring to your attention that you can leave money, business, profits and commerce as it is or has always been. All you have to do is use the Ten Golden Rules within your businesses or your relationships or your dealings with your neighbours, friends or fellow citizens. A peaceful existence will automatically follow. In other words, apply everything you think, do or say using these ten rules. If we can do it, so can you. It's up to every single one of you. When you start living this way, the rest will happen naturally. Money will become less important as peace and love take over your planet. Money will then automatically become a commodity of your past. Think about what I have just said carefully. The rewards for everyone on Planet Earth will be astronomical.

'I will now mention some of the technological rewards possible if you all make this a success. You will have extremely fast, totally safe T-Pod transport, resulting in no more accidents. You will have gene immunisation, resulting in no more unwanted diseases. Sickness will be a thing of the past. You will have sustenance pills that will provide you with a balanced diet keeping you fit and well without producing body waste. Eventually you will have interstellar transport that will provide Planet Earth access to the universe so you will actually be able to visit Univiah.

'You will also have access to our robots. They would be delighted to work on another planet and would serve you well. Those are the major changes, many more too numerous to mention are also possible. Take heed, everyone, an opportunity such as this will never come begging again. This whole scenario is for your exclusive benefit, in no way does it benefit Univiah, and it never will. Thank you for listening. I trust you have fully comprehended what I have told you. Goodbye for now.'

Following Chez's television broadcast, the share market started picking up, which strengthened Big Mal's portfolio as CEO thus returning him to a former glory no one thought possible. Profits were rising and Admin now settled into a better work environment, not that it affected Scotty or Alan. Big Mal hardly entered their thoughts or came near them. These days he never left Admin, which suited everyone except those working in Admin.

Alan met with the secretary of state. She was making enquiries about any data he might have before Internal Monitoring became involved. Alan told her he would look at his computer's history and get back to her.

Unbeknown to everyone, including Scotty, Alan had covertly set up two external hard drives, one of which was a backup for the other. All of the interaction between Univia, Galexiana and

Internal Monitoring was being stored on both drives, excluding Galexiana from accumulating data. The hard drives were physically visible to everyone, yet they sat partly covered by an array of multiple power point connections, cables and electrical cords surrounding his control room computer. Nobody had ever queried them, not even Scotty. His covert operation never interfered with Internal Monitoring as they could process and keep all data as it came to hand. Not so with Galexiana. Should Big Mal sack Alan again, he was making sure Big Mal and his treasured company would never capitalise on his work.

The secretary of state requested his presence again. Was there anything of further use in the stored data?

'Not really,' he commented. 'But wait, maybe there is. Chez did say something that intrigued me.'

'Can you remember what?'

Alan chewed his lower lip. 'She was describing how they sent out radio waves thousands of years beforehand. Something about throwing a stone into a still pool of water and comparing the speed the ripple moves from the area of impact to the ever-increasing area that is left behind.'

The secretary simply said, 'Interesting. Can you go back into your history and find it for me.'

Alan assured her he would do it before he left, breathing a sigh of relief she hadn't suggested sending the computer techs.

Scotty was having lunch when Alan appeared. 'Got a moment, mate? I'm on a mission for Internal Monitoring. Can you remember what Chez said earlier on about throwing a stone into a still pond of water.'

'Yes, to a degree. Why?'

'Maybe it means something.'

'It does, Al. It means you've disturbed every fish in the pond.'

Alan wasn't in the mood for jokes. 'Seriously, tell me what you remember.'

'It was something about comparing radio waves to the stone thrown into a pond.'

'Yeah, that's what I thought, yet didn't we get a bzzzzt type noise blocking the conversation?'

'You're right. I forgot about that.'

'They scrambled what Chez said, though I wonder why?'

Scotty appeared thoughtful. 'I don't know, but the Univians wouldn't have scrambled the conversation unless it was on the verge of supplying sacred information. Keep going, Al, you've sparked my interest.'

'So let's go back to the stone. Imagine we have a huge pool and we drop a stone, dead centre. The wave travels out in ever-increasing circles never changing speed. Now compare the area the wave left behind in the first metre of its journey to the area left behind for the tenth metre of its journey, taking into account there is no change in speed. Maybe that's what Chez meant when she said there is no distance between us, only area? I'm inclined to think it's all about the unbelievable speed they travel.'

'You could be right, Alan. Still how do you convert expansion of area to speed?'

'Let's leave it to the experts; meanwhile, I'll go look at the computer's history then talk with the secretary of state before she leaves.'

Alan found the conversation with Chez and copied it to a USB before heading back to Internal Monitoring, where he found the secretary preparing to leave.

Knowing her time was minimal, he gave her a quick run-down on his and Scotty's thoughts. 'It might have a bearing on how they manage to travel at such mind-boggling speed,' he informed her as he handed her the USB containing the conversation with Chez.

Before leaving, the secretary told Alan she would give the contents of the USB to the appropriate people in government scientific departments. 'Maybe someone will be able to decipher why the conversation was scrambled. Hopefully it leads to finding out how they travel so far in such a short time frame.' She slipped the USB into her front pocket.

Phil Muirhead

If only they could crack the formula, if there actually was a formula. Earth's future would be brighter with or without Univiah's help. Although if they did work it out, there was still the problem of inventing the further technology required to build an interstellar craft.

TWENTY-ONE

It was time for an official elder's meeting and drone report. Breno had previously summoned those who were monitoring the tiny bee-like devices, telling all drone operators to meet at one of the four venues. It had been six months since the elders last had a formal meeting, making him eager to see if progress was taking place on Earth.

Breno activated the virtual connectivity between all four Metropolis Centrals then opened the meeting. 'Our meeting today is designed to give us a better understanding of what makes our new friends do what they do. Your videos and observations will be crucial towards the destiny of our newfound friends. Don't be frightened to show anything you have even if you think it's irrelevant to our cause as it will inevitably provide a broad spectrum of their habits and behaviour as a society. Thank you for your attention.'

Elder Deco was the first to show his information. He had been flying his drone around Amsterdam and keeping an eye on the citizens. 'They all seem fairly peaceful,' he informed. 'They seem to work hard all day then relax in the evenings to enjoy a few beers and a smoke of some mind-altering substance. These humans seem to become more docile as the night goes on before dropping off to sleep, and a rather social bunch. I didn't come across anyone that wasn't enjoying their activities.'

Phil Muirhead

A female elder was next. She had been working her drone in a small village in Japan. Apart from the odd local getting intoxicated on rice wine, resulting in boisterous behaviour, she considered them model citizens. 'The people here are very courteous, and they look after one another, particularly the elderly,' she announced. 'They seem to live a cultured existence bought about by their Japanese forefathers.'

Another elder spoke up. 'Here we have a mountain, one side of which is a vertical cliff face, and the other side is a slight decline that can be easily walked up. Now watch this group of male humans who want to get to the top of the mountain. My observations were that they didn't know about the other side of the mountain or they would take a casual stroll to the top. Watch as they climb up the steep cliff face. I was in a state of distress watching them, which turned to relief when they reached the top safely. Thank God for that, I thought, at least they can see the other side and how easy it is to walk back down.

'Alas! Guess what they did next? To my disbelief they risked their lives again and struggled back down the same cliff face. Unfortunately. one of them fell, impaling himself on sharp rocks. Soon after, more humans arrived in the strangest vehicle I've ever seen. It hovered from rotating blades, and the driver manoeuvred it using a stick protruding from the floor. Then they tried to hook the climber off the mountain. Notice how those in the hover vehicle are all males. Invariably they're also trying to kill themselves, and it's the male of the species more likely to be involved in such antics.

'I'm wondering what these same males would get up to if they were custodians of our T-Pods. I can see them circumnavigating Earth to see who gets home quickest, or maybe turning them into snow ski racers. The only consolation would be that T-Pods have enough built-in technology they couldn't kill themselves, unless of course they fit cannons to them to kill off their sporting competitors. Anyhow I have no doubt my report will give you a lot to think about, and laugh about too. Thank you.'

'While we're on the subject of their crazy activities, take a look at this,' exclaimed Elder Joyco. 'These humans, mostly male, have some sort of backpack strapped to them. Watch as they all board this small plane. You'll never guess what they are about to do. I just got my drone on board before the plane took off. I couldn't believe it when they started jumping out of the plane. I thought they were embarking on mass suicide with their backpacks containing supplies for the expected afterlife. When the last one jumped, I flew the drone out after him. Here they are all dangling from multiple cords attached to some sort of canopy that slows their fall. Eventually they reach the ground. At first, I couldn't believe it then I couldn't stop laughing. Don't ask me what they're trying to prove, maybe they have a secret desire to be birds? I'm just grateful this mad species taught us to laugh. Without laughter I would have no idea how to react. I have never laughed so much since learning the art.'

Breno too was laughing, so was everyone present. 'Yes, they certainly are entertaining, and these are only some of the antics they get up to. I'm sure they have many more idiosyncrasies in store for us. Is there anyone else with similar observances?'

Elder Audro immediately put her hand up, stepping forward towards the stage. 'Take a look at these humans. They are riding below some sort of hollow, round-shaped fabric vehicle in a basket that dangles below from strands of rope. They keep it aloft by shooting a flame up the middle of it. How it doesn't catch fire is a mystery. You would think after risking their lives getting the cumbersome monstrosity airborne that they would go somewhere further afield, but no, they just go up, have a look around and come back down a short distance from where they started. What they've achieved is beyond me. From what I can work out there is no sure way of steering the confounded thing; it's pushed along by the wind. Too bad if you want to go in the opposite direction. Who in their right mind would get in that basket? It baffles me. I can't work it out. It's probably better I can't work it out, that way I can still sleep at night.'

Breno started laughing again. It was evident he was enjoying this segment of the meeting. 'Goodness me, does anyone have any more of these?' he asked enthusiastically.

'I do,' replied Elder Iano. 'Here we have humans stirring up a herd of wild animals with horns protruding from their heads. The idea is the wilder you get them the more fun you have. Notice the humans prodding them antagonistically before they set them free to a city street.

'Further down the street we have male humans everywhere waiting in anticipation. They're actually getting ready to outrun the animals when they come charging down the street. Look at this! Here they come! Galloping towards the running humans. Take a look at this lunatic, he's been picked up and thrown backwards, and is now getting trampled by the rest of the herd. And this one, the horned animal has him pinned up against a wall trying to gore him to death. Do you believe they do this voluntarily? Once again, they are males. Does this mean human males need to consult their female counterparts for some strict guidance?'

'The males need more than just guidance,' Elder Dano replied.

Elders everywhere were enjoying the newfound art of laughing, not sure whether the events they had been watching were meant to be funny or just plain stupid.

Meto was next to show his information, reluctantly starting up his video. 'Sorry, everyone, I hope you have enjoyed the lighter aspect of the meeting. Unfortunately, there's no lighter side to my video. I was working the drone in a city in America when I came across this atrocity that will live with me forevermore. Watch as this Earthling pulls up in front of a school then starts shooting at young children, apparently for revenge.'

Breno moved closer, transfixed by the footage. Innocent five-, six- and seven-year-old children who had never hurt a soul in their lives were being slaughtered by what Earthlings call a drug-crazed gunman, their tiny bodies scattered in the playground like disbanded ragdolls.

The Believer

Meto stopped to regain his composure then explained further. 'Apparently, the gunman's wife had left him taking his two children with her. In his deranged mind, he decided if he couldn't see his children then no one else should see theirs. Eventually someone shot him, bringing the carnage to a halt. Incredibly, a few of the children lived, yet the poor little souls who did live will have the ordeal of reflecting on this horrible event for the rest of their lives. I haven't slept properly for days. I doubt the children who lived will ever sleep properly again.'

Meto's video had a profound effect on every elder who saw the it. They sat motionless, unable to fathom how someone could commit such a despicable act. To peace-loving Univians it was inconceivable how this could take place. They reasoned it was so easily avoided by living to a simple set of rules.

'It seems to me this unfathomable disposition could be manifesting in their souls without them realising,' one of the elders suggested.

'Could it be brought about by their unwillingness to accept and believe there's only one universal God?' another asked. 'If so, I find it strange it only affects some of them. I wonder if the unaffected are those that practise God's given rules?'

'There seems to be a lot of factors at work here,' Breno advised. 'Maybe it's the fear their multiple religions instils in them. Can you imagine what it must be like trying to choose a suitable manmade God, knowing your peers worship another God portrayed in a completely different way. Fear no doubt plays a part in their religious upbringing, and somehow it is used as a tool to control and influence their followers, although it does seem that fear is more effectively used on humans who are vulnerable. Another thing I've noticed is the fearful are always the ones with negativity problems. Negativity is a form of fear within itself if you think about it.'

Another elder spoke up. 'I think their disposition stems from both fear and their gullibility of everything their particular God supposedly bestows upon them. I really don't think we're going to accomplish much unless we teach them how to use the free will God the Universe has set in place. Somehow, they have to be taught more meaningful ways.'

'How do you propose teaching them meaningful ways when God himself couldn't?' another elder questioned.

Breno kept thinking about Meto's video. 'Does anyone have any material showing compassion?' he asked.

'Yes, I do,' Elder Kello answered enthusiastically. 'Here we have loving humans working in a nursing home and caring for people who are ill, old or incapacitated. In direct contrast, they are caring for people to the utmost of their ability, giving them respect and love that are equal to if not more than we display among ourselves. It has me stumped. I have no idea why such contrasts of behaviour exist among them. Some crave killing and unrest while others go about their lives showing compassion, love and understanding. How do you work it out?' the elder asked everyone.

Nobody answered.

'I forgot something,' declared Meto. 'I have been monitoring television stations nearest the schoolyard massacre, and there wasn't a mention of those poor little souls being massacred at school. This brings me to believe they might be gift-wrapping their news. Usually they can't wait to tell one another of the day's horrific events, while all of the good news never gets a mention. Regarding their news, it also contributes huge amounts of gossip. Humans thrive on knowing what celebrities and the rich are doing with their lives. It seems gossip is purposefully aired to distract them from more important issues.'

'Breno, can we call it a day?' a few elders spoke up.

'We'll do one more then call it a day,' replied Breno. 'Does anyone else have anything to say regarding Elder Kello's description of compassion before I close the meeting?' Breno asked.

Elder Sopho raised her hand. 'I too have noticed compassion in varying degrees. Look at these lovely humans caring for the homeless and dispossessed. They will do anything to make their lives more tolerable. Don't be fooled though. I have noticed the very same people displaying anger. I don't quite know what anger is or how it permeates their soul, but somehow the angry ones can go from being compassionate to argumentative in an instant. They fall out with friends, family or anyone their thoughts wish to punish, sometimes forever. Usually it's over trivia. Whatever their problem is, I can assure you it is the opposite of compassion, and lots of humans have this disposition. I'm sorry, I have no understanding why.'

Breno thanked everyone for their input and declared the meeting closed.

TWENTY-TWO

Big Mal woke early. It was going to be a big day for his fifth Annual General Meeting. This time tomorrow, he would know if he had been voted back as Galexiana's CEO. Most workers at Galexiana hoped they would be saying good riddance to Big Mal, yet remarkably Galexiana's shares had clawed their way back to where they were a year ago. Clearly because Chez had instructed how Univiah only wanted Earth to live by ten rules and not necessarily replicate Univiah's existence in the short-term.

In Galexiana's case, the entire board of directors were all shareholders. Would they understand that the hiccup that took place a few months ago was due to unfortunate circumstances or would they blame Big Mal and appoint a new CEO? After all, a lot of shareholders got burned, mainly because they panicked and sold. Even a couple of Galexiana's directors felt the pinch, and they were using their shares as collateral in other ventures. Their shares plummeted, resulting in a panic sell to pay debt before the shares got too low. Eventually they recovered, yet would they blame the CEO or would they accept that everything was back to normal and leave Galexiana as it has been for the last five years?

Big Mal had some misgivings. He knew he should have seen what was coming. If Chez was consulted a month beforehand, the shares wouldn't have altered. Among other attributes, Mal had clawed back some impressive profit figures; he could now boast profits that were not only back to normal but increasing.

He walked into the meeting carrying an expensive leather satchel under his left arm. A few of the shareholders shook his hand and wished him well; others just said hello or avoided him altogether. In all, he was relieved the atmosphere seemed similar to the previous year's AGM. There was no way he wanted to replicate the last quarterly meeting of shareholders when Galexiana's shares plummeted.

One of the directors moved around and handed out the agenda for the meeting.

There was a call to order from the chairwoman. When the room silenced, she welcomed everybody declaring the meeting open. Mal didn't have to wait long before the chairwoman announced the CEO's portfolio vacant before proceeding to address the meeting.

'Before we vote I would like to bring to your attention Mal Roberts. As CEO, he has provided five years of solid financial growth to Galexiana. This year we did have a serious down period although I must say we have made a remarkable recovery. You may notice we have added review and performance to the agenda of electing CEOs. If any of you feel you would like say anything before we cast our vote, now is your chance.'

The room remained quiet – a sign Big Mal at the very least had a chance of surviving. No one stirred, prompting the chairwoman to go on. 'Today we are voting with the option of keeping the CEO we have had for the past five years or appointing another. If you decide a new CEO is warranted, we will be advertising in next week's journals. Please take the electronic device in front of you and press Yes if you want to keep the current CEO. Alternatively press No if you think we should leave the position open to make way for a new CEO. Do not press your electronic device more than once or your vote will automatically be void.'

The secretary of the meeting remained expressionless. She then printed the result and handed a single page to the chairwoman.

'Ladies and gentlemen, we will not be advertising the position of CEO. Mal Roberts remains the CEO of Galexiana, thank you.'

Everyone clapped then gathered to congratulate a relieved CEO.

Word was out in a flash. Alan received a text only minutes after Big Mal retained his position as CEO. It didn't worry Alan which way it went. His job was safe provided Univiah kept in contact with Earth, and so was Scotty's for that matter, provided Alan was still employed. Now that he had the news, he decided he would tell Scotty. Scotty was nonplussed, even though he didn't particularly like Mal.

They were more interested in talking about the possibilities of being able to turn the area covered into speed. Scotty said, 'I was lying in bed last night thinking about how far the first ripple on the pond would go in one minute. I'd say about the area of a city block, then by the end of the day it would have covered the whole city, expanding the area disproportionally to the speed travelled. Now if we make it travel the speed of light, we end up with the area coverage being incalculable because it keeps expanding so fast. Somehow the Univians seem to have worked out how to keep accelerating past the speed of light by using the area coverage.'

'Possibly, then again, we're using supposition. If you're right, the question is how?' Alan chimed in.

Scotty was mystified. 'I'm not sure, though I'll guarantee you whatever Chez intended saying before the conversation was scrambled would have given us enough information to formulate the way to travel faster than light, do you agree?'

Phil Muirhead

'I certainly do Mr Einstein. Seriously, Scotty, they were scrambling more than ripples on a pond. Whatever her next sentence contained was information so important that their computer or system managers shut down the conversation. I'm wondering if Internal Monitoring learned anything from the computer techs. I'll go find out and let you know.'

Alan arrived at Internal Monitoring just as Big Mal was leaving. Instinctively, he congratulated him on being re-elected. Big Mal just nodded.

Approaching an office worker, Alan said, 'I was wondering if the secretary of state was given any information from the people he supplied the USB to?'

'Not so far, but I did keep a copy of what you gave her if that helps?'

Alan agreed, saying it was better than him trying to find it again. He took the copy back to Scotty, suggesting they sit together to study the contents of the original conversation. 'We might just find out something incredible,' Alan said, plugging the copied USB into his laptop. 'OK, so the stone impacts the water, then she says the first wave increases in diameter as it expands, covering more and more area. Then she replaces the stone example and uses radio waves, so Univiah sent out radio signals that are still expanding to this day. These waves passed Earth more than a thousand years ago, yet the trick is to control the expanded area the wave leaves behind. This is easily achieved by keeping—'

Scotty interrupted. 'Let's think about this a bit more over a beer.'

'Good idea. I'll take a stroll back over to Internal Monitoring and give them back this USB then we can head off.'

Scotty and Alan entered the local bar. It was quieter than usual, which suited them. It had become a sacred meeting place whereby they could be left to their own devices. They were both sitting in their favourite out-of-the-way corner when Alan's phone dinged. On opening his phone, the text read, 'Hi Alan, this is Chez. Could you please contact me in the morning.'

'What the hell!' Alan said in surprise.

'What's up?' Scotty asked, concerned by Alan's reaction to the text.

I think someone is having a go at me. Take a look at this.

Scotty looked incredulous. 'Surely it's not Chez. How could she possibly know your number?' He suggested Alan press the number as a call back to see what happened.

'It says the number you are calling is disconnected, please check the number before trying again.'

'Maybe it is Chez? Looks like we'll have to wait until we get to work tomorrow to find out if it's authentic. More than likely she has come across a disused sat-phone number and worked out how to call out on it. It beats me how she found my number though.'

Scotty laughed. 'Easily compared to everything else she's done. I wonder who the call got charged to?'

Chez's text had Alan intrigued, so the next morning he decided it was time he got to the bottom of the mystery as he typed the password into the system.

'Hi, Alan, how clever am I! Did you like your surprise?'

He chuckled. 'Brilliant. How did you accomplish all that without me telling you my phone number?'

'Easy. I sifted through your phone provider's records.'

'That's illegal,' he informed her.

'Is it? Why? I only wanted your number to surprise you.'

'Never mind, Chez. Does this mean we can talk to one another directly without Internal Monitoring getting involved?'

'You're a fast learner, Alan.'

Alan sat staring at the microphone, coming to terms with another milestone in his friendship with Chez. 'Who in their wildest dreams would think we could talk to another planet via phone?' he kept asking himself. 'All of this brought to Planet Earth by a race of beings blessed with the most advanced technology in the universe. If this is what comes out of obeying a set of ten rules, bring on The Ten Commandments.'

The next morning at work, the president turned up unannounced. He'd had some feedback from the relevant government departments about their expanding area versus speed ideas. He mentioned if Chez could provide a few minor details, some guy in Houston might be on to something.

President Kennard wanted to speak to Alan before he departed for the White House. When he arrived at the observatory, his brisk walk was a tell-tale sign that he was in a hurry. 'Alan, we need an extension of time to implement the Ten Golden Rules. Most western countries are ready to conform though we are a long way behind taking into consideration third-world countries and the Middle East.

'OK, Mr President. I will put it to her tomorrow. Just remember it will have to go to a meeting of elders.'

'I realise that, Alan. I'd also like to inform you we have had some clever people working on your observations of area covered by speed travelled. There's an analyst in Houston who's ex NASA. He wants two snippets of information if Chez is prepared to tell us.'

'Go ahead. I can only ask.'

'OK, he wants to know if Einstein's theory of Special Relativity comes into play. If so, is time dilation a contributing factor? That's all he wants to know.'

Alan spluttered. 'That's all! He's full on into time travel by the sounds of it. I doubt Univiah will be handing out information along those lines. In fact, I doubt time travel comes into the equation if it exists at all. Then again, maybe it does exist considering the speed they can travel. Somehow they may be projecting themselves into the future for very small periods of time over and over again, creating huge amounts of velocity. I can't see it, though, but I'll do my best then let you know what she says. Oh, by the way, will a six-month extension period be enough?'

The president nodded. 'It should be, though we'll find out eventually. Thank you, Alan. Please keep in contact as we have a lot to do over a short period of time. God Bless.'

Scotty and Alan were surprised by the president's short but informative visit although it did add spice to their theories on how the Univians could travel so far in such a small amount of time. It also indicated the president's interest in Galexiana's new activities.

'Do you believe in time travel, Scotty?' Alan raised his eyebrows in question.

'I'm not sure yet I like to keep an open mind on these things. Why, what have you come up with?'

'This NASA brain from Houston wants me to ask Chez if Einstein's Special Theory of Relativity is known by Univians, and he also wants to know if they know about time dilation. I studied the Theory of Relativity, but did old Einstein really have a special theory?'

Scotty reflected on this. 'Yes, he did, though don't ask me why he called it such a benign name when it involves the subject of time travel. What do you think this analyst from Houston is on to?'

'I'm not sure, yet I'm wondering if he's thinking the Univians are projecting into the future for very small amounts of time then doing it over and over until they reach maximum speed.'

'What happens when they arrive? Won't they get there at a future point in time?' Scotty was perplexed.

'Not if they reverse the process at the end of the journey.'

'Alan, you missed your vocation in life. You should be writing science fiction novels now that you've progressed from "area covered" to "speed undertaken" to include "time travelled via time travel".'

'The problem is what I'm saying may be provable if this chap in Houston knows his stuff. After all, he is ex-NASA so he must have some qualified contacts too.'

'Possibly. Do you think Chez's conversation describing how the first wave increasing in diameter might have something to do with the waves it leaves behind?'

'Wow, Scotty, I never thought of that, but you could be right. Maybe the waves following indicate when the next acceleration process is commenced, like a type of galactic piggybacking so to speak.'

'Maybe, Al. Although maybe you and I are getting a bit carried away. I wouldn't be game to talk to anyone else like this.'

TWENTY-THREE

The time had come again for Alan to contact Chez. His first thoughts were to call using his mobile. It was the novelty involved. The problem with calling personally meant Internal Monitoring would miss the required information, so instead he typed in the password to alert Chez.

She answered as expected. 'How are you going with the reforms?' she asked, first off the bat.

'Not so well. We don't think we will make your twelve-month deadline,' he admitted.

'Why not?' she sounded mystified. 'All you have to do is change your ways. Surely it can't be that hard.'

'Most of us are ready, yet there are still a few diehards we have to convert. The president suggested I ask for more time.

'How much extra time do you require, Alan?

'Six months. If we haven't made it by then, we never will.

'I'll put it to the elders. There shouldn't be any opposition. Most of them have come to look at humans in a better perspective than they used to.'

'That would be great. Oh, and the president also asked me to ask you for two snippets of information if you would be kind enough to tell us.

'I'll be kind enough if the system lets me.'

'He wants to know if Univiah is aware of what we on Earth call "Einstein's Special Theory of Relativity".'

'Of course we're aware. We're also aware of time dilation if it involves your next question. Now are you going to tell me where this is leading?'

'We would like to know if you use Einstein's theories on time dilation to cover the massive distances you are capable of travelling in such small amounts of time?'

'Cheeky, Alan, very cheeky. I'd like to answer but I'll save my breath unless you like that Bzzzzzt Bzzzzzt noise.'

'I understand. I'm only doing what was asked of me.'

'I realise that, Alan. Perhaps you should put it on the back burner for a few years until your people have adjusted to God's given rules. I'm sure if you were settled into our lifestyle, the same information would be forthcoming without dispute. You have to get over your first hurdle before you start thinking of long-distance space travel.'

'I never mentioned space travel.'

'Admittedly, you didn't. One doesn't have to be too clever to realise why your friends require such information, nice try though.'

'Thanks, Chez. I'm going to have to go. Please let me know what comes of our proposal for extra time.'

Chez arrived at Metropolis Central to be greeted by QT42. QT took Chez by the hand and weaved his way through the crowd, taking an elevated narrow bridge to the other side of the landing gantry before proceeding through a series of tunnels that led to a lift going directly to the conference room.

'I see QT has brought you through the tunnel system,' Breno greeted as she stepped from the lift. 'Don't try it by yourself. I got lost down there for hours. Luckily another robot came along or I'd still be down there,' he exaggerated.

Chez was the only one at the meeting who was not an elder. It was her job to report and explain what had taken place via direct contact with the Earthlings. It was also her intention to ask for an extension of time before the elders made their final decision.

Breno opened the meeting asking everyone to be seated. 'I have asked Chez to come along to report on her direct interaction with the Earthlings. We will go to Chez first then I will ask elders who have videos and skits of information to come forward. We will then deal with domestic issues that have been brought to our attention. Chez, would you please address the meeting.'

Chez anxiously walked to the stage. It was the first time she had spoken publicly about her activities. 'Good morning, all. As you know, most of my interaction with Earth involves the astrophysicist Alan Holmes. Alan has asked for an extension of another six months, which will give them a total of eighteen months to implement the Ten Golden Rules. I therefore ask the elders to please decide whether an extension of six Earth months can be granted. Earth's inhabitants need more time to fully conform to our wishes.

'I have very little else to report except that I have noticed no bad news cropping up on their television networks. This is unusual considering they thrive on bad news, which indicates one of two things: either they're accepting reform or they are showing us what they want us to see. I will now leave it with the elders to decide if an extension of time will be granted.'

The elders deliberated, voting to grant an extension of time. The only proviso was that Chez must explain to the Earthlings there would be no more extensions granted, which virtually meant Earthlings must except and use The Ten Commandments by the due date or do without Univiah's technology.

The meeting continued, Breno calling for elders with new information to give their accounts. Elder Yano came forward. 'I have been doing an in-depth study of their religious institutions, and it seems some priests working within their religious schools interfere with little boys.'

'How do mean interfere?' Breno questioned.

'They expect sexual favours from the boys, who are too young to understand. The boys go on to live a tormented life, mentally confused because of maltreatment by those they trusted. It's hard to believe but not uncommon.'

'At least they're not killing them afterwards,' another elder commented.

Elder Yano paused, giving the audience time to decipher his commentary. 'What a depraved lot. What type of people condone this type of abhorrent behaviour?' he asked an astonished audience.

Breno gave everyone a perplexed look before asking another elder to come forward. The elder explained how he had been monitoring a police station. 'Some of them are as corrupt as the people they jail,' he assured. 'They are employed by their governments to uphold their manmade laws, though the whole procedure is questionable as most humans are terrified of their law enforcers.'

Breno butted in without warning. 'Does anyone here know how these people get the power to push other citizens around? How does such a system work?'

Elder Swino raised a hand, moving to the front of the meeting. 'We will never work it out properly although I know more than most as I've been studying their complex legal procedures since receiving my drone. This is how it works. Firstly, politicians get together to make their fickle laws. They too can be as corrupt as those who break laws and police them. To make it worse, they are among the greatest liars in their society.

'The next procedure that comes about is the laws are administered by their police. The police then hand their victims over to judges. The judges then decide the fate of humans that have broken the law the politicians have made. I'll turn on my video as it's quite entertaining in a macabre sort of way. First, look at the judges. They all have this ridiculous white curled hair draped over their heads. They wear long, loose black dresses and a ridiculous bow tie around their necks. You would think they're going to a fancy dress ball, yet they sit up on this throne-type seat and bang a funny wooden hammer on their desk. Take a look at this poor soul. The judge has decided to sentence him to death, so he bangs his hammer on his desk then the police arrive to escort him to jail to await execution.

'Now watch the next set of barbaric events. A month later a different type of policeman arrives to take this man to the executioner. On arrival at the executioner's gloomy parlour, an assistant helps the executioner strap the prisoner into a custommade chair and calls for a priest to give what they call his last rites. Don't ask me why religion has to get involved. This guy doesn't have any rights left. What the priest thinks he's going to achieve is beyond me, but he's probably paid to be there.

'Keep watching! Ka-zing. Except for a short period of convulsing, the man's dead. They've killed him with the flick of a switch. Watch as they disconnect him from the chair to be unceremoniously dragged outside by his legs and thrown into a box.'

The crowd stirred, looks of disbelief on their faces, some refusing to watch. 'Why did the judge kill him?' one of the elders wanted to know.

'He killed someone who killed his sister.'

'I don't get it. So you're telling us the judge killed this man because he killed a male who killed his sister?'

'Correct.'

'Why didn't the judge just kill the man who killed his sister before he killed him?'

'Oh, God love us. I don't know. I'd rather not know.'

An elder in the front row said, 'Please go on. Tell us what they did with the poor soul after they threw him in the box.'

'I didn't want to go there, but to relieve your curiosity, I will. The executioner called his family, who were beside themselves with grief. They were told to arrange to get him taken away within twenty-four hours or they would dispose of him themselves.

'At this point I couldn't watch anymore as this strange feeling overtook me. I couldn't believe it. I actually felt as if retaliation should be used on the executioner. It was a horrible feeling that I never want to experience again. I drove the drone away as fast as it would fly, deciding I would surrender my drone at this meeting. You can have it back as I don't wish to be involved with Earthlings anymore.'

'Oh dear, that'll do,' Breno announced, trying to forget about human laws. He pointed to a female elder at the back of the room.

'This is equally as distasteful,' she informed as she connected her video. 'I found this man at a train station. He had a backpack fastened over his shoulders, so I thought he was going to the nearest airport to jump out of a plane as in a previous video I saw, or perhaps this one's going to jump out of the train, I reasoned. Not so. He must have had an explosive device in his backpack, and found the most crowded area in the train. He then blew himself up along with a carriage full of people, mostly women and children. That was my last transmission as thankfully he blew the drone up as well. I haven't a clue as to why he did this, or what it was supposed to prove. Like the previous elder, I've had enough. I'm sorry about the drone.'

'You will probably find the human bomber was involved with one of their religions,' an elder shouted from the back of the crowd. 'I watched a human bomber too. They have all been brainwashed since childhood and are convinced they have been chosen by a higher power to perform these gruesome acts of insanity.'

'Are you still monitoring a drone?' Breno asked.

'No. After watching one of them blow up a building and kill those inside, I destroyed it by purposefully flying my drone into a nearby fire.'

'Fair enough,' was Breno's only reply. 'Next, please.'

'This is a bit different,' an elder explained. 'I followed a human lady who had just given birth to this lovely little boy. To my astonishment she opened a nearby drain and dropped him into it, walking away never wanting to see him again. Thankfully, someone heard the poor little thing's cries of distress, saving his life. He was taken in by another lady who couldn't have children.

I swear both ladies never knew one another beforehand, and I doubt they do to this day. I was going to forfeit my drone yet since this encounter along with my intrigue and fascination of humans, I will keep it.'

'Talking about drones,' Breno remarked, 'we will be monitoring the human species for years to come, so it's probably a good idea if we hand the drones around among ourselves if you have no more interest in monitoring them. Before we terminate this segment of the meeting, does anyone have anything good to report?' Breno asked.

'Yes,' another elder declared. 'I found these people who were desperately trying to help other humans who were involved in what they call a tsunami. A tsunami is a huge wall of water that engulfs human towns and cities. They are caused by an act of nature, but wonderful humans came from all over the planet offering assistance, some putting their lives on the line. They were marvellous, pulling victims to safety, providing food and shelter. I know this is in direct contrast to what has been shown here today; nevertheless, it is true. To me this goes to show there is compassion and love ingrained in all of them even if they don't practise it.'

The room went quiet with the elders comparing the tsunami video to previous videos. Breno gave them a little time before moving on. 'We have already voted on an extension of time for them to get things in order. We'll stay with it and make a decisive decision on technology when their allotted time is up. Meanwhile those with drones who no longer want to monitor them please hand them over to elders that do.

'Chez, next time you make contact with Alan, please tell him we have granted an extension of time. Please also tell him about our ultimatum: either they get their act together or the offer of technology from Univiah will expire. You may leave, Chez, if you wish, unless you want to be present for the next segment of the meeting which involves domestic issues.'

Chez elected to leave.

Phil Muirhead

When Chez arrived at home, her mother greeted her by holding her hands and generating the Univian sense of love. 'How are things developing with the Earthlings?' she asked.

Chez shrugged her shoulders before answering. 'Honestly, Mum, they are beyond fathoming, and I'm beginning to think they're beyond help. I now have the unenviable task of liaising between Earth and Univiah. We have given them an extension of time to get their act together, but for the first time I'm beginning to think it's all a no-win exercise.'

Her mother ushered Chez inside. 'Why's that?' she wanted to know.

'Because of their behaviour. I've been listening to and watching some of the reports the elders are providing, and human behaviour is certainly opening their eyes as well as mine.'

'They can't all be bad, can they?' Her mother frowned.

'They're not all bad, and that's what gets to me. I'm so confused. I do hope they see the light and reform their ways. They need our technology more than they could ever realise.'

Chez sat on her mother's couch and decided to contact Alan via text. It read: Please contact me; I have news for you.

Alan received the text just as he arrived at work. He immediately activated the password then waited for a response.

'Hello, Alan, that was quick. I have some good news for you, also some bad,' Chez said.

'I'm listening. I hope the bad isn't too bad.'

Chez continued. 'The good news is that you have your extension of time. Does that make you happy?'

'It certainly does, though what else did the elders come up with?'

'They came up with an ultimatum. Alan, if your people haven't mended their ways by the end of the extension period, Univiah will never reconsider providing you with the technological reform for a fleet of T-Pods.'

Alan was taken aback by this. 'What about the sustenance formula?' he queried.

'They aren't particularly worried about the sustenance formula because you can't kill one another with it.'

'I understand. I'm sure word is out and about as we speak.'

'I hope so, Alan, as I can assure you the elders aren't at all impressed with your people, for reasons I won't discuss at this stage.'

Alan could only agree with their sentiment. 'I can relate to what you're saying. All I can do is hope everyone on Earth understands the enormity of what's in progress.'

'If they don't, Alan, I can assure you there will never be another opportunity like this offered by Univiah. You should explain this in clear terms to each and every citizen on Planet Earth. Keep explaining there is no way we will provide technology to your species for you to turn it against one another, so it's now up to all of you. Live peacefully and reform your ways or do without the technology. I must go now. Goodbye, Alan.'

Alan sat there contemplating his conversation with Chez and wondering what the president would think when he heard the conversation through Internal Monitoring. He decided to ring him prematurely. The president answered immediately. 'Hello, Alan, do you have any news?'

'Only the news Chez just told me regarding our noncompliance to their wishes. I do hope your government isn't contemplating any form of trickery because there is no way it will work.'

'I'm not sure what you mean, Alan?'

I mean, Mr President, there is no room for complacency or hiding behind appearances. They're going to watch every move we make over the next seven months, and I'm not just talking about our television networks.'

'Are you saying they can actually keep track of us without using our satellites?'

'That's exactly what I'm saying, Mr President.'

'I fail to see how, Alan.'

'C'mon, Kennard. They're capable of travelling 1,695 light years in a few months, and are even capable of making phone calls from another galaxy. Do you really think we can put anything over them?'

President Kennard didn't sound so confident now. 'What makes you think we are?'

'Well, our news broadcasts have become remarkably serene lately, yet social media is still reporting murders, war and crimes all over the globe. I do hope you're not considering deceit as an alternative method to extract their technology because it won't work.'

'I'm not, although I do think a few small compromises are in order. Surely they don't expect every single one of us to undergo scrutiny?'

'They probably don't but they would definitely expect governments and world authorities to be complying. Put it this way: If a tribe somewhere along the Amazon weren't informed, I doubt they would care less.'

'I understand, Alan, and I will be doing my best to explain your thoughts to my colleagues.'

'Thank you. Please explain carefully that there is no way we can put anything over them. Also, could you tell me how that fellow from Houston is going with Einstein's Special Theory?'

'He's working on it, and he actually agrees with some of your analyses. Do you have any more thoughts or ideas you wish me to pass on?'

'Plenty!' Alan laughed.

'In that case, I will give you his number so you can talk to him personally. His name is Ron Hallerton.'

Alan typed Ron's number into his phone and called him immediately. 'Hello, Ron, I'm astrophysicist Alan Holmes,' he greeted.

'Alan, what a pleasure. I've heard quite a lot about your achievements. Do you have any more information for me?'

'Nothing you don't already know, yet I just want to shed my personal thoughts on Univiah's capabilities.'

'Go ahead. I'm more than happy to listen.'

Alan took a deep breath. 'As you know, the speed of light is approximately 300,000 kilometres per second. Multiply 300,000 by 60 twice, then multiply it by 24 hours, and you can work out how many billion kilometres light travels in one day. So they left Univiah on the 1st of June, arriving on Earth on the 21st of September, 113 days later. It simply doesn't add up. They would have to be travelling 15 light years a day. We both know if we use the laws of physics as we know them, it's impossible to travel 15 light years per day, yet the Univians visiting us gave us physical proof it can be done. Now if you really want to shake-up your brain, you can keep going and work out their travelling speed in kilometres per hour. How's that for defying everything you've learned about physics?'

'It's mind-boggling stuff, Alan. Any suggestions on how they could possibly be doing it?'

'Perhaps they're not doing it, Ron. If so, and it involves time travel, this is where you lose me. Mind you, Einstein himself was having trouble with time travel, so that's why I keep going back to our rock in the pool conversation with Chez. Whatever it was that they scrambled was probably the clue to how they achieve their unbelievable velocity and speed, at least that's what I think.'

'You could be on the right track, Alan. The burning question is how they go about it. At this stage we're creating more problems than we're solving, so leave it with me and I'll stay on the case or drive myself mad one or the other,' Ron chuckled.

'Thanks, Ron. Let me know of any new developments as they come to hand, and if I think of anything else I'll let you know.'

Another question Alan kept asking himself is why it took the Univians 113 days to travel to Earth. If they were using time travel, wouldn't they only use up a day or maybe two? Why 113 days. It had him baffled. Maybe they were using time travel in stages, like the area between the ripples on a pond, with each ripple becoming another stage whereby it all starts over again like a flat stone skipping over water? Only they skip across vast distances? What happened to the craft while time travel was taking place?

Phil Muirhead

'Where am I going with all this?' Alan asked himself, making his way to the coffee machine in a quest for a few minutes of sanity.

TWENTY-FOUR

Time marched on. There was little left of the extra six months granted by the elders. Humans were uniting all over the world, and everyday citizens were preparing for the day the world would be liberated for evermore. Judgement day was getting closer and closer, and the majority of humans were now living to God's rules in expectation of using Univiah's technology. They firmly believed a world of harmony, tranquillity and peace was about to begin. Peace that could be passed from generation to generation, ideals that could be embraced by everyone. Unfortunately, they were ideals a minority still refused to accept. Big Mal was a prime example, and there were many more like him.

Some of the deeply religious were expecting the second coming of Christ, which was reasonable considering the world was about to become a world of his teachings. The righteous and the good, who were the majority, were preparing with unsurpassed faith and conviction. For the first time since The Ten Commandments were presented to Moses, the world was poised for a new future.

Would the Univians recognise the failures of the minority and accept they could provide future correction and guidance, or would they refuse to supply technology for evermore? Would they compromise by supplying lesser technology or would they refuse to go any further leaving the Earth–Univiah relationship one of idle chat between Chez and Alan?

They would soon know the outcome. The Univians were busy preparing for the meeting of elders who would decide the quality of humankind's future existence forevermore. Earth's day of reckoning had finally arrived, and humans would know their fate within twenty-four hours.

TWENTY-FOUR

Chez arrived at the convention centre. She was again the only non-elder present, which made her nervous, particularly knowing it would be her who would relay Univiah's final judgement to Earth. Elders from all over the planet were gathering at all four Metropolis Centrals, all of which were linked together by virtual connectivity. A huge cinema screen split into four by a vertical and horizontal cross had been activated so all four Metropolis Centrals could watch the proceedings simultaneously, allowing elders to observe all four venues at once.

Breno, noticing Chez's arrival, signalled her from the other side of the room and beckoned her over to talk. 'Before the meeting, I would like you to do a preliminary talk with the elders of all four venues,' he explained. 'They need bringing up to date as a lot of them are less informed than those of us here, and you're the most informed of all. I notice connectivity with the other venues is already established so now's as good a time as any for you to get started. Don't worry if you are repeating what we have covered as there are bound to be elders at other venues who are not completely up to date.'

Chez had learned more about humans than most, which made her the ideal person to give an accurate account of human behaviour. She moved to the stage where she could be seen and heard more clearly. Breno spoke first, informing everyone he had asked Chez to give everyone a preliminary account of her observations. 'Please take notice,' he urged. 'Chez knows and understands Earthlings more than any of us, so if you have any questions don't be afraid to ask her.'

The elders in all four venues listened in rapt attention as Chez described human traits they hadn't previously considered or known about. One thing was certain, they would be listening to the truth. Chez embraced the microphone. 'Hello, everyone. Firstly, let me ask you not to think of humans in our own spirit, as they are totally different beings. They can be happy one minute and sad the next. They can be compassionate then turn to hatred whenever it suits. They forbid children to watch people making love on television yet the same children are allowed watch the violence and the carnage of war, so to our way of thinking their priorities make no sense.

'They have legal people called judges, but who judges the judges? I only recently learned that judges have the power to execute humans.'

Everyone spoke at once. 'What! That can't be right! Surely not! You're joking!'

'I would like to tell you I'm joking, but I'm not. I recently watched a video of an execution, and it was sickening.'

Gasps could be heard from all elders.

Chez continued. 'They have people they call terrorists that carry explosives strapped to their torsos. When the opportunity arises, they blow themselves up, taking many other humans with them.'

'No! My God! How can this be! Are you sure?' the elders cried in horror.

'More than sure,' Chez was ashamed to reveal. 'We have many videos as proof if you'd like to watch.' All elders vehemently shook their heads no.

'They have laws for their technology called patents, which can be bought by rich organisations that then withhold them from other humans who desperately need the new technology. One of their pharmaceutical companies has recently done just that, and not released the technology because it would affect the profits of the other products they make. Subsequently, thousands of humans remained in pain, with some even dying. A situation all caused by greed as unfortunately many of them idolise money.'

More horrified gasps were heard from all the Univian elders.

'If their animal pets have a terminal disease, they put them to sleep using a similar painless method we use when our time has come. In contrast, if a human is terminally ill and in severe pain, they keep them alive for as long as they can. The only reason they do this as I see it is because they can only make money from these terminally ill humans while they are alive.'

'Are you sure?' one of the elders protested.

Chez nodded sadly. 'It's true. Their so-called laws allow them to euthanise their pets yet not themselves, but I'll go on. They have governments who tax their citizens for their own wellbeing; per capita, most taxes are paid by the poor. Their whole existence seems to be about how much money they can accumulate. For some reason, the rich become celebrities who are looked up to. In actual fact, they are nothing more and nothing less than any other human, but they simply have more money.

'However, it's their warfare that revolts me the most. Humans take it very seriously, and they actually have a procedure called war games whereby they team up with so-called friendly countries, presumably to work out how to best annihilate their common foe. The procedure makes them more efficient if the game turns to a real war, and they gather ships, planes, missiles and huge cannons to play pretend war with their allies.'

'This can't be,' the elders cried. 'What kind of beings are these humans?'

'It's legal to kill fellow humans in warfare, yet they'll jail you for life or execute you if you kill a human who is not at war,' Chez explained further.

'Surely not!' the elders were aghast.

'You heard right. Don't try and work it out because you won't. Incredibly, they use legal documents to declare war or surrender to their enemy. Apparently there's no point in having a war or surrendering if it's not legal. The way I see it is that war is set in motion by the corrupt minority who never participate themselves. Unbelievably, they assume the right to start wars then rule with an iron fist, while in hiding themselves. They don't go into physical battle at all. How they get the better side of humanity to participate in such lunacy is beyond me.'

One of the elders couldn't help interjecting. 'Chez, this war thing you're claiming they do is absolutely insane. Surely there must be a reason they kill one another. No civil society behaves this way. What can they possibly prove by having wars? Surely there's an explanation?'

'I'm sorry, but I don't have the answers. Like most things they do, I'm at a loss for reason. Let me continue as I haven't finished with war yet,' Chez said ruefully.

'They also have a group of people who represent a conglomerate of armies. They are armed to the teeth in the name of separate countries who join their organisation. The idea is that they keep member countries safe if they encounter conflict. These are probably the same people who participate in war games. I have no notion or reasoning as to how it all actually works.

'Following the conflicts that cause the deaths of countless humans, they have people called lawyers who investigate war crimes. How this works is another mystery, considering the greatest crime in God's universe is wilful killing. The lawyers who do the investigating don't mind, as of course they are highly paid individuals who earn a living capitalising on the misfortune of others. Nothing they do can alter what has happened, no matter what they achieve. At best they should be put to use preventing war in the first place. At least that would make sense. I'll go on.

'If you are a soldier who excels in warfare, they give out prizes or medals as they call them. You would think it would be the other way around; surely, the medals should be given to those who avoid conflict and hurt no one. Imagine the medals Univians would have accumulated living in God's army of peace.'

The elders were stunned into absolute silence.

Phil Muirhead

'Humans have this special day to commemorate the soldiers who have fallen, fallen being a nice way of saying killed. On the eleventh hour of the eleventh day of the eleventh month of every Earth year, millions upon millions of Earthlings have a minute's silence for those who have been killed in warfare. What astounds me is that warfare is still taking place all over their planet as they take their minute's silence. I'm really not sure whether they understand that warfare is still taking place during their minute's silence or not. If they do understand, the procedure seems rather hypocritical. Perhaps they are devoid of memory or reasoning, but the whole procedure has a morbid fascination no Univian will ever understand.'

Chez noticed the dumbfounded expressions on the faces of those listening, prompting her to revert to less explicit descriptions of human behaviour. 'Remember, it is the minority who create wars and trouble; the same minority that control everything without interference from the majority. This minority will not conform to our requirements because it will affect their control, their decision making and their profiteering. Usually those in control enforce their cause by wearing uniforms. This is where their problem starts; it is obvious the majority of humans fear uniforms thus allowing the minority to control them. I really don't understand why.'

'What happens if the outcome of the meeting results in us abandoning them?' asked another intrigued elder.

'They'll go back to their usual ways, I'd say. Although you never know, now that the majority have started living to divine rules, they might just surprise us. Knowing them as I do, I very much doubt it. The minority always reign supreme. I've even thought of us frightening them into submission.'

'How would we do that?' the elder queried.

'I was thinking we should tell them we have the technology to blow Planet Earth to smithereens then threaten to do it if they don't live to The Ten Commandments. That would get the minority to conform. The problem is it would be telling lies, and we can't do that or we would be breaking one of the rules we are insisting they adopt.'

Breno signalled Chez, letting her know he was ready to formerly commence the meeting. He walked to the stage and beckoned Jenko to join him, the importance of the occasion obvious to every elder. The atmosphere was one of tension created by the uncertainty of what had already taken place. Breno sensed the uneasiness since Chez had given them her insights, deciding to set the proceedings in motion.

'Welcome, fellow Univians. Firstly, let me thank Chez for her impromptu information sharing. Also, I sincerely thank you all for taking the time to join in. I have never seen the convention centres so full with concerned Univians, so this alone indicates the seriousness of what we are embarking on.

'As you all know, we are gathered here today for a final evaluation to determine whether we release much-needed technology to Planet Earth. Before we go too far, I'll remind you Planet Earth is the fourth civilisation we have befriended. The other three have all been given our technology in one form or another without incident, although I must concede the task in front of us today is far more complex. Unfortunately, Earthlings are a lesser species than those we have previously helped, and it is also unfortunate that they need our technology more than previous recipients. From what we've worked out so far, the majority of Earthlings have reformed enough to be supplied some of our technology; however, we cannot ignore the minority of Earthlings who have rejected our offer of help by not cooperating.

'Could all of those who have been monitoring the drones prepare your notes and your videos then come forward please. Your information and video clips are crucial to our final decisions. As you know, the Earthlings were told of our ultimatum after our last meeting. For those of you who might have missed the last meeting, we gave the Earthlings a further six months' extension of time to further implement the use of the Ten Golden Rules. We will now view and discuss your videos. Elder Thelo, yours can be the first video and summary.'

Phil Muirhead

'Thank you Breno. I have been watching unfortunate humans who pay a lifetime's savings to criminals they call people smugglers. I'll turn on my video, but from what I can work out, the people smugglers take their money to organise a boat to take these humans to a better part of Planet Earth. It's a very questionable procedure, with men, women and children crammed into substandard vessels with little or no food and very little drinking water. According to my research, it's similar to behaviour they adopted years ago. Back then they called it the slave trade, whereby if you were a human blessed with money, you could actually buy and own another human. Incredible!'

'Are you sure?' one of the elders asked in disbelief.

'Very much so, though I can only go on their documented history.'

'How long ago did you capture the video?' asked another elder.

'About two Earth months ago,' Thelo replied.

Thelo returned to her seat, her oration lingering in every elders' mind.

'Does anyone wish to elaborate further?' Breno asked.

'I have something similar,' another elder replied. 'I watched people fleeing a war-torn country pay a truck driver their life savings to smuggle them to a safer neighbouring country. They entered a huge metal container with the promise of a better life, but out of sheer bad luck the truck broke down. The driver, frightened he would be caught, left them to die locked in a container in the hot sun. To make matters worse, these poor people were discovered four days later by soldiers, who elected to dig a huge pit then unceremoniously bury them in a mass grave. Did any of you see this incident on Earth's media networks? Our sustenance formula won't do these poor souls much good.'

Breno remained impartial, asking Elder Elmao to come forward. 'I have much of the same,' the elder proclaimed. 'These people are fleeing their homeland because of a raging war, yet they now live a substandard lifestyle in what humans call a refugee camp. It really is a pitiful sight, though somehow they

manage to feed them. However, nobody wants them permanently. Don't be complacent when making your decision today. The
human species we're dealing with are ruthless. These people are
still residing at the camp you're looking at as we speak. If anyone
needs the sustenance formula, these people do.'

Another elder took the opportunity to speak. 'I would like to
explain something, so please listen carefully. Since we befriended
the Earthlings, we have been in a slight state of disarray, and let
me tell you why. It's because we feel sorry for them – sorry because we know their suffering is unnecessary, sorry because it is
the young, innocent and poor who suffer most. However, the
problem with feeling sorry is it's starting to affect our thinking.
You may have noticed a new emotion creeping into our lives
called sadness. The sadness emotion is linked to sorrow, and it
was totally unheard of prior to our dealing with Earthlings. Sadness is slowly edging into our lives without us even realising. I
truly believe we should banish these beings from our lives forevermore before sadness takes a hold, becoming a systemic part of
our lives forever. That's all I have to say.'

'Would you agree to them having the sustenance formula?'
Breno queried.

'Definitely! But nothing more.'

Breno pointed to another elder he recognised. It was Meto.
'Good morning, everyone. Some of you might remember my
previous video of a schoolyard slaughter of innocent children. I
have since been accompanying an elder and monitoring his
drone in a quest to analyse human behavioural patterns. So far
we have learned that when we witness their loving and affection-
ate behaviour, it has no effect on us other than make us feel
good. On the other hand, when we witness their fighting and
their disregard for one another, we become stressed and desensi-
tised, making us feel hollow and unhappy. We're concerned we
are slowly becoming accustomed to insensitivity, stress and sadness. We suggest that elders seriously consider abandoning this
species before unwanted emotions penetrate the core of our very

existence. Give them the sustenance formula and not a thing more.'

The momentum of the meeting was changing, creating a distinct air of excitement as it progressed, prompting Breno to try another angle of enquiry. 'Does anyone have anything we haven't yet touched on?' he questioned. 'Something about their species we haven't yet discussed?'

Elda Sano spoke via virtual connectivity from venue three. 'After hearing about the adverse aspects of humans, I flew my drone everywhere searching for items of interest. Eventually, I came across this huge arched concrete structure holding back about three trillion gallons of water. It's a dam that was built a long time ago when their technology levels were lower than they are now. Take a look, it's quite a magnificent feat of engineering to say the least, so it just goes to show there are some very clever humans among them.

'Bear with me, and I'll show you another structure. Here we go, this bridge is called a suspension bridge, and it crosses a huge expanse of water. It's 220-feet high and is over one-and-a-half miles long. The centre span is three-quarters of a mile long. It was built at approximately the same time as the dam I just showed you. It too is a superb feat of engineering, and as a species, there must have been some very clever humans involved in creating this structure too.

'Now, can anybody watching tell me why such clever beings can be so stupid? If they are clever enough to build such majestic structures and go to their moon, wouldn't you think they would be clever enough to look after one another and not have wars? You would also think they'd be clever enough to adopt ten life-changing rules? Thank you.'

'Before you go,' Breno interrupted, 'you never mentioned whether you'd agree to provide the sustenance formula. I won't mention T-Pod technology as I can't see anybody considering it.'

'I see no reason not to provide the formula,' the other elder agreed.

Breno signalled for another elder to speak. 'I thank you all for giving me your time. Mostly I have been monitoring Earth's politicians and religious leaders. Both professions are similar, and when analysed there's very little difference between both professions. Earth's politicians have unlimited power, and they make laws based on money, greed and fear. As far as I'm concerned, there is an element to them that should be inside the very jails they legislate to control. I wonder what God thinks about them making millions of laws without taking into consideration they only need ten laws that actually work.

'Now let's talk about religion. It's even more fascinating than their politics. As you no doubt know, they have thousands of different religions scattered all over Planet Earth, all in God's name, supposedly. How does that work, you may ask, when there is only one God governing the universe? Extremely well, it seems, provided your followers are forever providing money towards the religion you have control over. Somehow, they brainwash their followers to the extent they think they can't do without the religion that serves them; it's an incredible process based on fear. Believe me, if any of their thousands of religious groups gets a say in our technology, they will convince their flock it is technology sent by the God they worship, not technology freely given by us.

'Politicians will use our technology as an instrument that plays the tune of war, profit and control. Mark my words, those in power will play out the technology in every form they can think of. They'll sell it to those less fortunate, taxing their newly found good fortune as a means of extracting more money towards their greedy cause. As far as the sustenance formula is concerned, I say give it to them as a parting gesture.'

Breno announced that everyone should take a break.

Chez decided to give Alan an impromptu call during the break. She was lucky to get through as his phone hadn't stopped all day. Leaders from all over the world had been continually calling, wanting the latest news from Univiah. He had just finished talking to the president when he received the call.

Phil Muirhead

'Greetings, Alan. I know you would rather talk through Internal Monitoring but I don't have time.

'I understand, Chez. How is the meeting of elders going?'

'I wouldn't like to build your hopes up, but from what I'm hearing, I'm almost certain they will provide Planet Earth with our sustenance formula. No one on Earth will ever go hungry or malnourished again, and the poorer people on Earth will be the big winners,' she said.

'What about your T-Pod technology? Are they considering favourably?' Alan pressed.

'I wouldn't say so. They seem convinced you will turn them into military machines, yet we're only halfway through the meeting. Maybe they will decide in your favour with certain provisos.'

'You don't sound too positive, Chez.'

'You are a species hard to be positive about, Alan. There is a minority within your species who will never reform, and it is this minority we are discussing. We don't come close to understanding why the majority of you put up with them. We wouldn't understand even if you could explain.'

'I'm sure given time we can overcome the problems we are facing.'

'You were just given time. I have to go, Alan, as the next segment of the meeting is being called to order. Please call me the minute you get to work tomorrow. I'll have judgement from the elders prepared for you. Goodbye, Alan.'

Alan immediately rang the president explaining how the meeting of elders was progressing. 'There's hope,' he told him, 'although they are not happy about the minority among us who somehow control the world, hence control weaponry.'

The president responded sheepishly, 'Do I come into that category?'

'You certainly do, Mr President. After all, you're a very powerful politician with unlimited control.'

'This is not always the case, Alan. You know that.'

'I know one thing, Mr President. We're not going to get what we want, although Chez did say they would probably supply us with the formula for sustenance pills, so no one on Earth will ever go hungry again. Think about it, sustenance pills would solve major problems all over the world. Landfill from food packaging would become a thing of the past, food production would cease, alleviating the necessity for people to be continually working, body waste would no longer occur, solving sewerage and pollution problems worldwide, and society would be totally restructured in a manner nobody at present would consider possible.'

'Have you thought about the adverse implications, Alan?' the president asked.

'Such as?'

'Such as the economy, food supply chains, farmers, industry, commerce. We would go broke on a scale never seen before.'

'So it all gets back to money! You're sounding more like Big Mal every time we speak.' Alan was fuming but tried keeping his tone civil.

'I'm just pointing out the obvious, Alan.'

'Your obvious is quite an admission, Mr President, one I doubt the Univians would take too kindly. Pray they aren't monitoring our conversation as successfully as they let you monitor our conversations with them.'

Suddenly out of the blue, the president stopped talking, the silence broken by a series of loud bangs and wacks that sounded like someone bashing a rolled-up newspaper against a wall, over and over. Alan heard the sound and wondered if the president was in an altercation with a staff member. 'Are you alright?' Alan yelled into the phone.

There was no answer. He could still hear the commotion taking place in the background, then finally it stopped.

'Alan, are you there?' the president asked, puffed and out of breath.

'I am, though what happened on your end?'

'I'm allergic to bees, but I've had this odd-looking bee flying around here for a couple of days. Poor little thing, I just bashed it so hard it disintegrated. Now where were we before that pesky bee appeared?'

'We were talking about how you should pray Univiah isn't monitoring you as successfully as you are allowed the pleasure of monitoring them.'

'Is it possible they could be monitoring me on a personal basis aside from Internal Monitoring?'

'Not possibly, Mr President, probably, considering what they are about to embark upon.'

'So you're thinking they don't trust me?' the president was affronted.

'I'll guarantee they don't, though if you think about it, you get all of your information through Astrospace Galexiana, which is controlled by a CEO who hasn't cooperated in the slightest. Big Mal is a prime example of why they distrust us. He's been in a position to be a perfect role model, yet instead he's opposed everything we've tried to achieve, all in the name of Galexiana's profits, with not a thought going to anyone but himself and his shareholders. To make matters worse, everything Big Mal has done has happened right before their eyes, and your eyes too.'

'I understand, Alan. We could go on forever, yet what's done is done, and we can't alter the past. Please call me immediately when you know their final decision. Before I go, please contact Ron Hallerton in Houston. He has been making headway.'

As soon as Alan hung up, his phone rang. It was the Australian Prime Minister asking the same questions as the US President. Alan gave him a general run-down, telling him the same story he had just told the president.

TWENTY-FIVE

Meanwhile back at Metropolis Central, the meeting was starting to gather momentum, and Breno's mind was working overtime. 'Please, have your say,' he urged, prompting an elder who had just walked forward.

'I'll be quick and to the point. I too go along with providing the sustenance formula but I'm afraid that's it. There is no way I will condone supplying any other technology.'

'Keep your thoughts coming,' Breno said, pointing to a female elder.

'Hello, I'm Cheto. This human male considers himself a cult messiah. He has brainwashed his subjects to the extent they can't live without him. For some reason, his followers gave him all their money, sold their houses and donated the proceeds to his cause. Most left behind loving families and handed control of their lives over to this man, convinced he was a messiah sent to help them. Eventually, the authorities became aware, so he lured everyone to take a cyanide pill as apparently he would lead them into the afterlife. Only he forgot to tell them his capsule contained sugar!

'You certainly wouldn't want him distributing sustenance pills, nor would you want him working in the factory that makes the sustenance formula. Seems to me it doesn't matter what technology we give them, they'll find a way of using it against one another. Regardless of what I have said, I still think we should supply the formula, and if sometime in the future they revert to lacing the formula with poison, it will be on their conscience not ours.'

Breno's thoughts shifted to another level. Previous to Cheto's observations, he had never considered the sustenance formula could be used adversely. 'Does anyone else think they would consider using the sustenance formula against one another?' he asked. 'Give me a show of hands if you think they will use it detrimental to their cause.'

Every hand in all four Metropolis Centrals shot skyward.

'If this is indicative of your thoughts, I would like to know more. Give me another show of hands if you would still give them the sustenance formula knowing they could misuse it.'

The same show of hands took place, prompting an elder who had his hand raised to address the meeting. 'I look at it this way. If we vote for them to receive the formula, we have done so from our hearts. If they use it to kill one another, it's out of our hands, as we've done nothing wrong by trying to help them. Give them the formula and leave the rest to God the Universe to sort out.'

'Next, please,' Breno announced, noticing the elder who came forward was slightly agitated. 'I hope I can get through to you, Elder Breno. While I appreciate you would like to help these wayward humans, have you not noticed we are unknowingly being consumed by an Earthly emotion called anger? For the first time in my existence, I have actually been affected by anger. Univians thus far don't know what anger is, so let me explain how it creeps into your soul. Listen carefully!

'After witnessing people dying of starvation while fellow humans nearby were oversupplied with every conceivable luxury known to mankind, I felt this strange emotion coming over me. I felt like killing the affluent humans who weren't helping their unfortunate fellow humans. It was a frightening experience, and one I never want to experience again. You can have your drone back as I've had enough. Do whatever you like with it. You can also do whatever you like with the subspecies in question, but I refuse to vote or have further involvement, so do not try to include me again. I don't care whether you give them the sustenance formula or not. I never want to hear about humans again.'

Breno instinctively knew and understood how he had become emotionally overwhelmed by the proceedings taking place. The elder's analogy of anger was one Breno was starting to understand himself, and he had never even been in control of a drone. Walking towards the audience he announced there would be one more short recess.

'Please mingle with other elders to discuss why and how you will be voting,' he told them, 'and don't be frightened to voice your opinion. After the break we will come back and prepare for the final deciding vote. Before we vote, I will be calling on Elder Jenko to summarise the meeting and also to advise those who have any further questions.'

Recess was quite a scene, the spontaneity of the meeting livening debate between the elders who were now talking loudly out of turn, waving their hands in an erratic fashion not familiar to the species. Originally, every elder present was prepared to get involved in Earth's future for no other reason than the benefits Univiah could provide humankind, yet would this still be the case?

Univians were now in the final throes of deciding whether to supply humans with technology they could only dream of. Technology they were considering withholding due to a minority of Earth's people who refused to comply with ten simple rules. A minority element was responsible for humankind's pathetic past, which was created because nobody questioned this evil minority who have insisted since time immemorial to control by fear and stealth instead of compassion.

Elders gathered in groups in the four Metropolis Centrals, all discussing the events that had taken place. The humming sound of too many people talking at once filled the air. Hands were waving, arms outstretched, indicating gestures of heartfelt concern. Breno and Jenko stepped down from the stage and joined four female elders. Joyco, Thelo, Audo and Elmao were the most boisterous of the elders present. They were well-known to Breno and Jenko as all four of them had never missed an elder's meeting in fifty years. Somehow they always attracted attention, and not one of them were afraid to tell it as they saw it.

Joyco threw her arms in the air and told everyone her thoughts in no uncertain terms. 'I'm sure Earthlings all have learning and memory problems,' she protested. 'Somehow they aren't capable of looking at the past to rectify their future; otherwise, they wouldn't keep doing what they do. Perhaps they're genetically dysfunctional? Whatever their problem is, we don't need it. Do the rest of you agree?' she shouted to be heard above a chorus of inaudible chatter.

Elders were butting in excitedly throughout each venue trying to get their point across, and comments were being heard in tandem. All four venues were now alive with noisy debate, with different points of view all being spoken at the same time.

'They're beyond redemption! There's no helping them! No one in God's universe does this! Why would they hurt one another? Is it a genetic complication? Banish them! They must like mistreatment! Give them the formula no more! God the Universe tell us why! Be rid of them! They have unsolvable problems! We're just trying to help! We will never work them out! No more! We're doing this for them not us!'

The meeting was now becoming unruly and needed toning down. Breno sensed the urgency of the situation and intervened, urging fellow elders to settle. 'Please! Please! Will you all quieten down as we are achieving nothing. Order! Order! I ask all four venues for silence! Silence, I said! Please listen! Thank you. I understand how you feel, as there is nothing worse than trying to help those who for reasons beyond our understanding won't help themselves.

'I realise your Univian upbringing compels you to want to help the Earthlings, yet you must be guided by your conscience and common sense. The type of behaviour you're displaying is akin to the very people we are debating, which is not a society as sophisticated as ours. That alone should tell you something about how you should vote. Now let's get back and listen to Elder Jenko's summary, then get this meeting over with. I for one have had enough.'

Jenko walked onto the stage, joining Breno and a group of elders who had been discussing the unfolding events. Suddenly without notice, Quino, one of Univiah's oldest most prominent and respected elders, slowly shuffled across the stage unannounced. Breno, Jenko and the group of elders stood aside, wondering what he was intending. There were six elders either side of him, and they were all looking towards Quino, some with their arms stretched out towards him as if to say, 'What's Quino doing?'

Quino, uninvited and without consulting anybody, addressed the elders in his own poignant style, his speech slow but concise. 'My life as a compatriot and elder is spent, but please listen carefully. I'm 303 years old and about to terminate my existence. I realise I am frail, yet my mind is complete. This has been the most futile elder's meeting I have attended in 103 years of eldership. I'll get straight to the point as we have wasted enough time on this unfortunate species. It is obvious to the keenest of intellects that a species who won't help themselves can never be helped. Be rid of them before irreversible damage takes hold. If you don't, I can assure you, you are all setting yourselves up for total chaos. Chaos that will result in your demise, with the end result being that Univians will suffer the same emotional problems as Earthlings. Feelings of insecurity will slowly creep into our lives, so too will fear, stress, worry, loneliness, greed and hate, as will depression, remorse, anxiety and anger. We've already had an insight into how this happens. Before we befriended Earthlings, we never knew such emotions existed. We must not, I repeat must not, let these insipid Earthly emotions infiltrate Univian society. Be rid of them before we too learn the art of crying.'

Quino simply about-turned and shuffled towards one of the convention centre's perimeter exits. It was a powerful moment that his fellow elders would never forget. Quino wasn't just leaving the meeting, he was leaving to keep a long-awaited appointment with God the Universe. Every elder present pondered Quino's formidable words, his impromptu speech lingering in their minds as they watched him disappear through one of the perimeter exits.

Jenko broke the profound silence, signalling his intention to give his summary of the meeting. 'Fellow elders, as you already know, Earthlings have not lived up to expectations. I notice there is a strong favour to supply the sustenance formula and nothing else. I personally will vote in favour of suppling the sustenance formula, and Breno tells me he too will vote this way. It seems everyone's consensus is we should give them the sustenance formula; nevertheless, it is every elder's prerogative to vote according to their reasoning. However, we must not take this approach when considering any other form of technology.

'Their disposition within the universe is hard for us to understand, and the majority of Earthlings may want to live in peace and harmony. Unfortunately, there is a somewhat disproportionate sector of their society we have to consider. Please take into consideration that the people we are dealing with can fix their plight overnight if they wish. However, they have a problem within their midst caused by those who are tyrannical. Somehow the tyrants are the minority who master control. For some reason, the same minority consider themselves above God the Universe while the majority are prepared to let them reign supreme.

'Please remember they were issued with same rules countless years ago that Univiah uses, but decided to disobey them. It is no longer our business to further advise or confront them, so please consider what I have said before you vote. I sincerely ask you take heed of Elder Quino's final words. Do you have any questions?'

No one stirred. A decision was imminent, and it would be relayed to Earth through Chez in the morning.

TWENTY-SIX

Alan and Pam woke simultaneously thanks to a day-breaking call from Ron Hallerton.

'Sorry for the early call, Alan, yet something important has come to mind since we last spoke. I only have one question.'

Alan looked at Pam, raising his eyebrows as if to say 'Why this early?'

Ron asked his all-important question. 'Can you tell me, did anyone get a look on board the interstellar craft when you were in Australia? I think we're onto something.'

'No. Why?'

'We have come up with a few new ideas concerning photonic laser propulsion and anti-gravity.'

'Go ahead, Ron. This sounds more feasible than time travel.'

'It's probable that Univians have no conventional power source on board. Instead, they would use an energy propulsion device, and according to this theory, they simply project themselves forward with photonic propulsion that uses particles of light to propel the craft. Given that light particles have no mass but do have the energy to push, it is quite plausible to assume this is how they travel at such incredible speed. On top of that, they could be putting the craft into an anti-gravitational state, which would cause photonic propulsion to be super effective.

Phil Muirhead

'There's no logical place or space on board their interstellar craft for any type of sizeable propulsion system let alone a fuel source, are you with me?'

'Yes, and it makes more sense than time travel.'

'Tell me, Alan, what have you learned so far about the sustenance formula?'

'I've learnt it creates no body waste, which is a big plus if you have eight people on board an interstellar flight for 113 days. I've also learnt the sustenance formula nourishes their organs and keeps them healthy in case for some unknown reason they have to revert to solid food again. If you think about it, the sustenance formula is as important as finding out how they reach such astronomical speed. Seriously, Ron, take my advice and wait for the outcome of the elders meeting before you go any further.'

'You're probably right, Alan,' Ron relented.

'I'm sure I'm right. If you're contemplating space travel on a scale the Univians practise, you're going to be needing Univian knowhow, like it or not.'

Ron reluctantly agreed.

'Today's the big day, isn't it?' Pam asked

'Yes. I have to contact Chez as soon as I get in. It will be a relief to know one way or the other. I'm sure they'll give us the sustenance formula although it's the rest of their technology we need most. Chez was rather aloof last time we talked, and it worries me.'

'Never mind,' reassured Pam. 'What will be, will be. Perhaps Univiah will provide nothing more than a philosophical look at our own failings.'

'In that case, you will be first to know, and I will be the first to go, leaving Galexiana forever.'

Pam sat on the side of the bed, contemplating what Alan had said. 'What are you going to do if you leave Galexiana?' she asked, concerned by Alan's words.

'I don't think it's called leaving, love, although I'll guarantee Big Mal won't get the pleasure of firing me.'

'What do you intend doing if Chez gives us a full negative?'

Alan chewed on his inner cheek. 'I'm going to exit so fast Big Mal will see nothing but the dust I leave behind.'

'What about Scotty and Willy? They're in the same boat as you when it comes to Big Mal.'

'I'm not sure what they intend doing. I guess it's up to them.'

'We shouldn't be considering the negative, Alan, as there is no reason they won't supply us with the sustenance formula,' Pam soothed.

'I agree. I'm just a bit anxious, that's all.'

After breakfast, Alan headed into work. He entered the control room and decided to give Scotty a call before he contacted Chez. 'I'm about to make contact with Chez. Just wondering how things are with you and how you feel given the circumstances?'

'Nervous, Al. And you?'

'Same, Scotty. I need to get this over with.'

Alan went to the window overlooking the car park. Big Mal had just arrived. It was the first time anyone had seen him arrive riding his Harley Davidson. Two other bikies, both riding Harleys, were accompanying him. Alan immediately recognised his accomplices; they were the same two body guards he used when he first sacked Alan. Mal had obviously prepared for the day's unfolding events, completely aware of the magnitude of the occasion. He walked towards Admin carrying a leather satchel, both of his bikie mates following close behind. Alan's observations were such that he couldn't help thinking how well-dressed and business-like Big Mal looked compared to his ruffian mates.

If Univiah refused point blank to co-operate further, he figured it would take ten minutes for Internal Monitoring to inform the president and the Australian Prime Minister. Big Mal and the rest of the world would be informed soon after. In a worst-case scenario, Mal would mobilise his mates then come knocking.

Alan reasoned it would take about five minutes at the most to remove his paper files and external hard drives, then drive out before Big Mal arrived to sack him. It should be just enough time for him to make a smooth exit if necessary.

If Univiah refused to cooperate on all fronts, he wouldn't leave a trace of information for Galexiana to capitalise on. Taking every skerrick of information with him would be a silent legacy Alan would leave Big Mal, a last-minute statement without him having to be there.

Alan decided the time had finally come. He entered the control room then removed his paper files from his locked filing cabinet. He then unravelled the leads and connections to his external hard drives, the contents of which he had been very careful to keep separate from Galexiana's data. The external hard drives were now ready to be quickly removed for a fast getaway. His only task left would be to delete his unimportant day-to-day content from Galexiana's computers. 'I sure hope I don't have to make a quick exit,' he told himself, 'but there is nothing like being prepared. Surely at the very least they will provide us with the sustenance formula, which will no doubt keep me employed here for a few more years.'

He sat in readiness, hesitant to activate the password, his thoughts roaming back to the schoolyard where it all began in 1969. He could still remember the day like it was yesterday. Little did he know where it would all lead.

He went to activate the password, then stopped, reminiscing on more past events as they unfolded within his mind. Dad would be pleased, he said the authorities would make everything go away, though I bet he's up there proudly looking down on me because I proved him wrong. As for Mum, if she's been looking down on me, I bet she believes in aliens now.

He realised he should have updated his sister and daughters about everything, yet knew they would be patiently waiting for him to reveal the outcome. He wondered if God chose him to be instrumental in the whole procedure, or was it just fate? He found that incredibly hard to believe. He also realised he could have had such a fulfilling life if he hadn't pursued his DEMC. Then again, maybe he'd pursued his dreams as God the Universe expected. He sure hadn't appreciated the last bit of the journey, but perhaps God was trying to test him by seeing how much angst and stress he could cope with, and perhaps the next segment was just about to begin.

Poised to activate the password, he hesitated again, thinking of the moments he'd spent with the Univians at Quinella Downs. What an incredible few days. If only it had lasted longer. He wondered if there could be another meeting with the Univians sometime in the future.

Alan sat perfectly still, mesmerised by his thoughts, then suddenly snapped out of it, realising it was pointless delaying the inevitable. He typed Univ-Al, cracking his knuckles anxiously while awaiting the connection.

'Greetings, Alan.' Chez's twangy voice sounded a softer tone than usual.

'Hello, Chez. Do you have a verdict?'

'I do,' she said meekly, 'but before we go any further, I want you, Scotty and Pam to remember as time goes by the decision-making process has all been decided by the elders.'

'I understand, as will Internal Monitoring.' Now Alan was very anxious.

'Firstly, I have a message to deliver. The elders told me to sincerely thank humankind for introducing Univians to hugging, clapping, laughing and music. These aspects of your lives have become so endearing to us. I will now get straight to the point. Unfortunately, Alan, the elders have decided to stick with their original requirements. They are withholding all technology until such times as Earth is living and complying with The Ten Commandments or Golden Rules.'

'When you say all technology, does that include the sustenance formula?'

'I'm afraid so, Alan.'

'Chez, you said Univiah would consider releasing the sustenance formula and also some of your lesser technologies.'

'I know I did, yet the elders voted otherwise. They all agreed there will be no release of technology in any form until all of you are living in harmony as we do.'

Alan thought for a few moments, debating in his mind whether he should ask about anti-gravitational laser propulsion. He had nothing to lose. 'Chez, we think you are conjointly using laser propulsion and anti-gravity to propel your interstellar craft, could you possibly give me a simple yes or no answer?'

'My answer to your question is Bzzzzzt.'

I expected that, but can you tell me what happens between us from now on?'

Unfortunately, nothing, Alan.'

'Are you saying there will be no further communication?' Alan was aghast.

'I'm afraid so, although the elders did agree Univiah would monitor Planet Earth at yearly intervals.'

'What will that prove?'

'If we ever notice you are all using God's given laws instead of your hapless manmade laws, we will make amends.'

'In what way?' Alan wanted to know.

'You know how it is. Discard your manmade laws, none of which work, and adopt the ten laws that do. Then we will help you. Let me remind you that helping you at a future point in time is your only salvation. During the meeting, most elders wanted to sever our connection with Earth forever.'

'So you're saying we will never speak after today until mankind adheres to your rules?'

'I'm afraid so. Incidentally they're not our rules, they are God's rules.'

Alan was speechless but pressed forward anyway. 'Chez, we have formed a wonderful friendship over the last couple of years. I would like it to stay that way even if we only speak once a month.'

'We have indeed formed a unique friendship. Unfortunately, it has to be cut short unless humankind can change its ways.'

'Do you agree with the elder's final decision?' Alan wanted to know.

'Unreservedly, although I did ask the elders if I could be the person who monitors Planet Earth at the specified yearly intervals. They said I'm a glutton for punishment but agreed I could do so.'

Alan was inconsolable, although he understood where all the Univians were coming from. Humanity was not to be trusted at this point in time.

'All I can say is that I will be doing my utmost to rectify everything over the next year to make sure reform takes place.'

'It won't, Alan. From what I've learnt, your people will never reform to a peaceful existence.'

'Chez, please stay in contact with Pam and myself. You have my phone number, and surely it wouldn't hurt to talk to me or Pam occasionally?'

'I am forbidden to communicate after today until you all start living as we do, which means we will never communicate again unless somehow you all miraculously reform.'

'Chez, please see if the elders will allow an occasional phone call even if it's only at Christmas. We've grown so fond of you.'

Chez was resolute. 'Alan, please listen, it's not going to happen. Accept how it is, and let go graciously. You are making me sad, and I am also experiencing anger due to the stupidity of your people not conforming. These are emotions I cannot fathom nor do I ever want to. They are emotions I have started to learn from Earthlings, emotions I intend banishing from my life forever. Please give my love and say goodbye to Pam and also to Willy and Scotty. Unfortunately, our friendship has come to an end for now.'

'Chez, Chez, wait, please wait! Don't go, please don't.'

'I'd like to say I'm sorry, Alan, but I won't allow myself. Goodbye, my friend!' Bzzzzzt Bzzzzzt Bzzzzzt Bzzzzzt Bzzzzzt Bzzzzzt Bzzzzzt ----

And like radio waves released, there's.... No end.

ACKNOWLEDGEMENTS

Please let me thank my editor and independent publisher, Dr Juliette Lachemeier from The Erudite Pen, who transformed my roughly written manuscript into a novel I'm proud of. To Judith San Nicolas who created *The Believer's* cover design. To Nicholas Rothwell, a journalist, author and nearby neighbour who encouraged me to keep working on the manuscript. To George Ahlers, who piqued my interest in UFOs. To Ron Scomazzon and Brad Bell who I used as critics while the manuscript was in its infancy. To my two wonderful daughters Sophie and Kelly, and to my five lovely grandchildren, Bonnie, Madison, Tyler, Lucas, and Kody, who were always trying to drag Poppy away from his computer to play.

ABOUT THE AUTHOR

Philip Muirhead was born in Atherton, Far North Queensland in
June 1950. He attended Atherton State School where telling
stories became essential to the non-conformity that caused his
regular visits to the headmaster.

After leaving school he started a carpentry apprenticeship. He
then went on to work for himself in the building industry until
retirement.

Phil remembers watching television at the end of the Vietnam
War when perfectly good helicopters were being thrown from
ships into the ocean. This was when he first thought, *I wonder
what another highly intelligent civilisation would think if they were watching
us? If other beings were taking a peek, we must surely be a source of superb
entertainment.* Then came the still inner voice that whispered, 'You
could write a book about it.'

Phil knew a cattle station owner who was adamant he had witnessed a UFO event at his property's homestead. To this day, after listening to his account, Phil firmly believes him.

Looking back over his life if he had to sum up his past, Phil would describe it as a life of 'colourful turbulence'. Turbulence out of which the compelling Univian series arose.

Enjoyed the book? You can contact the author at:

Email: philipjmuirhead@gmail.com

Website: www.philmuirhead.com

Facebook: facebook.com/philmuirhead.author

If you liked the book, please leave a review on Amazon,
Goodreads or with the author directly. Reviews are invaluable in
supporting an author's hard work
and are greatly appreciated.

THE UNIVIAH NOVEL SERIES

Book 2

What awaits Alan Holmes and Planet Earth in the sequel to *The Believer*?

In the year after leaving Astrospace Galexiana, Alan has increased his endeavours to encourage the Univians to once again make contact. On Earth, some incredible changes are taking place. The determined astrophysicist has instigated events to eliminate the controlling factors that have for so long been kept in place by the influential elite minority.

To achieve this, Alan, along with his inner circle, has founded the People's Movement, a movement that uses nothing more than peaceful people-power to achieve its revolutionary outcome.

The People's Movement insists on four common denominators before they will again ask Univiah for their coveted technology: (1) The military will have to be dismantled; (2) Governments need to be abolished; (3) Religion must use one God and obey the Ten Commandments; (4) The elitist oligarchs of the world must be stripped of their ability to dominate others.

Receiving Univian technology will be the catalyst that transforms humanity into an advanced society previously only dreamt about. Can the People's Movement overcome the elitist stranglehold over the world's consciousness, freeing the majority from the insidious groupthink that has kept Earth's civilisation in chains for aeons? Or will warmongering, selfishness, greed and survival-of-the-fittest mentality ruin humankind's second chance for a faster-tracked evolution?

Find out in Book 2 of The Univian Novel Series, out towards December 2022.